Vanessa Del Fabbro

Fly Away Home

D1550799

Steeple
Hill®

Published by Steeple Hill Books™

STEEPLE HILL BOOKS

Steeple
Hill®

ISBN-13: 978-0-373-78628-2
ISBN-10:   0-373-78628-X

FLY AWAY HOME

Copyright © 2008 by Vanessa Del Fabbro

Printed in U.S.A.

Books by Vanessa Del Fabbro

Steeple Hill

The Road to Home
Sandpiper Drift
A Family in Full

*A Monica Brunetti novel

For Emma and Juliet, with love

Acknowledgments

I would like to thank my agent, Helen Breitwieser, for her years of enthusiastic support, and my editor, Joan Marlow Golan, for everything she has taught me over the course of writing the Monica Brunetti series. These two gracious women took a chance on me, and for this I will forever be grateful. To the rest of the team at Steeple Hill Books, thank you for your help and kindness. And lastly, thanks to my husband and young daughters, for their love and encouragement.

❧ Chapter One ❧

Monica imagined her little girl. She'd have blond hair, just like her own, but rather than straight it would be curly, like Zak's when he let his grow longer than an inch. When Monica had first met Dr. Zak Niemand, she'd thought he could have passed for a military man. Dark eyes were dominant, so it was likely the baby's eyes would be brown like Zak's and not green like hers. She hoped the baby would inherit Zak's complexion, too. He tanned easily, while her pale skin turned bright pink and peeled if she was exposed to too much sun.

"I wonder what's taking Mandla so long," said Zak, looking through the windshield toward the front door of their house for the appearance of their eight-year-old adopted son.

Monica knew better than to share her baby fantasies with her husband of three years. He would say—and rightly so—

that they were premature. But what was the expression Ella, Mandla's biological mother, had always used? She had felt premonitions "in her bones." After more than two years of trying to get pregnant, Monica could feel in her bones that today was the day the doctor would confirm a tiny baby was growing inside her.

Mandla ran toward the car and hopped into the backseat. "What's Sipho doing?" Zak asked him.

"Still studying," replied Mandla in a tone that suggested his older brother was engaged in a distasteful pastime. He leaned over the front seat and gave Monica a quick hug. Mandla wanted this baby as much as she and Zak did.

Earlier this afternoon after school, Mandla had snuggled up next to Monica on the sofa and allowed her to hug him as though he were still a baby. If a stranger were to see these tender family scenes, Mandla might seem to be the more sensitive of Monica's two boys. But, in fact, it was fifteen-year-old Sipho who was the more gentle natured. Mandla resembled his late mother, Ella Nkhoma, whom Monica had met in a Soweto hospital. Monica had been shot by a carjacker while working as a journalist, and Ella had been in the ward for what she'd said was "a touch of bronchitis," but was actually AIDS. Like his mother, Mandla had a personality magnetic enough to fill any room, and people gravitated toward him like ants to spilled juice. At the outdoor concerts in Lady Helen, the little town on the West Coast of South Africa where Monica had moved her family more than five years ago, Mandla always got as close to the stage as possible and sang in accompaniment at the top of his voice, while playing an imaginary guitar or clapping to the music. At church or in a restaurant, he'd call out to people in greeting, shake hands as though he were a politician running for office, and slap backs as he said goodbye. Sipho had always been shy—Sipho, with his big eyes inherited from his father, Themba, who before his death and during the struggle against the apartheid government had been a member of the armed wing of the African National Congress. Themba had infected his wife, Ella, with the HIV virus. Now they were both deceased and the boys had been living with Monica for seven years.

Zak turned onto a smaller road and for a while the car headed straight toward the whitecaps of the agitated ocean. Just as they drew close enough to get a whiff of salt spray, he turned south onto the road that climbed the koppies surrounding Lady Helen. Monica remembered when she'd brought the children to Lady Helen to live. They had driven all the way from Johannesburg and arrived during the middle of a ferocious and unseasonal thunderstorm. The view that had captivated her on her first visit, when she'd come to film a report for the television news program, *In-Depth,* had been completely obscured by driving rain. Monica's housekeeper, Francina, who had agreed to make the move with the family without having laid eyes on Lady Helen, was prompted to say, "You never told me we were coming to a swamp."

The view of Lady Helen from on top of the koppie always reminded Monica of looking down on a coral reef from a glass-bottomed boat. Cerise, orange, pink and red bougainvillea covered every available surface, so that the town was almost entirely concealed from view except for the tops of the palm trees and the peaks of brightly colored tin roofs. To the north of town, a lagoon stretched inland, in the shape of a giant horizontal question mark, its surrounding brown and blond like the mane of an aging lion. Bougainvillea didn't like wet feet.

The attractive, dark-haired doctor, who had been too busy delivering twins during Monica's first visit to grant her an on-camera interview about the Lady Helen Hospital's new burn unit—and had not been allowed to forget it since—now drove down the other side of the koppie and joined the main road to Cape Town.

"Everything's so green with all the rain we've had," he remarked, looking at the low scrub bushes of the enclosed national park that stretched up the coast.

Unlike the rest of the country, the Western Cape received its rainfall in winter. During the summer, Monica missed the smell of damp soil and crushed flowers that followed the daily afternoon thundershowers in Johannesburg. When it rained in Lady Helen in winter, you wanted to snuggle indoors under a blanket.

If Sipho were with them, he'd be pointing out birds and flowers, using both the common and scientific names. But he had too much homework to get through this afternoon, he'd said. Monica suspected he was nervous about the result of her pregnancy test. Everyone in the family had been disappointed so many times.

The first time Monica laid eyes on Sipho he'd been watching a wildlife program on television and wearing a Bafana Bafana T-shirt his mother had bought in an attempt to pique his interest in soccer. To this day, he was not the least bit interested in the national team.

The streets of Cape Town in winter were much quieter than in summer, when thousands of European tourists descended.

"The mountain's wearing its tablecloth," said Mandla.

Monica looked out of the car window at the iconic flat-topped mountain that stood guard over the mother city and had once been a welcoming beacon to scurvy-ridden explorers and spice traders en route to the New World. She didn't see a tablecloth but a baby's blanket.

In the waiting room of the reproductive endocrinologist's office, Monica picked up the worn photograph album she had perused many times before. Zak looked over her shoulder at the snapshots of twins, triplets and even one of quadruplets. Thank goodness he realized on this day that it was better not to joke or tease about wanting two little Monicas.

"Monica?"

Ivy, the nurse who had been working with Monica for over two years, wore her usual implacable smile. Did she know the results yet? Or would she be in the office and just as suspended in anticipation when the doctor opened the envelope and read the findings? Positive, negative. Two mundane little words, so undeserving of the impact they might have on the lives of a yearning couple.

"Is it still blowing a gale out there?" asked Ivy.

Monica was grateful when Zak answered; she did not feel capable of speech.

Surely Ivy wouldn't be making small talk about the weather if she knew the results of Monica's pregnancy test.

"Will you be okay out here in the waiting room?" Monica asked Mandla unnecessarily. The last thing the boy wanted to do was accompany them into the doctor's office.

Monica and Zak slipped through the swinging doors

and followed Ivy down the carpeted hall. The nurse knocked lightly.

"Come in," Dr. Jansen called in his deep voice.

As Ivy held the door open, the doctor rose to greet them, hand outstretched. Monica wondered if he was aware of her trembling as his fingers closed over hers.

"Please sit and I'll tell you what you've come to find out." Monica and Zak sat down on the upholstered chairs.

Dr. Jansen opened the creased folder of Monica's medical report and cleared his throat. As Zak shifted in his seat, she felt the blood pounding in her ears. She stared at the frames of the doctor's wire glasses and at the beginnings of a bald spot on the top of his head. *Please God,* she prayed, *let him say, "I have good news."* The doctor's pale lips started to move. "I'm sorry, Monica, Zak. The result is negative."

Monica covered her eyes with her hands. She felt Zak's warm hand on her knee and her eyes filled with tears. He put his arms around her.

"We'll let your body recuperate for a couple of months and then we can try again," said Dr. Jansen. "Ivy will make arrangements with you to come in and receive a fresh supply of fertility drugs."

But Monica knew that she could not handle flipping through the calendar for a suitable date. She needed to be outside, to feel the air on her hot face, to hear the wind howling up the sides of Table Mountain...like a woman wild with grief.

Ivy held the swinging doors open for them, as though they didn't have the strength to do it themselves. Mandla, looking up from his homework as they entered the waiting room, saw Monica's face and immediately began stuffing his books back into his bag. He would not cry; he would hold in his churning disappointment and fury. Normally Monica would tell him not to be so rough with his schoolbooks. But not today. While Zak settled their account, she took Mandla's hand and led him toward the elevator.

Like most of the homes and buildings in Lady Helen, Monica and Zak's house had a tin roof. It also featured green lace filigrees, shutters, wood-frame windows, whitewashed walls and a porch with a polished concrete floor. It was the house that Monica had bought for her little family, but it had been expanded after her marriage to Zak by the addition of a new master suite. The boys each had their own bedroom and there was an extra room for Yolanda, Zak's daughter, who came on weekends from Cape Town, where she lived with her mother. There was also a new garage to replace the one that had been converted into a studio flat for Francina, who was now married and living on Main Street above her shop, Jabulani Dressmakers.

Francina no longer worked as a housekeeper; word of the magic she could weave with a bolt of fabric and a needle had spread as far as Cape Town. She had even been profiled in a national lifestyle magazine. She did, however, still collect Mandla and Sipho from school every afternoon. She'd told Monica more than once how much she dreaded the day when Sipho would go away to university and Mandla would be old enough to take care of himself while Monica was at work at the *Lady Helen Herald*.

The second Zak pulled into their driveway, the front door opened and Sipho ran out, all arms and legs, to greet them. He had his birth mother's height and his father's slim build.

It was Mandla who'd inherited Ella's broad shoulders and muscled frame. Sipho searched Monica's then Zak's face, and found the answer he was looking for.

"I'm sorry," he said, in his new man's voice that Monica thought she'd never get used to.

"What's that behind your back?" asked Mandla.

"Nothing," said Sipho.

"What is it?" persisted Mandla.

"Just a letter. I'll show you later."

Mandla made a grab for it, but Sipho sidestepped him. Monica and Zak looked at each other in surprise. Sipho did not have any friends elsewhere in the country. Who would have written to him? Perhaps it was from Monica's parents in Italy. Mirinda and Paolo Brunetti spent a few months every spring and summer in South Africa, staying in the Old Garage, as Mandla had christened the studio flat. Because of these extended visits, they had become very close to the boys. But Sipho would not hide a letter from their grandparents from Mandla.

"I was going to show you if…" Sipho let the sentence hang in the air, but Monica knew what he'd intended to say. If they'd come home with good news.

"Show us anyway," she said.

She could see him struggling to suppress a smile. Obviously the news in the letter was so exciting he could not keep a solemn face.

"I've been accepted," he almost shouted. "I'm going to be an exchange student in America for a year!"

Monica wondered if her mind was capable of absorbing this fresh bad news. She had helped him with the application, but when she'd signed her name on the form, she'd prayed that he would not be accepted. She didn't want Sipho to go halfway across the world to stay with a family of strangers, no matter how good the experience would look on his application to medical school in a year's time.

She put her hand to her mouth, to stop any words she might regret saying. But there were none. For the second time that day, her eyes filled with tears. She hurried inside.

"Mom?" called Sipho.

But she couldn't turn around. She locked herself in the bathroom. Finally, a private place to grieve.

Chapter Two

Francina stopped hemming for a moment to study the bowed head of her adopted daughter, who was sewing beads onto a wedding dress for a lady from a town north of Lady Helen. The poor bride was going to stagger under the weight of a thousand imitation pearls, but Francina always said that she would gladly shave her head if she came across a bride who was not prepared to suffer for beauty on her big day. A groom wouldn't wear shoes that pinched his toes, or a hairstyle that pulled so tight the corners of his eyes lifted, or a shirt so snug across his stomach he couldn't eat a morsel from the menu that had been so painstakingly chosen.

Unlike some of the other fourteen-year-old girls at Green Block School, Zukisa wore her hair in the natural style of proud African women. Sometimes Francina would braid it, but the girl complained that it pulled too tightly on her scalp.

Perhaps Zukisa would one day be the first bride Francina had ever met who was not willing to suffer for beauty.

"Am I going too slowly?" asked Zukisa.

"No, not at all. I was just admiring the neatness of your rows."

Although Zukisa and Francina were not related by blood, they both had high cheekbones, aquiline noses and, up until Zukisa became a teenager, the same flawless complexion. But their eyes were different. Francina knew that people were unnerved by the way her left eye stared without blinking. Her first husband, Winston, the son of the chief of the village where she'd grown up, had once beaten her so badly that doctors had had to replace her left eye with a glass replica. Children, more openly curious than adults, frequently requested that she take it out so they could study it, and she often obliged them.

Francina's mother-in-law, Mrs. Shabalala, would normally be in the shop in the afternoon, while Francina and Zukisa supervised the boys at Monica's house, but today Monica had taken Mandla with her to an appointment in Cape Town, and Sipho, at fifteen, was perfectly safe on his own. After some initial fine-tuning, Francina found that this shift arrangement worked well for Jabulani Dressmakers. In the mornings, Francina measured clients for new orders and did most of the sewing. In the afternoons, Mrs. Shabalala balanced the accounting books, ordered fabric, thread and other supplies, wrote invoices, met clients to hand over their completed orders, and cleaned the shop. Though Francina had given her mother-in-law many lessons in sewing, Mrs. Shabalala's most valuable contribution would always be her cheerful manner, which could soothe even the most agitated client if an order was not ready on time. Jabulani, the name of Francina's village in the Valley of a Thousand Hills, meant happiness in the Zulu language, and with the division of labor as it was, the atmosphere of the shop always lived up to its name.

Since coming to live with Francina after the death of her mother, when she was ten, Zukisa had shown an eye for design. The meticulous stitching had come later, after patient tutoring from Francina, but from the start Zukisa had known which colors complemented each other, whether a fabric would look better cut on the bias or not, whether a client would look elegant or ridiculous with ruffles. A year later, she was sketching her own designs and cutting out pattern pieces from newspaper. Some of her early efforts had made the mannequin look dressed for a pantomime, but now clients came in just to see the latest design it displayed. At times, Zukisa needed encouragement to keep working on her creation until it was completely hemmed and pressed, but that was understandable for a teenager. Francina was pleased at her daughter's dedication to the tedious job of sewing beads onto this wedding gown, when other girls would be wandering idly up and down Main Street with their friends.

"My aunt couldn't come to the phone this afternoon," said Zukisa.

Francina did not allow herself to ask about Zukisa's weekly phone calls to her aunt, and instead waited patiently until the girl offered her tidbits of information.

"Was she working an extra shift?"

Zukisa's aunt cleaned a restaurant frequented by men of the nearby dockyard. After the death of her mother from

AIDS, Zukisa had gone to live with her aunt, where she helped out taking care of her aunt's grandchildren while the woman was at work. Zukisa's aunt said that her daughter— the mother of the children—had fallen through the cracks of life and could not take care of them.

"She didn't just fall," Francina was fond of telling her husband, Hercules, "she lost her balance because she raised a bottle to her mouth." Francina could not understand how a woman with three beautiful children could abandon them for a life of sin, when she, Francina Shabalala, a woman who had passed her prime early and could not have children of her own, managed to live a decent life and put the violence she'd suffered at the hands of her first husband behind her.

"Not everybody is as strong as you, my dear," Hercules would say. "Addiction is a medical problem." The worst of it was that the wayward mother had joined the oldest profession in the world so she could afford her liquor.

Zukisa had stopped going to school in order to take care of her sick mother, and didn't go back when she moved in with her aunt. Zukisa had been another mouth to feed, another child who needed school fees paid and school uniforms. The aunt's meager state pension was just not enough.

Now, four years after Zukisa had come to her, Francina still thanked God daily for His gift of the child.

Zukisa stopped sewing and looked at Francina. "My aunt is sick."

From the anxiety in her eyes, Francina could tell that Zukisa believed the same disease that had taken both her parents would now take her aunt.

"No, it can't be what you're thinking," she replied in a gentle voice.

Zukisa's expression relaxed a bit. Her adopted mother had never lied to her.

"Are the boys looking after their baby sister?" Francina asked.

Zukisa shook her head. "Those two wouldn't know how to look after a dog, never mind a five-year-old girl."

Francina saw the question on her daughter's face. She took a deep breath. "We can drive down on Saturday if you want."

Zukisa smiled. "Thanks, Mom."

Francina did not know why, but she still lost sleep over her daughter's monthly visits to her blood relatives. Zukisa had come into Francina's life so unexpectedly and with such ease that it seemed likely the girl could leave it in the same way. But God wouldn't grant Francina happiness only to take it away one day, would He?

Footsteps sounded on the stairs leading down to the shop from the family's two-bedroom flat. It was Francina's husband, Hercules. His mother, bless her heart, made her impending presence known with greater volume. Ever since Francina had met her, Mrs. Shabalala had been trying to lose weight. Some months she'd be successful, but her close friendship with Mama Dlamini of Mama Dlamini's Eating Establishment was her downfall. Mama Dlamini's cakes and pies could melt the resolve of even the most motivated dieter.

"When are my girls going to call it a day and come up and see my new painting?" Hercules said, entering the shop.

Francina had met her future husband at a choir competition in Ermelo, a small town east of Johannesburg. Her fellow choir members had mistakenly left her behind at the hostel when they'd hurried off to the church hall. With only thirty minutes before the performance started, and nobody else around, Francina had accepted Hercules's offer of a ride. He'd gone back to the hostel because he'd forgotten his retractable baton and never conducted his choir without it.

When he'd come over to her in the dining hall after the competition, she'd been impressed that he didn't talk about sports as most men did, but about his mother, who was going to be disappointed, he said, that his choir had not won the competition that year. Francina had permitted him to join her at the table, partly because she was in the company of three of her choir sisters and felt that it was proper, and partly because a man who talked of his mother deserved to be treated kindly. She'd agreed to go for a walk with him that afternoon, and not once had she caught him staring at her glass eye the way most people did when getting to know her.

Back in Johannesburg, she'd looked up the name Hercules in Sipho's encyclopedia and had been amused to discover that a tall, pointy man with no meat on his bones could be named after a Greek who looked like a white version of a Zulu warrior. With a name like Hercules, what else could he have become in life but a history teacher?

When Francina and Zukisa were working in the shop, Hercules spent his free time painting. Lady Helen had become a respected center for the arts after a famous artist, S. W. Greeff, had rediscovered the crumbling and deserted town on a walk up the West Coast. Hercules, the dear man, had thought that he could add to the town's reputation, but his first efforts had caused Francina a crisis of conscience; she didn't want to hurt him but she never lied. In the end she had reluctantly—and gently—told him the truth. Now, after four years of art lessons, Hercules had disproved the theory that talent could not be taught, and every space on the walls in their flat was taken up by his paintings. Francina could not think of a scenic spot anywhere in the surrounding countryside, including on any of the koppies, that he had not captured in watercolors. He had recently hung a large painting of dairy cows in their bathroom, and Francina found, to her annoyance, that she could no longer relax as she soaked in her tub, not with six pairs of large brown bovine eyes staring at her.

"Why don't you have a show and sell them?" Francina had asked Hercules time and again, but he did not believe that his work was good enough to be seen by the public.

Hercules's mother would never utter a word of criticism of her son, though Francina had seen the look of irritation on her face when she knocked into one of the many works hanging in the narrow hall to the bedrooms. The small flat felt even more confining with walls of vivid color.

This tall, skinny history teacher, who Francina's choir mates had once likened to a giraffe, was a man of surprises. Those silly girls had quickly lost their smiles, though, on the weekend when she and Hercules had their first official date, in Pongola, a small sugarcane farming town near the Swaziland border, and his choir had taken first place in the competition and won the trophy. Her choir hadn't placed, but she had snagged the greatest prize of all—the man who would become her husband.

"While I was painting I was thinking back to the choir competitions," said Hercules.

Francina knew her husband was leading up to something. Unlike her, Hercules never made idle conversation.

"I think our choir could do well."

Francina couldn't have been more shocked.

"Our choir? Traveling in a minibus taxi to sing in a scout hall and stay in a school dormitory? Hercules, have you gone mad? It took those white ladies five months to get used to wearing their African-style tunics. And now you want them to go and sing Zulu praise hymns. I think that the fumes from your paint have gone to your head."

Zukisa giggled.

"We don't have to go in a taxi. The ladies have cars. We could travel in convoy. And stay in a hotel. You'd like that, wouldn't you, Zukisa?" He looked beseechingly at his daughter.

Zukisa looked from her mother to her father and nodded slowly.

"They'd be inspired by the other choirs, Francina. Don't you remember how we used to feel the music, feel it reverberating off the walls of those shabby halls?"

Francina thought about those times with her people more often than she cared to admit. Sometimes her dreams were filled with voices praising God in the beautiful words of the Zulu language.

"But we'd have to sing in English."

Hercules shrugged. "We'd manage a Zulu song or two, as well."

Hercules, who could coax beauty even from the most reluctant voices, could surely manage it. He'd converted the sick-bird singing of the choir of Lady Helen's Little Church of the Lagoon to a glorious wall of sound that brought people to their feet, clapping and stomping and reveling in the presence of God.

This year, the town of Lady Helen would elect a new mayor. Hercules would make a good mayor. He wasn't a politician as Mayor Oupa had been, or a showman like the current mayor, that brightly attired artist, Richard, with his thick shoes made from recycled car tires and his short pants that exposed his calves. Why the residents of Lady Helen had elected him Francina would never understand. No, Hercules would be the best sort of mayor: thoughtful, rational, fair and accessible. He said he was not comfortable talking in front of a crowd, but didn't he talk all day long to a classroom full of children? He said he wouldn't know how to draw up a budget and stick to it, but wasn't that what he did for his family every year? Lady Helen would benefit from Hercules's gentle wisdom, and Francina planned to ensure that the town was given the opportunity. So far there was only one candidate, and that was the incumbent mayor.

Francina snipped off the thread of the completed hem on Ingrid van Tonder's dress. She had lost count of how many dresses she'd made for Reverend van Tonder's wife, her first ever paying client. Ingrid looked far more elegant and comfortable in Francina's flowing designs than in the poorly made synthetic fire hazards she used to wear.

"Why don't you go up to the flat," Francina told her daughter. "Delicate work like sewing on beads is hard on your eyes."

Zukisa hung the dress on the rail reserved for unfinished orders. "Thanks, Mom."

Francina and Hercules watched her skip up the stairs, on her way, no doubt, to join her grandmother on the couch watching television. The old woman and the young girl shared a bedroom and a love of soap operas.

"None of what you see on the screen happens in real life," Francina would tell them with a mock-stern look on her face.

"Oh, yes, it does," Zukisa would reply. "These shows deal

with all sorts of problems." Too real or not real at all, Francina believed firmly that they'd all be better off without what she saw on that little gray screen.

From upstairs came the muffled sound of Mrs. Shabalala greeting her granddaughter.

"What's wrong?" asked Hercules.

Francina had done nothing to make him suspect that anything was wrong, but with the same intuition that made him the only teacher at Green Block School who the students found impossible to trick, he could always tell her moods.

"Zukisa's aunt is sick."

Hercules nodded slowly. They both knew the full import of these words. Zukisa was fourteen years old and totally capable of looking after a family. She'd done it when she was ten; she could certainly do it now. And the family that needed her were blood relatives.

"Perhaps it's not serious," said Hercules, seeing the fear in his wife's eyes.

Zukisa was a girl of high moral principles; if her family needed her she would help them, even if it meant dropping out of school and moving back to Cape Town. It was not unusual in this country for a child to be the head of a household.

"Those children have a mother," said Francina, pushing the chairs under the tables with more force than necessary.

Hercules shut the front door of the shop, flipped the Closed sign around and turned off the light. Then he put his arm around his wife's shoulders.

"It will all be okay, you'll see."

"I hope so. I can't stand the thought of—"

"Shh…don't say another word. Let's go upstairs and see what drama those two are watching now."

Zukisa looked surprised when Francina joined her on the couch. "You don't like soaps, Mother," she said.

Francina took Zukisa's hand and for a moment was too overcome by emotion to speak.

"What's wrong?" asked Zukisa, her voice full of concern.

"Nothing, sweetheart," replied Francina. "I'm just happy to be with you."

✧ Chapter Three ✧

Monica saw the question in Dudu's eyes the moment she arrived at work the morning after her trip to Cape Town to see the fertility doctor. In some places it might be inappropriate for an editor to divulge the details of her private battle with infertility to the receptionist, but this was the *Lady Helen Herald*. And besides, Dudu not only answered the telephone, she was the director of design in charge of the weekly newspaper's layout.

Monica shook her head sadly.

Dudu rose from her desk. "I'm sorry. I've been thinking of you all night."

"I've been thinking of me all night, too."

"Will you try again?"

Monica shrugged. How could she adequately explain to a woman who had three children the toll—emotional, physical and financial—that this problem was taking on her and Zak? There were the daily injections, the forced immobility as she lay on a gurney while the ultrasound technologist counted and measured the follicles, as well as the financial drain. Thankfully, she and Zak did not have to go into debt to pay for it, but the weight of it all was sometimes too much to bear. She might not have mortgaged her house, but it sometimes felt as though she'd mortgaged her soul. They'd started trying to have a baby immediately after their marriage, and when their first anniversary had come around with no sign of a pregnancy, they'd gone to a reproductive endocrinologist in Cape Town.

Unexplained fertility. What sort of a diagnosis was that? How could anything be unexplained in this day and age? Scientists were able to clone sheep, for goodness sake. Almost every organ could be transplanted. Why couldn't someone just identify what was wrong with her? Zak obviously didn't have a problem. He already had a daughter. For two years, it had felt to Monica as though she were living suspended in time.

"If you and I both spent last night thinking, then maybe I should make extra strong coffee this morning and not rooibos tea."

Monica nodded and managed a smile. Practical Dudu was a blessing to this office. While her colleague went to make their drinks, she walked into her office and looked at the to-do list she had compiled the previous day. Flower show in Darling. How delightful that had sounded with the prospect of a tiny seed growing in her belly. Now it sounded tedious.

She looked out the window at Main Street. Mama Dlamini was setting out her tables and umbrellas on the sidewalk. Lately, she had taken to leaving the café in the hands of Anna, one of her long-time waitresses, and no one knew where she went. Not even Francina, whose mother-in-law was a good friend of Mama Dlamini.

Main Street ended in a park that ran along the beachfront for about a quarter of a mile, palm trees forming a natural break between the neatly mowed lawn and the white sand. In the middle was a gently sloping grass amphitheater, and behind it a rock garden that flourished with poker-red aloes, pincushion proteas and African heather. Last week, at a concert at the amphitheater, Monica had felt a twinge of nausea that had filled her with hope.

Now she noticed Anna walking up Main Street toward Mama Dlamini's, her youngest child—an eighteen-month-old daughter—wrapped in a blanket on her back. Sighing at the sight of the baby, Monica turned away from the window and sat down heavily in her chair as Dudu walked in with the coffee.

"I'm going to try something new with the layout of this week's issue," said Dudu. "I'll do it early so I can change it if you don't like it."

Monica had noticed lately that Dudu had stopped reporting the escapades of her children. Monica didn't know what was worse, casually curious people who unthinkingly asked when she was going to have a baby, or the unnatural caution of those like Dudu.

"What's Phutole been up to lately?"

Dudu's youngest had been diagnosed with attention deficit and hyperactivity disorder in his second year of school.

"His teacher says she couldn't ask for a more disciplined child. I'm going to take him to Dr. Niemand to see if it's time yet to reduce the dose of his medication."

Dudu never used Zak's first name. Most people in Lady

Helen were on first-name terms, but some felt that doctors ought to be the exception.

Dudu didn't offer any more information about Phutole. Monica was about to tell her that Sipho had been accepted as an exchange student when the switchboard telephone rang, and Dudu hurried out to answer it. Sipho had only two days to decide whether to take the opportunity or not. Even at her strongest, Monica would feel panicked at the thought of letting him go, but as fragile as she was now she could barely bring herself to even consider it. Last night in bed Zak had pulled her close, but he knew her well enough not to rehash the events of the day or offer words of hope for the future, and so he'd merely held her until he'd drifted off to sleep.

She looked at her watch. Nine o'clock. He would be in his office drinking a cup of coffee and checking his mail after his morning rounds. She dialed his number.

"Will going to America really help Sipho get into medical school?"

Monica heard Zak swallow a sip of coffee before answering her. In other countries, students completed a bachelor's degree before applying to medical school, but in South Africa students went to medical school for six years straight out of high school.

"His grades are good enough to get in, but he doesn't have any other interests."

"What about wildlife?"

"Yes, but that translates into hours wandering around in the bush alone, examining insects, birds and plants, and then coming home and studying books."

"He's in the Young Conservationists Club."

"But the members don't really do anything, aside from

sitting around talking about dwindling species. If Sipho goes to America it will show that he has a sense of adventure, that he's up to the challenge of living with people he's never met before, that he has inner strength."

"Mr. D. said his grades are the best in the province."

"Sipho wants to go, Monica."

She was silent.

"The two issues are not related, sweetheart," said Zak softly.

She began to cry. "I know they shouldn't be. It's so hard."

"I feel it, too."

Monica sniffed. "He'll be devastated if we say no."

"He's a good boy. If we have a valid reason to say no, then he'll come to understand."

"But we don't, do we?"

"A mother's concern is valid."

"But he'll be staying with a mother, his host family's mother."

Zak was so good at this—making her fill in the holes of her own argument.

"And we could visit him. I'll find a locum to replace me at the hospital."

"But what about Sipho's end-of-year exams?"

The South African school year, which had started in January, was more than halfway through, but the American school year started in just over a month's time.

"You know Sipho, he could take his exams now and still get straight A's."

Monica heard another voice in Zak's office.

"Sweetheart, Daphne needs me in the ICU. We'll talk when we get home."

Zak's nurse, Daphne, had a three-year-old son, Victor, who was in awe of Mandla. Another eight-year-old might find the attention of a toddler tedious and embarrassing, but not Mandla. He'd showed Victor how to fly a kite, how to play "Row, Row, Row Your Boat" on a drum set of kitchen pots and pans, and he was currently encouraging Victor to take the training wheels off his bike—which made Daphne very anxious, but Victor was itching to do it.

Monica replaced the telephone receiver and looked at her to-do list again. Nothing piqued her interest. Where had her predecessor, Max Andrews, obtained his inspiration all the years he had been editor of the newspaper? If he would just finish writing his memoirs she would find out. He'd been working on them since she took over his job five years ago, and Monica sensed that he didn't want to complete them because he feared that as soon as he did his life would end.

She got up and looked out the window again. The wind must have picked up, since Mama Dlamini had taken down the umbrellas. Spring was still at least a month away, but the warm sunshine had obviously fooled Mama Dlamini into thinking that it might be close. Spring officially started in Lady Helen the day the migratory birds returned to the lagoon. Usually that was after the first of September, and so, while the rest of the country marked the change of season by the calendar, the residents of Lady Helen eagerly scanned the skies for a sign of the homecoming. Sipho would miss the return of the birds this year if he went to the United States. Since coming to live in Lady Helen he had always been at the lagoon when the birds made their return, except once.

Spring was nature's perfect time for birth, but clearly, not for her. And perhaps not ever. She had to consider that it might not be in God's plan for her to give birth. Eggs would be hatching, on Peg's dairy farm there would be glossy-eyed new calves, but Monica's store of lovingly collected baby receiving blankets, booties and onesies would remain in their hiding place, on the top shelf of her closet behind her sweaters, gathering dust and tempting fish moths.

Making a face at her list, she pulled on her jacket and buttoned it up to her chin. She needed a walk in the park, with the wind blowing her hair into the crow's nest that always made Mandla laugh.

Her friend Oscar was leaving the park as she arrived. In the days after her arrival in Lady Helen, he had been a comforting source of help and advice, and he had remained close to the family after Monica and Zak's marriage.

"The wind's unpleasant here, Monica," he said. "What's up?" She shrugged.

"You aren't going for a walk in this weather because you're bursting with the joys of life."

Oscar knew things without being told. And he never repeated anything when it was confided to him. She explained about Sipho, but didn't mention the failed fertility treatment.

"I hitchhiked all the way to Egypt the year I finished school," Oscar said. "My mother didn't get a letter from me for six months."

"Sipho will be with a family."

"My point exactly. You could phone him whenever you wanted. It will be good for him."

It was no secret that Oscar found Sipho a trifle studious, whereas Oscar and Mandla behaved like raucous sailors when they were together. Ever since Mandla first laid eyes on the tattoo of Medusa on Oscar's forearm, he had been intrigued by the man.

"You've got to let them go sometime."

Oscar had no children. He had never even married. But he was probably right.

Oscar had once been in love with a woman from Trinidad, but her father would not let them marry. Since Oscar, a white man, was not allowed to marry a black woman in his home country, the father felt Oscar should not wed his daughter in Trinidad. And then Oscar had fallen in love with Francina while tutoring her for her school exams, but Hercules had snatched her away. He'd arrived in Lady Helen to ask her to give him a second chance, and Francina had agreed.

"Sipho will hold it against you for the rest of his life if you don't let him go," Oscar said now.

"Thanks for the advice," said Monica. She waved and walked off into the wind.

It was colder out than she had anticipated. Winters in Lady Helen were often mild, but there seemed to have been more biting cold days than usual this year. One morning, snow had even appeared on top of the koppies. To Mandla's disappointment, the sun had melted it before the end of the school day. Monica wondered if there would be changes to the weather this summer, which was usually perfect, with hot, dry days, a natural drop in temperature at dusk and cool ocean breezes.

She had forgotten her sunglasses, a necessity even in winter in Lady Helen. The achingly bright light always made the landscape look as though it were begging to be painted. Within fifteen minutes, she could no longer feel her toes because of the cold. She turned and, with her hands stuffed deeply into her pockets for warmth, trudged back to the office.

Sipho didn't say a word about the exchange program when she returned home that afternoon, and for a while she wondered—and hoped—that his enthusiasm had dimmed. But then she saw the acceptance letter waiting for her on the dining room table, which he'd set for dinner. She took her time preparing the salad.

Monica was the last to sit down at the table. Sipho and Zak were staring at the letter. She shook her napkin out slowly and placed it in her lap. Then she poured a glass of water for herself from the carafe.

"I hope I didn't put too much balsamic vinegar in the salad again tonight," she said.

"Mom, please tell me. Am I going or not?"

Monica looked at Zak. Mandla stopped pouring chutney onto his bobotie.

"Do you really want to?"

"Last night I almost chickened out." Sipho's voice caught. "It will be hard for me to leave."

"We're coming to visit you at Christmas," said Mandla.

Zak put up his hands. "I said *if* Sipho went we could visit."

Sipho smiled broadly at his brother.

"You can go," said Monica quietly.

Sipho turned his smile on her, but it was not as broad this time. "Thanks, Mom."

She heard the nervousness in his voice and reached across the table for his hand. Now that the decision had been reached she had to make an effort to bolster his courage.

"It will be an experience you'll remember for the rest of your life."

Monica hoped and prayed that his memories would only be happy.

❧ Chapter Four ❧

On Saturday morning, Francina awoke to the sound of rain falling, and hoped that Zukisa would call off their visit to her aunt in Cape Town. She did not want to leave the warmth of her bed, where Hercules lay as still as a post with the heavy down duvet pulled up to his ears. Francina would never get used to rain in winter. It just didn't seem right. How could the rest of the country get rain in summer and only a small part along the southwestern tip get rain in winter? She hurriedly wrapped herself in the thick cotton dressing gown she had made, while her feet found the fluffy slippers Zukisa and Hercules had given her on her last birthday, and then she left the bedroom, closing the door quietly behind her.

"Good morning, Mom."

Zukisa was already dressed in a corduroy skirt, thick tights and a sweater knitted by Mrs. Shabalala. The sleeves were a little long, the body a little short, but Francina would never have thought of pointing out these faults to her mother-in-law when the creation had been a labor of love.

"I've made porridge, but I didn't want to start the eggs until you and Dad were both up."

Zukisa did not need to mention her aunt. She was ready and eager to depart for Cape Town.

"Should we phone your family to warn them we're coming?"

Zukisa blushed. "I already did. My aunt said to come anytime."

"I'll wake your father then."

Entering her bedroom, Francina felt trepidation, which she tried to brush away by remembering that it was perfectly normal for a good girl such as Zukisa to want to visit her sick aunt. As a Zulu, Francina understood the pull of blood ties. She didn't often dwell on the fact that Zukisa was not her biological daughter, except for times like these when she experienced an irrational fear that the situation could rob her of the girl.

While Hercules dressed, Francina ate the porridge Zukisa had prepared. Mrs. Shabalala emerged in her dressing gown and joined them at the dining room table with a sigh.

"Bad dream?" asked Francina.

Mrs. Shabalala shook her head. "I wish Mama Dlamini hadn't given me such a big slice of cake last night. I didn't sleep well because of it."

Francina wanted to tell her mother-in-law that she didn't have to eat the whole slice, but instead she just smiled. It was difficult for a woman continually trying to lose weight to be close friends with the owner of the best restaurant in town. As two of only a small group of Zulus in Lady Helen, it was obvious that Mrs. Shabalala and Mama Dlamini would become friends, but Francina sometimes wondered if her mother-in-law would make an effort to see her friend every day if the visit didn't include cake and pie. Mrs. Shabalala's marketing always ended with a stop at Mama Dlamini's to catch up on the day's news. Whatever weight Mrs. Shabalala lost through honestly valiant attempts at dieting never stayed off.

"Do you want to come with us to Cape Town, Gogo?" asked Zukisa, using the Zulu term for grandmother.

"I can't. I have to help out at Mama Dlamini's. She's…" Mrs. Shabalala gave a sheepish smile and didn't finish her sentence.

Francina was able to read people, despite her lost eye, and she could tell that her mother-in-law wished that her tongue had not slipped and mentioned Mama Dlamini.

"Why does she need extra help at the café?" she asked casually.

"Oh, it's going to be busy today."

"Is something special going on in town that I don't know about?"

Mrs. Shabalala concentrated on stirring two tablespoons of brown sugar into her porridge.

"Is there something on at the amphitheater today?" Francina persisted.

"Promise you won't tell anyone," said Mrs. Shabalala, looking directly at her.

Francina thought of the irony of needing to keep a secret about Mama Dlamini, who was the town's most efficient reporter of everyone's personal news. "What's Mama Dlamini up to then?" she asked.

Mrs. Shabalala lowered her voice as though there might

be someone listening at the second floor window. "She's moonlighting as a chef at the golf resort."

This was news Francina did not expect. "She's working for Mr. Yang, the fraudster who tried to have everyone evicted from their homes in Sandpiper Drift so he could build another golf course? I thought he was in prison."

"He just got out. His sentence was shortened for good behavior."

"I wonder if Monica knows," said Francina.

Monica, who had helped uncover the fraud that had almost caused the residents of the small neighborhood on the inland edge of the lagoon to lose their homes, had been banned from the golf resort for life. A hostile standoff had existed between the residents of Lady Helen and the resort management ever since Mr. Yang went to prison. Even the two residents of Lady Helen who had washed dishes at the resort and acted as the town's spies had been too disgusted to return. What on earth was Mama Dlamini doing fraternizing with the enemy?

"If she performs well she'll be made head chef of the five star restaurant," said Mrs. Shabalala, answering her daughter-in-law's unspoken question.

"I see," said Francina, when, in fact, she didn't.

"You of all people should understand what that might mean to a woman who grew up poor in a village in KwaZulu-Natal."

There were still mornings Francina wanted to pinch herself to make sure she wasn't dreaming when she saw the shadow cast on the shiny floor of her shop by the gold lettering of the name on the window. But her mother-in-law's observation was only partly astute, because Jabulani Dressmakers was more than enough for Francina, and the café should have been enough for Mama Dlamini. If the woman became head chef at the resort, where would she set her sights next? On cooking for the president? Francina was in favor of ambition if the goal was self-improvement, but runaway ambition was dangerous. And it appeared that Mama Dlamini was afflicted with the dangerous kind. How could Francina not tell Monica?

The flat-topped mountain rising above Cape Town, with its veil of soft white clouds, never failed to impress Francina. Johannesburg had its flat-topped golden mine dumps, but the sight of them had depressed Francina whenever she'd returned from a visit to her beloved province of KwaZulu-Natal. Johannesburg had been her address for more than twenty years, and yet it had never been home. She had resided there to earn a living, because there weren't any jobs close to her village. Her situation had not been different from that of thousands of men who had left their families in the villages to go to Johannesburg to work underground in the gold mines.

It was not natural for men to live in dormitories, separated from their wives for eleven months of the year. Johannesburg was full of girls who had forgotten the lessons their mothers had taught them back in the villages, who did not think twice about going out with another woman's husband. A girl could be seduced by a man who offered a distraction from a life of drudgery pushing a broom down deserted office corridors. How different things might have been if people did not have to leave home to find employment. How many individuals might have been saved from this terrible disease, this pandemic that was stealing more than eight hundred people a day, most in the prime of life?

Hercules said that one day this would all be a chapter in a history textbook, the type of textbook that he used in his classes, teaching his pupils. People didn't realize, he claimed, that they were a part of history in the making, and that the course of history could be changed. If Francina gave Hercules half a chance, he could go on for hours about how this war could have been avoided if only so-and-so had done this instead of that, or the citizens of that country could have been living like kings if only they'd realized sooner that their such-and-such head of state was leading them toward starvation. But to change the path of history, Francina believed, required strong leaders, and no matter where in the world you looked nowadays you could not find ones like the Zulu kings of the past.

Francina smiled at her daughter, who had sat in silence for most of the way to Cape Town, thinking no doubt of her sick aunt. Today might hold a major shift of direction in the history of Francina's own little family. Would she be able to change the course of events, or would the ties she had to her daughter be insignificant compared with the ties of blood?

Cape Town no longer seemed the innocent city where Francina and her family had whiled away happy hours wandering through museums and browsing at outdoor markets. Now it threatened to be forever remembered as the site where the family that Francina had waited half her life for had slipped from her grasp. Johannesburg would seem joyful in comparison. She squeezed her daughter's knee. Zukisa's worried smile only made Francina more uneasy.

The area where Zukisa's aunt lived was undergoing a half-hearted renovation. The blocks of government-subsidized flats were being given coats of fresh paint, teams of municipal workers were attacking the graffiti that lay over the neighborhood like cobwebs, and potholes were being patched. The local government's efforts had been spurred by vocal residents who, sick and tired of the gang activity in the area, had vowed to take the law into their own hands if the authorities didn't act. In other sections of the city, similar groups had burned down houses where suspected drug dealers lived, and so, wanting to avoid such actions, the authorities had promised more frequent police patrols and had thrown in the renovation as an act of good faith.

Hercules parked next to the stairwell that led to Zukisa's aunt's flat. Extra police patrols or not, Francina knew that he would worry about his car until the visit was over.

Zukisa led the way, taking the stairs two at a time. She had already knocked on her aunt's door by the time Francina caught up. From inside came the sound of a blaring television. Zukisa's aunt's grandsons would never do well at school with the amount of television they watched.

Zukisa knocked louder. Still there was no answer. Hercules tried the door. It was unlocked. Francina reminded herself to scold those boys. Imagine leaving the front door unlocked in a neighborhood such as this. Francina and Hercules looked at their daughter. It was her decision whether to enter the flat uninvited. Zukisa pushed open the door.

What Francina noticed first was the smell. Zukisa led them into the kitchen and closed the open cupboard doors. In the sink, a pile of dishes was stacked precariously on top of a roasting pan filled with rancid fat, the source of the stench. Francina rolled up her sleeves and began removing the dirty dishes so she could fill the sink with hot water. Hercules gave her a rueful smile, recognizing this as the first of many contributions his wife would make today, and then followed Zukisa into the living room.

After putting the rancid fat into a plastic bag and sealing it, Francina quickly realized that the roasting pan and dishes would not come clean without a long soak in soapy water. When the sink had filled with hot water, she dried her hands on her dress, since the dish towel was crusted with old food, and hurried to join her daughter and husband.

She found them in the living room, attending to the youngest of Zukisa's aunt's grandchildren, five-year-old Fundiswa. The little girl was eating peanut butter out of a jar with a spoon and watching men wearing only tight pants and masks fight each other in a ring surrounded by thousands of screeching fans. Francina picked up the seat cushions from the floor and put them back on the couch. Zukisa had ascertained from Fundiswa that the boys had not returned since going out the previous night, and that her aunt was sleeping. From the child's delight at seeing Zukisa, it was obvious that the little girl spent a lot of time on her own.

Zukisa looked at her mother, the question clear in her eyes. Francina nodded and followed her toward her aunt's bedroom. Zukisa did not want to be alone when she opened the door.

When Francina saw the figure of Zukisa's aunt asleep on the bed, she was reminded of her father lying in a hospital bed next to a window with a view of the ocean that he never saw. Illness, she had learned, made people seem shrunken, like children again. The last and only time Francina had seen Zukisa's aunt, terror that the woman would not allow Zukisa to be formally adopted had filled her. But although Zukisa's aunt had given the appearance of a strong, gruff lady, underneath she was like every woman trying to make it alone in

the world with too little money and too many responsibilities. She had agreed to Francina becoming Zukisa's
adoptive mother.

"Hello, Auntie," said Zukisa, touching her arm gently.

Her aunt awoke, saw Francina, and for an instant
seemed confused.

"My mother and father brought me to see you," explained Zukisa.

The wonderment of hearing herself called "mother" had
not dimmed over the past years, and Francina doubted it
ever would.

Zukisa's aunt coughed and the wheezing sound made
Francina wince. Zukisa shot Francina a look of helplessness.

"It's my heart," whispered the ill woman. "The doctor
called it congestive heart failure."

Francina had never heard of this disease, but judging
from the tone of her voice and the pallor of her face, it was
serious. Serious enough to warrant full-time care. Full-time
care from a girl who already knew firsthand the commitment
and endurance that would be required. Full-time care from
a girl who should be at school.

In the vain hope that she could distract her daughter
from swirling thoughts of sacrifice, Francina moved around
the room, collecting dirty glasses and a half-empty plate.
Someone—perhaps one of the elderly woman's grandsons—had brought her food, but not stayed to see if it was
eaten. Francina left the room and almost ran into Hercules
outside the door.

"Is it bad?" he asked. For the first time in her life, she
heard fear in her husband's voice.

She nodded.

"Where are those boys?" he asked. "They should be looking after their grandmother and their sister."

The couple looked at the little girl, who waited shyly in the doorway to the living room. Her face and hands were now clean, but her dress needed to be changed. Mercifully, Hercules had turned off the television.

Dear, sweet Hercules. He was the only man Francina knew who thought boys had just as much responsibility as girls to care for an ailing relative.

"They'll come home sooner or later," she said. But her tone was flat, because she knew—as did Hercules—that the kind of boys who left their young sister and sick grandmother and stayed out all night would not be competent caregivers.

"Nothing has been decided yet," said Francina, looking intently into her husband's eyes.

Hercules nodded, but she could tell he didn't buy it. She didn't, either. Before something was said that would make her cry, she hurried to the kitchen to discard the half-eaten food and wash the soaking pan and dishes. When she came out with bacon and cheese sandwiches for Zukisa's aunt and Fundiswa, Hercules was sitting on the couch reading a story to the little girl. Francina wondered if Zukisa's aunt, even when she was well, had had the time to do this. Looking after three grand-children was not easy for a woman her age, especially when she had to keep a job to supplement her meager pension.

When the story was finished, Francina led the little girl to the other bedroom and hunted for a clean dress. There were boys' clothes in all the drawers but not a sign of any dresses. Hercules, aware of her search, began looking around in the living room.

"Found her clothes," he called.

Francina and the child joined him in the other room, where he had discovered a box containing girl's garments on a bookshelf piled with pirated videos.

Francina took the little girl into the bathroom, bathed and dressed her in a clean skirt and T-shirt. As Francina's hands worked, her mind was on another girl, only a few years older, who undoubtedly was contemplating her future.

"That's better," said Hercules, when Francina led the little one out of the bathroom.

At the same time, the door to the aunt's bedroom opened and Zukisa stepped out.

Francina took one look at her face and knew immediately that Zukisa felt she ought to stay. But there was no time for Francina to try and change her mind, because at that moment the boys walked in, bringing with them a stale odor of sweat and cigarettes.

"Howzit going?" the eldest boy asked Zukisa.

He was three years older than her, but only one year ahead of her in school.

"Where have you been, Xoli?" Francina demanded.

Xoli looked at her with surprise, as though she were a bird that had flown through the window. Neither he nor his brother, Bulelani, answered her question.

Francina did not try to drag an answer out of them. "How can you leave your sick grandmother alone all night? And what about your sister? The front door was unlocked. Do you know what could have happened if she'd wandered outside on her own? Are you listening to me?"

Xoli turned on the television.

Francina snapped it off. "This is serious," she yelled.

Zukisa, who rarely heard her mother raise her voice, bowed her head.

"We're going to come back here next week to check on you, and we better find this place in better shape," said Francina.

The boys gave halfhearted nods, but would not meet Francina's eye.

"Let's go, Hercules, Zukisa."

Hercules patted the little girl on the shoulder and took Zukisa's hand.

Before Francina closed the front door, she gave the boys one last searing look and shook her finger at them.

"That should sort them out," she said, going down the stairs.

Zukisa was silent in the car on the way home, and Francina knew she was thinking about moving to Cape Town to help her aunt.

Forgive me, God, my selfish thoughts, Francina prayed silently, *but I cannot bear to think of life without my precious daughter.*

❧ *Chapter Five* ❧

Monica stared at the clock on the kitchen wall, wondering what would be an appropriate time to call a stranger in the United States. The boys were clearing the table after dinner. In America, it would be noon. What time did American church services end? She did not even consider that the family might not attend church.

It had been three weeks since Monica had given Sipho permission to go. The days had passed quickly—too quickly—and now only four remained before his departure, on Friday morning.

Although Sipho had expressed only a casual interest when Monica had mentioned that she'd like to talk to the lady who was going to be his host, she knew that he was curious about the family. Monica hoped she'd be able to form an accurate opinion from her voice alone.

She dialed the string of numbers and waited for the phone

to ring on the other end. It wasn't long before a young person answered, perhaps the boy with whom Sipho would be going to school. He sounded polite and agreed to call his mother. Monica heard high heels clicking on a wooden floor.

"Hello?" The word sounded long in the lady's accent.

Monica explained who she was, and was astonished at the enthusiastic reaction she got.

"I'm so happy you called," said the lady. "I would have done the same in your place." She insisted Monica call her by her first name, Nancy.

Monica did not know how to proceed without making Nancy feel as if she were being interrogated, but there was no need to say another word because the woman spoke enough for both of them. She told Monica all about Houston, about the school Sipho would be attending, the curriculum, sporting activities—Monica didn't have a chance to tell her that these wouldn't be necessary for Sipho—and about the church the family attended.

"He won't object to coming to church with us, will he?" Nancy asked.

"Oh, no," said Monica. "Actually, next year he's going to be a Sunday school teacher at our church."

Monica could only conclude that, aside from the sporting activities, Sipho's life would follow much the same pattern in the United States that it did in South Africa.

The conversation lasted for almost twenty minutes. Nancy did most of the talking. Monica didn't mind, since the purpose of the call was to learn about Sipho's host family. When the two women finally said goodbye, Monica was as reassured as possible for a mother whose son was about to travel thousands of miles away from home.

Sipho was hanging around the doorway to her bedroom when she got off the telephone.

"What did she say?" he asked.

"Phew, a lot. But she sounds nice. And you might not approve, but you will be thoroughly supervised."

"What about her son?"

"He plays a lot of sports."

"Oh." Sipho sounded disappointed.

"But he has other interests. Debating, charity work. Actually, I don't know when he has time to eat, with all his activities. And you don't have to join in with anything you don't want to."

She hoped that he would understand that this piece of advice applied to more than extracurricular activities.

"Did she say if I needed warm clothes?"

Monica laughed. "By the sound of it, Houston might have a shorter and milder winter than we have here on the West Coast. But school uniforms aren't required like here so you need some extra clothes."

"Can you just pick them out?"

Sipho hated shopping. He'd be content if she bought him five identical pairs of pants with five identical shirts. Mandla, on the other hand, always wanted to choose his own clothes. When he was little, he'd refuse to wear anything decorated with tractors, cars or sports logos. The design had to be plain, the fabric soft and nonirritating against his sensitive skin.

Monica had already decided to take off Thursday to help Sipho get ready, and she bargained on getting him to miss school that day. She put the idea to him now.

"I suppose so," he said. "But it will only take ten minutes to throw some clothes into a suitcase."

Most children she knew, Mandla included, would jump at the chance to miss school, but Sipho was a dedicated student. To him, schoolwork was not a chore but a long task to complete before he could do what he really wanted, which was study medicine.

Monica thought that she and Sipho could spend most of the day engaged in their favorite activity: walking, either up the koppies or along the beach. Sipho was an informative companion on these walks. He could name every bird, animal and sea creature that came into view, as well as their diet, habitat and method of reproduction.

"Thanks for letting me go," said Sipho. "I know you don't really want to."

Monica gave him a weak smile. "You'll understand one day when you have children of your own."

"What would my mother have done?"

The question did not take Monica off guard as it had when Sipho first started asking it, when he became a teenager. For years, his own memories of his mother had been enough, but then it seemed to Monica that he had begun to worry that they were becoming hazy, and so he'd started drawing her into this game of hypothetical parenting. She had never sought to eclipse Ella's memory, so she went along with it, even when she wasn't quite sure of the answer. This time, however, she was.

"Your mother lived in South Africa, Zambia, Canada and Cuba. She and her parents left their country of birth against their will, but your mother was an adventurer and made the most of it. She would have wished her sons to do the same, if that's what they wanted."

Sipho nodded, and Monica wondered whether the vision

he had of his mother right now was of her lying sick in bed, or when she was still capable of hiding the disease from her family and friends.

"Can I tell you a secret, Mom?"

"Of course, sweetie."

"I know I should go to America, but I'm not so sure I want to." He searched her face to judge her reaction.

This was one of those moments, Monica knew, when her mettle as a parent was being tested. She wanted to say, "Don't go, stay here with me." But Monica the parent had to weigh her words. She didn't want Sipho to one day regret a missed opportunity. He was scared, understandably so. In his place, Mandla would not be, but Sipho was more cautious. Any change he made was because he had thought it through and made a considered choice to fulfill a purpose.

"You don't have to stay there if you're unhappy," she said.

His eyes lit up. "You won't be disappointed if I want to come home after a month?"

Monica shook her head. The expense of airfare was unimportant. She would be proud that he had conquered his fear of trying something new.

"Well, then that's different," he said.

They heard a car in the driveway. Zak had returned from taking his daughter to her mother's house in Cape Town. The constant moving between two households had, at first, upset Yolanda, and her schoolwork had suffered. But now, at seventeen, in her second to last year in high school, she'd mastered her dual lives with ease. She no longer even bothered to pack a bag, but kept clothes and toiletries at her father's house.

Yolanda's mother had married the man for whom she had left Zak, and although Yolanda had once left home and come to stay in Lady Helen for a while because she did not get on with him, she had learned to live in peace with him. She said, however, that she would never love him because he hadn't respected the sanctity of her parents' marriage.

Zak came through the front door, rubbing his hands together.

"It's freezing out there," he said. He kissed Monica and sat down next to her. "So what have you been doing while I was away?"

"Sipho and I have been talking about his trip to the United States."

"Are you sure you'll be able to get someone to replace you at the hospital over Christmas?" asked Sipho.

Zak nodded. "I'm already looking into it. Don't worry, we'll be there."

"Good. Well, I'd better finish my homework."

"Where is your brother?" asked Zak.

Sipho rolled his eyes. "Writing to one of his pen pals, a girl who lives in Australia. He'd be better off studying."

Mandla was not as committed a student as Sipho, but his report cards were well above average. It had to be difficult having a brother who was the best student in the history of Green Block School.

Sipho went to his bedroom and Zak pulled Monica close. "Are you feeling okay?" he asked.

She sighed. "It's going to be horrible to say goodbye to him."

"We'll see him in four months."

"I know."

"And what about…?"

Monica knew what Zak wanted to ask. "I'm trying not to think about it," she said.

He put both his arms around her. "It'll work out in the end."

She nodded. There was no reason not to believe him. They were both young, both healthy. She leaned her head on his shoulder. The only bright spot in this whole mess was that they were together. Infertility could put tremendous strain on a marriage if both partners weren't in agreement on how much they could take. And she and Zak were both in it till the end, whatever that might be.

The next morning, Monica received yet another call at her office from Ivy, the nurse at the reproductive endocrinologist's office. Ivy wanted to set up an appointment for Monica to collect her medication for the next round of hormone shots.

"I don't know when I can make it to Cape Town," Monica told her.

"You've been putting me off," said Ivy.

Monica explained about Sipho leaving, but even to her this sounded like an excuse.

"Is there anything you want to talk about, Monica?"

"No, nothing's changed. I'm just—"

"You're scared it won't work again."

"Yes," said Monica miserably.

"That's perfectly understandable. But if you don't try, you won't get pregnant."

"I know, I know."

"Call me this afternoon," said Ivy.

"Okay," she agreed.

After she'd put down the telephone, she threw herself into a story she was writing on a local man's research trip to the

Antarctic to study the effects of global warming on seals. But Ivy's words kept coming to her. *If you don't try you won't get pregnant.* Ivy was correct, of course.

At lunchtime, Monica took sandwiches to the hospital and met Zak in his office, intending to discuss Ivy's call. He was exasperated because the hospital's plumbing was acting up, and if the plumber didn't arrive soon the place might be without water by the end of the day.

"Sooner or later we're going to have to lay new pipes," he said.

In the past, Zak had conducted his own fund-raising to finance various pieces of medical equipment, since the government health department's funds were stretched thinly, and needed more urgently in underprivileged areas. It wore him out, though he would never admit it. Monica often suggested he ask someone else to do it for him, but they both knew the benefactors' response to a professional fund-raiser would never be as generous as it was to a desperate doctor. Now it seemed Zak would also be required to raise money for basic infrastructure.

Eating her chicken sandwich, Monica decided this was not the right time to bring up Ivy's call. Neither she nor Zak was in the mood for that conversation.

That afternoon she did not call Ivy back. She left the office early, picked the boys up from home and took them to Main Street to buy new shoes. Sipho couldn't arrive in the United States, the home of designer sneakers, in the worn ones he favored. Mandla, of course, had to have a new pair, too. He joked about using his brother's room when he was gone, and Sipho gave a feeble smile, but Monica could see he was upset to think of life here going on without him. She assured him that upon his return he would find his room exactly as he'd left it, but she was similarly disturbed. Nine months was a long time.

She could tell that Mandla had not yet grasped what it would be like to be separated from his brother. Yolanda would be with them on weekends, but during the week Mandla would be the only child at home. Thank goodness for Zukisa, who Francina brought with her every afternoon.

Three more days and Sipho would be on an airplane flying over thousands of miles of ocean. Monica tried to focus on the wonderful opportunity this trip was for him, but she could only imagine how she'd feel walking into his quiet bedroom when he was gone.

Please God, she prayed, *when the time comes, give me the strength to be able to let Sipho go.*

৯ Chapter Six ৯

Monica heard the alarm go off. She opened one eye and saw Zak standing beside her. He put his palm on her cheek.

"It's time," he said softly.

She groaned. This day had arrived too quickly. She was not ready for it.

"We can't be late," said Zak. "Sipho's already up."

She sat up in bed, realizing that every moment spent here was one less moment she could spend with her son before he left.

It took her only ten minutes to shower, pull her shoulder-length hair into a ponytail and then dress in a suitably somber brown skirt, beige sweater and boots. She appeared in the kitchen with a fake smile on her face to bolster Sipho's confidence, which she knew might be flagging.

"Why can't I go to America, too?" asked Mandla.

Sipho poured milk into his cereal. "Because you're too young."

"I can't have both of you leaving," said Monica, getting out a frying pan to make bacon and eggs. Sipho could not get on a flight with only cereal in his belly.

"Do you promise we'll go at Christmas?" persisted Mandla.

"Of course," said Monica.

When the eggs and bacon were ready, Mandla wolfed his down as usual, but Sipho said he wasn't hungry.

"Come on, eat," she said, feeling for some ridiculous reason that all would be okay if he just ate this plate of bacon and eggs.

He ate slowly, eyeing the clock on the kitchen wall.

"I smell bacon," said Zak, taking a seat beside Sipho.

Monica put two eggs in the pan for him. She looked at the three of them around the breakfast table, the site of so much banter as well as serious discussion in the morning. It would be a long time before they'd all be together here again. Would Sipho come back the same boy he was now? And would she be the same? Or would she be an expectant mother? So many times in the past she had pictured milestones in the future, and she always had a baby with her, or was pregnant. It had seemed easy, a matter of course. Now it seemed possible that Sipho could return from his time abroad to find her as before, unchanged, not pregnant and with no hope.

"Eat up," she urged him. "You don't want to miss your flight."

"Remember to phone us collect when you get to Washington," said Zak.

"Washington, D.C., Dad," said Sipho. "Washington is a state in the Northwest."

Monica was not happy to be reminded of her son having to make a connecting flight all on his own. Zak had told her that Sipho was perfectly capable of finding the gate, and that she was worrying unnecessarily.

"I wonder what kind of car the family will be picking you up in," said Mandla. "They drive *huge* cars in America."

"And don't forget to phone us when you arrive at their home in Houston," said Monica.

"I won't."

"I'm sure the family will allow you to make one international call. After that you can buy a calling card." Monica knew that she had gone through this many times before with him, but she could not help herself. She thought of the time she'd said goodbye to her parents when they'd left South Africa for Italy. She'd returned to her car and sobbed for ages. And now, for a few months every summer, they took up residence right here in the studio apartment in the Old Garage. Her father had never admitted that he could not readjust to the winters in Italy after decades of living in South Africa, but her mother had told Monica of his grumbling. Now, for him every year had two summers: one in the northern hemisphere, where he harvested grapes and vegetables in his small garden and went out fishing in a small boat with his brother and cousins; and one in the southern hemisphere, where he fished with his grandsons from shore and tried to teach them Italian, his mother tongue.

"Are there cowboys where Sipho's going?" Mandla asked curiously.

"Of course not," answered his brother.

"Except when the rodeo comes to town," said Monica. "Your host mother said it was the highlight of the year." She hated calling Nancy that, but that's what she would be for the time Sipho was in the United States.

"Let's load up the car now or we'll be late," said Zak.

It was a ninety-minute drive to the airport in Cape Town. Sipho's airplane would take him first to Johannesburg to pick up more passengers, and then to Dakar, Senegal, where they would land to refuel, but not be permitted to disembark. Twenty-one hours after leaving Cape Town, he would arrive in Washington, D.C. Fortunately, there were many flights from there to Houston, in case he missed his connection.

The boys watched for tortoises on the road to Cape Town, and just after passing the entrance to the nature reserve their vigilance was rewarded with a whole line crossing the road. Zak stopped the car and waited for the stragglers to clear the asphalt.

"Can you imagine if you missed your plane because we had to wait for the tortoises?" he joked.

The West Coast tortoise was a common sighting within the nature reserve, but for some reason the creatures tended to wander outside the boundaries, and the results were often tragic. When he was younger, Sipho would cry when he saw splintered shells scattered across the road.

Mandla was more excitable than usual this morning. Monica wondered if he was anxious about his brother leaving. The boys had never been separated. They'd never expressed the desire to be away from home or each other.

The airport parking lot was full and attendants were directing cars onto a grassy field outside the perimeter fence. Zak lifted Sipho's new hard-shell suitcase out of the trunk, and its wheels sank deep into the mud that remained after an overnight sprinkling of rain. Sipho noticed but did not appear fazed. Grumbling under his breath, Zak carried the suitcase the rest of the way and, once inside the terminal, tried to remove the worst of the mud with tissues. The family joined a long line of passengers that had formed in front of a baggage screening machine.

When it was finally Sipho's turn, Zak heaved the boy's suitcase onto the short conveyor belt and was told by the security staff member to collect it at the other side and then proceed to check-in.

The lady at the check-in office was sympathetic to Monica's pleas to notify the flight attendants that Sipho would be an unaccompanied minor.

"Yes, mam," she said, "it's stated on his ticket."

"I just want to make sure that they know," said Monica defensively.

"I'm fifteen, Mom," Sipho whispered fiercely.

"Yes, a minor," she replied, "and unaccompanied."

Zak put an arm around her shoulders in the same way that Monica's father did whenever her mother was upset. It was strange how one's parents' habitual gestures became one's own. Sometimes she was horrified to find herself commenting on Zak's driving, just as her mother always did with her father, but that was the extent of the similarities between herself and her mother. Mirinda Brunetti was in a class of her own, one that Monica had never aspired to join. The older woman was well-dressed, her graying hair was regularly restored to its former flaxen glory, and, to anyone who didn't know her well, she was completely unaware that she was no longer the femme fatale she had once been when she'd left her small Karoo desert town to become a model in Johannesburg. Her daughter's lack of interest in haute couture had always irritated her, but after years of fruitless cajoling, Mirinda had given up. In private, Zak told Monica that he preferred Monica's natural look to her mother's manufactured one.

The ticket agent leaned over the counter and fastened a colored paper bracelet around Sipho's wrist, identifying him, in large letters, as an unaccompanied minor.

"Happy now, Mom?" he asked with a wry grin.

They stepped aside through the crush of departing passengers and their families, and found a quiet corner to say their final goodbyes. Zak had warned Monica not to prolong this parting or Sipho would be upset. He was right, of course, but it would take considerable effort on her part.

"Take care of yourself," she told Sipho, before wrapping her arms around him.

Despite the change in his voice, he was still a young boy. Well, outwardly anyway; he had always seemed wise and mature beyond his years.

"I'll miss you, Mom," he whispered in her ear.

"We'll see you soon," she whispered back.

It was Zak's turn to hug him next. "Goodbye, Sipho," he said in a voice full of emotion. "We're here for you, so phone anytime."

Mandla and Sipho's goodbye was awkward since they were not used to hugging each other. Sipho looked genuinely sad about leaving his brother, but Mandla pulled away, smiling and talking about his own trip to the United States at Christmas. His sibling's absence would sink in over the next few days, Monica suspected.

Sipho, always a worrier, did not want to go to the boarding area at the last minute, and so, although they could have spent more time together, the family escorted him to the security checkpoint through which only travelers could proceed.

Monica stole one more hug before he joined the throng showing passports to a uniformed security guard. Sipho turned around and waved once. Monica fought back her tears.

Zak put an arm around her shoulders and Mandla took her hand. "It's only four months," she murmured. But it was not only the time, it was the distance, too, and the fact that Sipho was going to another country. In his luggage was a collection of his favorite books on African animals and marine life, as well as a photo of his family and one of his late mother, Ella. How would her son cope in a new place, where these things were of no importance to anyone but himself? He would truly be alone.

Mandla wanted to watch Sipho's plane take off, but since that wouldn't happen for at least an hour, Zak suggested they watch another plane instead.

"It's not the same," said Mandla, accepting the deal.

Despite his grumbling, he was thrilled by the sight of a massive airliner leaving the ground, and all the way back to the car he complained about the unfairness of Sipho going to America and not him.

"Aren't you a little young to think about leaving us?" asked Monica, expecting him to give his usual sheepish smile before hugging her and promising her his undying love.

"I suppose so," he said, carefully weighing his answer. "But I might have to go one day."

She shot Zak a tearful look, but he was engrossed in rifling through his pockets for the parking ticket. If she had been alone, she would have locked herself in the car to sob her eyes out, just as she'd done the day her parents had left South Africa.

Monica and Zak were both quiet on the return journey. Zak knew better than to try to cheer her up by telling her that four months would pass quickly, that Sipho would adjust, that he was a resilient boy. But Mandla could not bear the silence and filled it with his chatter. Nothing escaped a comment from him—other cars, shacks built close to the freeway, people trying to cross the highway on foot. And when they turned onto the road that led north to Lady Helen, he attempted, without much success, to recall the names of the birds he spotted, the plants Sipho had identified for them on countless other trips, the insects that spattered against the windshield.

Monica and Zak dropped him off at school just as recess was ending, which caused him to groan in disappointment.

Zak then drove to Monica's office on Main Street.

"Will you be okay?" he asked tenderly.

She nodded. "I'll be busy, which is good."

"Do you want to come to the hospital for lunch?"

She patted his hand. "You've missed your morning rounds. You'll need the time to catch up. Really, I'll be fine."

He kissed her and waited until she had opened the front door to the newspaper office before driving off.

Monica had wondered how long it would take Mandla to feel his brother's absence, and was surprised when he started moping around the house after only three days. Sipho had called from Washington, D.C., to tell them that his flight had been uneventful, and then he'd called again from his host family's home to say that he'd been met on time and made to feel welcome. Their family car, he'd told Mandla, was an enormous sport utility vehicle with three rows of seats.

Mandla asked Monica to rent a movie filmed in Houston so that he could see where his brother was living, but she couldn't think of any. She showed him pictures on the Internet instead.

Francina reported to Monica on Monday evening, after Sipho's first weekend away, that Mandla had begged Zukisa to play games with him, and although Zukisa had taken as much time from her homework as she could spare, it hadn't been enough for Mandla.

"He's like a fisherman without a boat," observed Francina.

Ivy called again to tell Monica that it was too late to start her treatment this month, but if she collected her medication soon could start giving herself shots next month. Monica managed to put the nurse off by saying she needed to discuss matters with her husband, although she couldn't seem to force herself to broach the subject with Zak. And Zak never mentioned it, either. It was as though they'd lost the road they were following, but neither of them had the courage to admit it.

❧ Chapter Seven ❧

The telephone rang early on Saturday morning, two weeks after Francina and her family's last visit to Zukisa's aunt, and before Hercules had even picked it up, Francina knew that was who was calling. Hercules listened for a minute and then went to wake Zukisa.

"Is she okay?" Francina whispered to her husband, as Zukisa took the receiver.

"I don't know," he whispered back.

They watched their daughter's bowed head as she talked quietly to her aunt and then replaced the receiver with care. She took a long time to face them, so long that Francina knew what to expect.

"My aunt wants me to look after her," said Zukisa quietly. She waited for them to react, and when they didn't, she added, "She said family comes first."

Francina felt as though she might faint. "We are your family, too," she said in an unsteady voice.

Hercules took her hand.

A sob caught in Francina's throat. "We have court papers to prove that you are our legally adopted daughter."

Zukisa began to cry, and Francina realized that she had been wrong to show her distress. She gathered her daughter in her arms and wiped the tears from her face.

"I don't want to go, Mom," she whispered. "But my late father would expect me to look after his sister. She was very good to us when my mother was sick."

"I know, I know," crooned Francina, rocking Zukisa like a baby.

"I'll fall behind in school. What if I can't go back?" she lamented.

"Over my dead body," said Francina, and then immediately regretted her choice of words. She softened her tone. "You're not going to end up like me, a woman without an education, cleaning, washing and cooking for someone else. You might have to repeat the year, but you will be back."

"Don't worry about your education," said Hercules. "I will bring you the course material and, if you have time to do homework, I'll take it to your teacher. We'll all get through this. Won't we, Francina?"

"Yes, we will," she said in a strong voice that belied her trepidation.

As Hercules drove them to Cape Town, Francina thought of Monica's trip to the same city one week earlier, to take Sipho to the airport. Fifteen years ago, when she was still a housekeeper in the employ of Monica's mother,

Francina would never have thought that she and Monica would ever share common experiences, but now they both, with heavy hearts, had to drop their children off in Cape Town with a suitcase full of clothes. God certainly worked in mysterious ways.

Zukisa's aunt's flat was again unlocked, even dirtier than the last time, and as before, the boys were nowhere to be seen. Fundiswa, dressed in a grubby nightgown, was asleep on the bed next to her grandmother.

Zukisa's aunt held out her hand to her niece. "Thank you for coming," she said. And then, addressing Francina, she said, "Thank you, my dear, for bringing her back."

Francina felt tempted to remind the woman that this was only a short-term arrangement, but thought better of it because of the larger significance her words might take on. The aunt's time left on this earth might be short.

The boys arrived home after Francina and Hercules had spent an hour cleaning the flat.

Francina wanted to shout, "Where have you been?" but she allowed her daughter to lead the conversation.

"Granny didn't take her medicine last night," said Zukisa.

Xoli shrugged. "I put it next to her bed."

"Yes, but she needs water to take it," answered Zukisa.

He shrugged again. "I can't be expected to think of everything."

"And how can you leave your sister alone?"

Francina had never heard Zukisa use this tone of voice with anyone before. From the boys' expressions, they were as surprised as Francina.

"Things will have to change around here," Zukisa continued in the same tone. "Granny has been looking after you for most of your life, and now it's time for you to do something for her. And you'll start by cleaning this flat. It's filthy."

"Who put you in charge?" asked Xoli.

"I put myself in charge," said Zukisa. "Now start cleaning."

Complaining bitterly, the boys shuffled off to the kitchen.

"Good girl," said Francina, hugging her daughter.

She noticed Hercules blinking furiously and knew that he was more upset than he would let on to be leaving her here.

"How long—?" he began in a strangled voice.

And in the silence of his unfinished question, Francina felt God directing her toward the answer. He wanted her to find the children's mother, Lucy, and bring her back. But how could that be? Lucy was a drunk. She couldn't take care of herself, let alone three children and her elderly mother.

Francina told Hercules what she believed to be God's plan. "The person who should be caring for Zukisa's aunt and the children is Lucy, the woman who abandoned them four years ago."

His face showed incredulity. "But the children have not seen her since she left, when Fundiswa was one year old."

Lucy had divorced the boys' father years ago and he had not been heard from since. Nobody knew the identity of Fundiswa's father.

Francina saw that Zukisa's eyes had brightened at the possibility of Lucy's return, and she realized how hard this all was for her daughter.

"I don't know why God is directing me to find a woman with a drinking problem," said Francina, "but perhaps it's in His plan for me to help her. We have to start searching immediately. Zukisa, can you see if your aunt has a photograph of her daughter, and also try and find out her last known address."

Zukisa bustled off to her aunt's room.

"Are you sure you want to start the search today?" Hercules asked his wife.

"The sooner we find Lucy, the sooner we can…" Francina didn't say what was in her mind: *…the sooner we can take our daughter home.*

"And how will we persuade this woman to come back and give up drinking? She has an addiction that has kept her from her children for years."

Francina would not allow her practical husband to dampen her enthusiasm. "This is God's plan. He will help us," she replied in a firm tone.

Hercules knew better than to argue with that.

Zukisa returned with a dog-eared photograph of a woman smiling dreamily at the camera. In her arms, she held a newborn baby, her daughter.

"My aunt says that the last time she heard from her she was staying at the Dorchester Hotel. But that was more than a year ago, and she doesn't have the address."

"Well, that's where we'll start then," said Francina. "Will you be okay if we leave now, Zukisa?"

The apprehension on her face belied her confident nod. Francina pulled her close and kissed her on the forehead. "You are a good girl."

Zukisa wrapped her arms around Francina's neck. "I love you, Mother."

"I love you, too."

Zukisa hugged her father's middle. "I'll miss you."

"Don't worry. We'll be here more often than you can imagine."

His tone was jovial, but Francina could tell that her husband was deeply disturbed.

"Don't go outdoors," he told Zukisa. "We'll bring you groceries, and if you need anything in an emergency, send one of the boys to get it."

Zukisa nodded.

"And don't open the door to anyone."

"Yes, Father."

The boys appeared from the kitchen, Xoli with a broom, Bulelani with a mop. From the way they held them, like swords, it was clear that cleaning was a new experience.

"You start on your bedroom," Francina instructed Xoli. "And Bulelani, you can put down that mop and get a duster."

The youngest boy dropped the mop on the floor where he stood, and stalked back into the kitchen. It was obvious that Zukisa had a challenge on her hands.

"We had better start our search," said Francina, taking the photograph. She bent down and stroked Fundiswa's cheek. How different this little girl's existence would be if her mother came back into it. There were many things in life that one could not change, but this was one instance where Francina and Hercules might make a difference.

They stood at the door, hugging their daughter in unison, neither wanting to pull away. Then Zukisa's aunt called from the bedroom. In the end, it was Zukisa who broke from the embrace.

"Every night I thank God for bringing you to me," she said. "Now you'd better get going so I can lock the door behind you."

Francina and Hercules raced down the stairs with surging energy. The sooner they found Lucy in Cape Town, the sooner they'd get their daughter back. Neither thought about what would happen if Lucy didn't want to return, or how difficult it would be to help her to give up drinking.

✎ *Chapter Eight* ✎

Francina and Hercules did not have a street address for the Dorchester Hotel, but she called the one person who could find anything if she put her mind to it: Monica.

Five minutes later, Francina's cell phone rang. Monica said that the hotel no longer had a number listed, but she had an address for it.

"Why are you going to that part of Cape Town?" she asked worriedly.

Francina explained the situation briefly.

"Be careful. That's a drug neighborhood."

Francina assured her that they would get a police escort if necessary. Monica took particular care about where and when she drove. She knew firsthand the trauma of having a gun pointed at her face, and being forced out of her car. Francina still could not think about Monica's carjacking without choking up. The Brunetti family had almost lost their daughter that day. If a kind taxi driver had not found Monica lying wounded on the side of the road, and taken her to the hospital, she would have died.

Francina relayed Monica's warning to Hercules, and his knuckles whitened on the steering wheel. Francina reminded him that they could ask for police help if they thought they needed it.

"I doubt they'd waste manpower on a search for a woman who has not been taken against her will," he said.

He was right, of course, but this was the only way they'd get their daughter back.

Monica was correct about the neighborhood; the Victorian facades of the buildings were covered in colorful graffiti and the little park at the corner was overrun with weeds and filled with rubbish. Francina tried to imagine elegantly dressed women strolling down these sidewalks in a different era. Some would say a gentler era, but not those who'd lived in poverty and oppression, without any rights in their own country.

Hercules drove slowly down the street, looking for numbers on the buildings, but most of them had disappeared.

"We can ask someone," ventured Francina.

There was not a soul about.

"Stop at that corner shop."

Hercules parked the car outside the store and insisted on going inside with Francina.

There were bars on the windows. A loud bell sounded when he pushed open the door. A petite Indian man behind the counter asked if he could help them.

As soon as Francina mentioned the name of the hotel, the shopkeeper shook his head. "That closed down two years ago," he said. "Someone set fire to the top floor. The owners were charged with insurance fraud, but the case was thrown out because of a lack of evidence."

Francina's heart sank as she saw their only lead come to nothing.

"There are still people living there," added the shop-keeper. "Legally, illegally, I don't ask questions."

Buoyed by the prospect that their search might not be in vain, Francina looked around the shop for something to buy so as not to appear ungrateful for the man's assistance. She selected a packet of butterscotch drops and took two cold drinks from the fridge. After paying and thanking the shop-keeper, she and Hercules got back into the car and drove slowly down the street, looking for the building with the burned out top floor. It did not take long to find it, but Hercules drove straight past when a group of young men who had been walking down the sidewalk stopped outside. There appeared to be an argument going on; eight youths were shouting at once. Hercules stopped the car a block away from the building, and he and Francina turned and watched.

A punch was thrown and the group jostled into a circle to give two combatants a stage.

"What if one of them takes out a gun?" asked Francina.

"Then we drive away as fast as we can," replied Hercules.

But that didn't happen. The cries grew louder and louder, and then Francina realized she was hearing a different voice, that of a woman. On top of the short staircase leading to the front entrance of the hotel, an elderly woman was waving a rifle at the young men. The two youths who had been fighting stopped rolling on the sidewalk and stared at her in astonishment. The group grew silent and Francina and

Hercules were able to hear what the woman was saying. Her language was crude, but her meaning was clear: if the youths didn't go away she would shoot them.

The young men on the ground picked themselves up and the whole group skulked off. When they were several yards away—in line with Francina and Hercules's car—they shouted obscenities at the lady and promised they'd make her sorry for threatening them.

The old woman took aim, and the gang took off, running. Francina watched her go back inside the building, her shoulders shaking with laughter.

"She's the one who'll help us," said Francina.

Hercules let out a slow breath as he turned the car around and drove back to the burned out hotel.

The smell of cooking meat hung in the air as Hercules and Francina stood outside the door. They decided that this was probably the entrance to a common area in the building, and Hercules tried the door handle. It was locked. He knocked. When there was no reply, he knocked again, more loudly. A key turned in the lock and the nose of a rifle appeared through a crack in the door.

"If you've come back for more, then that's what you'll get," screamed a voice. A string of profanities followed.

The door opened wider, and Hercules and Francina found themselves staring into the wild eyes of the old lady.

"What do you want?" she asked.

Francina thought it better if she, and not Hercules, explained the reason for their visit.

"I remember that one," said the lady, looking at the photograph. "But she's not here anymore. I run a clean house and she wouldn't play by the rules."

"The rules?" said Francina.

"No drugs, no alcohol. I'll take you in if you're poor, but I won't tolerate any nonsense."

The hotel had been abandoned by its owner after the fire, and the old woman had moved in as its unofficial new manager. She cooked and cleaned, and residents paid her whatever they could afford. Zukisa's cousin had been able to pay her way, but her money, said the lady, was dirty. The words she used to describe what Lucy did for a living made Hercules blush.

"Do you know where she is now?" asked Francina.

The woman shook her head. "She was involved with a bad character. Her room was always full of stuff—stolen stuff. She told me he had a business in Orange Grove. Business, my eye!"

Francina looked at Hercules. The name of the area meant nothing to him, since he had lived most of his life in Dundee, KwaZulu-Natal, but she knew that it was a neighborhood in Johannesburg. Her heart sank as she thought of leaving Zukisa in that flat.

"Is there anyone here who might have her address?" asked Hercules.

"No, my tenants move all the time. Sometimes they go back to their families. Sometimes they find a job in another town."

Francina and Hercules thanked the old lady and returned to their car. As they drove down the street, they saw the same group of young men sitting in the park, passing a carton of liquor around, cigarettes dangling from their lips, the fight— and perhaps the old lady—forgotten.

"Can we go to Johannesburg tomorrow?" asked Francina.

"I'll have to speak to Mr. D., the principal, tomorrow morning before he leaves for church. If he can't substitute for me on Monday, then I'll have to wait until a replacement can be found. Who will look after Mandla?"

"He can go to Monica's office after school. She'll understand how important the search for Lucy is."

They didn't speak much on the journey back to Lady Helen. Francina knew firsthand how big Orange Grove was. Looking for Lucy was going to be like looking for a single locust in a whole hillside of mielie plants.

Hercules's mother was sweeping the shop when they arrived home. "How long is Zukisa going to be away?" she asked.

"I don't know, Mama," said Hercules. "Her aunt is gravely ill."

"But what about the grandsons? Why can't they manage? You would have been able to at their age."

Hercules smiled weakly. "Yes, but not all boys were raised by a mother like you."

Mrs. Shabalala was not to be appeased. "Why should we have to give up our child?"

Francina gently touched her mother-in-law's arm. "Zukisa came as a gift to us from her aunt. We have to remember that."

Mrs. Shabalala nodded, as though in agreement, but Francina had never seen such agitation on her face before. She explained the plan for finding Lucy and helping her, so that she could take care of her family.

Mrs. Shabalala's eyes lit up as she listened. "Yes, yes. You must go to Johannesburg and find her. Leave tomorrow morning. I'll pack you breakfast and lunch so you won't have to stop for food."

"Thank you, Mother," said Hercules. "I'll have to speak to Mr. D. first."

"He'll give you permission to go, if he knows what's good

for him. You're the best teacher the school has." Mrs. Shaba-lala picked up her broom and started up the stairs to the family's living quarters. "Hurry up," she called. "You have to pack your suitcases."

Francina and Hercules looked at each other. It was real. They were actually going off to Johannesburg tomorrow morning to comb the streets for a woman they had never met and who might not wish to speak to them, never mind come home with them. But this was God's plan. He would help them in their search. Francina was certain.

⁂ Chapter Nine ⁂

Monica sat at her desk, reading the week's letters to the editor. Sometimes these were reactions to a story she had written in the previous issue, other times they were complaints—about potholes, the postman missing a day of work, the high price of drinking water, all of which would be better directed to the mayor. Only three letters to the editor made it into the pages of the newspaper each week, but Monica still tried to answer all the others personally, even if only with a line or two.

Francina and Hercules had left yesterday morning for Johannesburg, and Mandla was looking forward to coming to her office this afternoon after school. The first week without his brother had been tough on him, and now that he wouldn't have Zukisa to pester every afternoon, Monica would have to work hard to amuse him. She hoped that Francina and Hercules would find Zukisa's cousin and manage to help her give up drinking so that she was capable of returning to look after her children.

Shortly after she and Dudu had finished their tea break, Zak arrived at her office.

"To what do I owe this honor?" she teased.

He closed the door so Dudu wouldn't hear their conversation, then he sat down heavily in the chair across the desk from Monica.

"Jacqueline and her husband want to move to Australia." His expression was deadpan, but Monica knew his emotions always roiled when he was forced to deal with situations created by his ex-wife.

"And Yolanda?"

Zak took off his glasses and rubbed his eyes, as he often did when he was exhausted. "Jacqueline asked me if they could take her along."

"You'd never give permission, would you?"

He shook his head. "I told Jacqueline that. But she's the most manipulative person I've ever met. We both know she's not to be trusted."

This was the first time Zak had spoken openly of his ex-wife's infidelity. His reluctance to do so in the past had never bothered Monica, because she did not want to be reminded that he had once been perfectly happy with Jacqueline.

"But she can't take Yolanda out of the country unless you agree."

"Monica, what if Yolanda chooses to go with her mother?"

Monica moved around the desk and took his hand. "I can't believe she'd ever leave you."

Zak sighed. "I'm going to phone her this afternoon when her mother's at work and tell her to find her passport. And then I'm going to drive to Cape Town to get it." He sounded so tense Monica wondered how he would make it through the hours until it was time to go.

Later that afternoon, he phoned to report that Yolanda had searched for her passport and it was not to be found.

"I knew Jacqueline would try something," said Zak. "I'm going to call the police."

"Are you sure that's—"

Zak didn't allow her to finish. "I can't do nothing."

She had only wanted to ask if that was the appropriate first step. Perhaps he should consider speaking to Jacqueline first. If his ex-wife knew that he was onto her plan, then she might not carry it out.

"What about talking to Jacqueline?" Monica said quietly.

"You don't know that woman. When her mind is made up, nothing can change it."

His words stung; Monica knew he was referring to the efforts he had made to hold his first marriage together, even after he'd discovered that Jacqueline had been unfaithful.

"Maybe I should pick up Yolanda on Saturday morning as usual and then never take her home."

This was the most irrational statement Monica had ever heard Zak make. He was more upset than she'd thought.

"Do you want me to come to the hospital now?" she asked.

"No, we'll talk about it tonight. I have patients to see."

Monica hoped that he would calm down enough to do his work with a clear head.

That evening Zak announced that he was going to have a word with Jacqueline and scare her out of doing what he knew she was planning.

"Good," said Monica.

For the rest of the evening, he didn't say another word about it. But Monica could tell the situation still played heavily on his mind, from the way Mandla had to keep reminding him it was his turn in their board game.

✤ Chapter Ten ✤

The sound of doors slamming woke Francina from her deep sleep. For a few seconds she could not remember where she was. Then she recalled the long, tedious drive to Johannesburg and checking into this hotel near the airport. The room, not much bigger than an office cubicle, was fitted with a bunk bed, a dresser and a tiny television. There was no en suite bathroom, but Francina had noted the communal facilities when they'd arrived last night, after midnight. Now, leaving Hercules asleep on the top bunk, she hurriedly pulled on her clothes, grabbed her toiletry bag and left the room, taking care not to let the door slam. The bathroom was entered by pushing a button on the outside wall, which not only unlocked the door, but, to Francina's shock, also started the shower inside. In an instant her clothes were drenched. On the wall was an automatic soap, shampoo and conditioner dispenser, and a timer ticking down the minutes from ten. Afraid of not finishing in time and being left all soaped up, Francina quickly undressed, hung her clean clothes on a hook out of reach of the spray, and stepped into the shower.

After she was done, she left the bathroom and heard the water inside go on at full force. Wondering if she had done something wrong in this fancy, futuristic bathroom, she tried to go back in, but the door remained locked.

"It's disinfecting itself," said a bemused woman walking by with a little child. "I almost jumped out of my skin when I first heard that noise."

"I wish I could get my bathroom at home to do that," replied Francina, chuckling.

She quickly found her room and entered by waving a hotel ID card at a flashing pad next to the door. Hercules was awake and checking the weather on the television.

"I thought that the beds might have made themselves while I was away," said Francina. She told Hercules about the shower.

He didn't find it amusing. "There are a lot of people out of work in this country. I don't know why the government allowed this foreign hotel chain to establish here, if it wasn't going to hire locals."

Sometimes Francina wished that Hercules's could just laugh without thinking. Delayed laughter was never as good. Hercules, of course, would say the opposite, that nothing could be more amusing than an intelligent joke.

The weather that day would be mild, and since it didn't rain in Johannesburg in winter, in Francina's opinion there had been no need for him to even check the weather. But that was Hercules: always prepared.

As she tidied their belongings—just in case the room decided to vacuum itself while they were away—her thoughts turned to Zukisa, who would be preparing breakfast right now for those infuriating boys and their sweet little sister. At fourteen, Zukisa was more capable in the kitchen than some adults, but Francina still worried about her daughter. The scars that ran from Zukisa's chest to her knees were a reminder of how this little girl had always assumed roles beyond her years. Her injury had happened when Zukisa had been boiling water to make pap for her family and had tripped over a dish towel.

"For breakfast, shall we finish the leftovers from our trip?" she asked Hercules, knowing he would say yes because he hated to waste food. The faster they got to Orange Grove to look for Zukisa's cousin, the faster they'd get home to Zukisa.

They ate the cheese, nuts and crackers in silence, Francina thinking of the words she would use to persuade Lucy to come home, Hercules poring over a map of Johannesburg and plotting his route. Francina admired his courage for undertaking to drive in a city he did not know. She didn't drive, but if she did, she wouldn't be inclined to do it in Johannesburg, where drivers flashed lights for cars to move aside, tailgated and used the emergency lanes for passing. Whenever she'd traveled by minibus taxi in Johannesburg, she would shut her eyes and pray.

Orange Grove might once have been a rural area east of downtown Johannesburg, befitting of its name, but the land was now divided into postage stamp-size lots. The main street through the neighborhood was a blur of restaurants, nonprofit organizations, music studios, dance halls and barbershops.

Francina rolled up her window and instructed Hercules to do the same.

"Look at all these men wanting to wash our windshield," she said. "Any one of them could be a crook who'll grab my purse."

"Or they're just honest people who can't find work and are doing the best they can," said Hercules.

Francina shot him a warning look and he rolled up his window.

"Where on earth do we start looking for Lucy?" she moaned.

Hercules stopped at a red light and a man began to wash their windshield.

"We just got it cleaned two blocks back," yelled Francina through the closed window.

The fellow ignored her and continued swiping away at the soapy suds with a rubber squeegee. Hercules opened his window and dropped some coins into the man's upturned hand. The light changed before he could begin clearing the passenger side, and Francina was furious to find herself peering through a curtain of white soap.

"I don't know why you pay these people," she muttered. "Look at this. I can't see where we're going."

"Would you like to argue with them?" Hercules asked calmly. "They might throw a stone at the back of our car if I don't pay."

"Extortion. That's what it is. Everywhere I look nowadays I see extortion. From these guys to the so-called parking attendants."

"According to that sign we just passed, we've left Orange Grove," said Hercules, ignoring his wife's tirade. "I'll turn around, and we can start at the first business establishment, working our way back down the road."

Francina was grateful to have levelheaded, practical Hercules to bring her to her senses. There was something more important at stake than menacing panhandlers. She took the out-of-date photograph of Lucy from her purse and handed it to Hercules. Until she calmed down, it would be better if he did the talking.

A barber shook his head and said that he'd never seen Lucy before. "You should come back at night when all the runaway kids are sleeping in the doorways," he said.

Francina examined the photograph again. Zukisa's aunt had said that Lucy had been twenty-eight when it was taken, but the barber could not be blamed for presuming that she was a kid, because she looked no older than fifteen.

"Lucy's not a runaway," she told him. Not technically, anyway. She hadn't snuck out in the dead of night; she'd calmly told her family that she was leaving to live on her own in Cape Town. Which, in Francina's mind, was even more cruel.

Three hours later they had entered every establishment on one side of the main road in Orange Grove. Nobody had laid eyes on Lucy. Francina was close to tears. What if she had moved on from here? A person could disappear for good in the huge black hole that was Johannesburg.

"Let's have something to drink in that café," said Hercules, pointing towards the other side of the street. "And then we can carry on the search."

Francina leaned heavily on his arm as they crossed the road. She felt weak from thirst and disappointment at not finding a single lead. Each day spent away from Zukisa was a day too long. She knew her thoughts should have been more compassionate, but she could not understand how Lucy could have walked out on her children.

"Everybody deserves a second chance," said Hercules as they sat down at a round table covered with a red-checked, plastic tablecloth.

"What was that?" asked Francina, thinking that either her ears had deceived or her husband had gained the power to read her mind.

Hercules pointed at a headline on a newspaper next to the shop counter: Fraudster Pays Back Millions to Scam Victims.

"Humph," said Francina. She was so eager for the cold drink Hercules had taken from the refrigerator in the café that she chose not to comment.

They sipped their drinks and stared glumly out of the window at the pedestrians on the street. The task of finding Lucy was beginning to seem so monumental Francina wasn't sure they'd have time to tackle it properly. Hercules couldn't stay away from Green Block School for more than a week.

"I'll do the talking this side of the street," she told him.

He agreed without an argument, which told her that he, too, was growing frustrated.

The café owner was no help, nor were the employees of the next four stores. When Francina showed Lucy's photograph to a lady wiping tables outside an Italian restaurant, there was a brief flash of recognition in her eyes.

"I think I've seen her before," said the waitress. "But that photo was taken awhile ago. She looks very different now."

"You mean like a drinker?" asked Francina.

The lady nodded.

This was the fragile thread they'd been hoping for. Lucy had been here, after all. Their journey had not been in vain.

They continued their search with renewed energy, suggesting to everyone they approached that the young woman in the photograph looked older and a little worn now. After ten more stores, two beauty salons, three restaurants and a church, their hope had dwindled.

Francina was so exhausted she longed to go back to the car to nap, but there were three more blocks to explore.

"If only we had a more recent photograph," she lamented.

Outside an electronics store, an elderly lady sat on the sidewalk behind an upturned milk crate, with small bags of potatoes and onions for sale. Francina watched in resignation as Hercules held Lucy's photograph out to her. What was the point, Francina wondered, in showing it to someone with only a makeshift business in the area? And why bother even carrying on, when the whole exercise was turning out to be pointless?

"Pretty girl," said the lady, studying it closely.

Yes, yes, thought Francina, *but we don't have time for a chat.* The poor woman was probably lonely. Why was she out on the street trying to earn money at her age? Nice sons and daughters she had. Francina longed to sink into the passenger seat of their car and rest her aching feet. She wished Hercules would retrieve the photograph so they could leave. Standing still was even harder on her feet than walking.

"Terrible, terrible," the vegetable vendor was muttering.

The poor woman was losing her mind. Francina sent Hercules a look imploring him to move on.

"What was terrible?" he asked.

Oh, Hercules. It's sweet to offer an ear to a lonely soul, but not now.

"He didn't even stop." The lady clicked her tongue in disapproval.

"Who didn't stop?" asked Hercules gently.

"The driver who hit her."

Francina moved in closer. "The woman in this photograph was hit by a car?"

The woman nodded. "Right in front of my eyes."

"But nobody else mentioned that," said Francina.

Seemingly unperturbed that the veracity of her words was in doubt, the lady continued in a quavering voice. "I arrive here early each day, at about five. I don't know why she was still drunk at that time of the morning, but she stepped right in front of the car. The only people around were some street children and a boy selling newspapers."

The woman was telling the truth, Francina suddenly knew. Her ability to read people the instant she met them had let her down for the very first time.

"Did she die?" Francina held her breath, waiting for a response to her question.

The lady shook her head. "She was still alive when the ambulance took her to the hospital."

Francina sighed with relief. "When did this happen?"

"Maybe two, three months ago."

Francina's heart sank. Lucy would have already been discharged from hospital. Their search had come to another dead end.

Hercules asked if the lady knew which hospital Lucy had been taken to, but, of course, she didn't.

"We'll try them all," he said.

Francina's mood brightened as she realized that the hospital might have an address on record for Lucy.

"Thank you, for your help," she said. "We'll buy all your potatoes and onions." She turned to Hercules. "Please pay the lady."

Both Hercules and the woman looked at her as though she had appeared in town wearing pajamas. Hercules's raised eyebrows said, "What are we going to do with fifteen bags of potatoes and onions?"

"You should go home and rest," Francina told the lady. She came close to expressing her outrage that the woman was sitting out here in the first place, but she didn't want to hurt her feelings. No matter how ungrateful her children were, the lady loved them as any mother would.

Hercules handed over the money.

"God bless you, my children," the vendor said, as Francina and Hercules left with all her vegetables.

At the car, Hercules set down the bags so he could find his keys. "What on earth are we going to do with all these potatoes in a hotel room?" he asked.

Francina lifted her shoulders then dropped them. "We'll make a plan."

They spent the rest of the afternoon visiting the hospitals closest to the site of the accident. None had a record of Lucy ever being admitted.

That evening, at their space-age cubicle hotel, they locked the vegetables in the trunk of their car. They were exhausted and would have been despondent if they didn't still have Johannesburg's largest hospital to try the next morning.

"She must have gone there," said Francina, as she got into the lower bunk.

Neither mentioned the real possibility that even if Lucy had been admitted to this hospital, she might not have survived.

For Zukisa's sake, thought Francina—for *all* their sakes—Lucy had to be alive.

❧ *Chapter Eleven* ❧

Johannesburg's main hospital sat high on a ridge overlooking the leafy neighborhoods north of downtown. As Francina and Hercules crossed the parking lot to the reception area, she thought of the day she had stepped out of a taxi after traveling all the way from Lady Helen to Durban to see her father in the tall hospital that overlooked the ocean. He had held on to life until she arrived.

Francina's only other experience with a hospital had been after her first husband, Winston, beat her so badly that doctors had to remove her left eye. At that time, hospitals were segregated, and an ambulance for blacks had taken her more than twenty miles, to a black hospital, even though there had been a white hospital within spitting distance.

Francina watched the elegant young woman behind the reception desk purse her painted lips as Hercules put forward their request. "Are you family?" she asked.

Francina knew that an explanation of the facts would be confusing and only bolster her resistance to helping them.

"Yes," Francina stated. If not by blood, they were family by law.

"Wait over there," said the young woman, pointing at an alcove next to a window.

Francina and Hercules found a sleeping man stretched across all five of the chairs, so they leaned against a wall close by and prepared to wait.

Francina was a tangled ball of nerves. What if Lucy hadn't survived? Did that mean they'd have to leave Zukisa with her aunt?

"Mr. and Mrs. Shabalala?"

They had not noticed the man approach. He wore a crisply ironed white shirt, black pants and a name badge on his pocket that identified him as a clerk in the medical records department.

Hercules shook his outstretched hand, which was quickly withdrawn. *Old-school,* thought Francina, but not being one for shaking hands herself, she didn't mind if the man left her out.

"Follow me," said the clerk.

He led them to a large office divided into cubicles containing other clerks in identical dress, most pecking at computer keyboards. The man found his cubicle and indicated for Francina and Hercules to sit down in the plastic chairs in front of his desk.

Hercules read over the document that the man gave him to sign, then shot Francina a desperate look. It asked his exact relationship with the patient for whom records were being requested, and required a signature to the sworn statement at the end.

Francina took the pen from Hercules's hand and wrote, *Adoptive parents of cousin of patient.*

She could have lied, but her principles would not allow it.

The clerk took the document from her, read what she had written and frowned. "I'm sorry, but I can only give out information to immediate family," he said.

"We don't want any medical information, only her address," explained Francina.

"Oh, medical records can only be released to the patients themselves, unless, of course, they're deceased."

"She's dead?" asked Francina, putting her hand to her mouth. "Oh, Hercules, she's dead."

The clerk shifted in his chair. "I didn't say she was dead."

"Then she's alive?" asked Francina.

"I didn't say that, either."

"Well, either she's dead or alive. So which is it?"

The clerk sighed heavily. "The rules state that—"

Francina did not allow him to finish. She knew she had made him uncomfortable, and took full advantage of it. "How can you let us suffer like this?"

The clerk leaned back in his chair and glanced toward the cubicle on his left, then his right. Then he leaned forward and dropped his voice. "She was admitted to ward 310. Ask for Sister Agnes. She's nice."

Francina was ecstatic. Lucy had survived—at least long enough to make it from the emergency room to a ward. And ward 310 sounded a whole lot better than the intensive care unit.

The clerk brushed off their thanks and stood quickly to usher them out.

Since morning visiting hours had begun, Francina and Hercules were not deterred from wandering up and down the corridors in search of ward 310. The hospital was much bigger than the one in Durban and nobody approached them.

Finally, they reached their destination and discovered it was for surgery cases. Lucy had undergone an operation and had made it back to this ward. Francina flashed Hercules a broad grin.

Sister Agnes wouldn't be in until noon, they were told by a nurse, at which time visiting hours would be over. They were welcome to come back during afternoon visiting hours.

Francina and Hercules found a place to sit and wait.

"If she's as nice as that clerk says she is, then she'll give us five minutes of her time even if it's past visiting hours," Francina commented.

It was warm with the sun streaming through a window behind them, and before long she found herself dozing in her seat. She awoke to feel Hercules nudging her in the ribs.

"It's almost noon," he said. "Most of the visitors have left. We'd better pretend we're leaving, too."

But their subterfuge wasn't necessary, because just then they saw a nurse entering ward 310 with a heavy sweater over her white uniform and a handbag over her shoulder.

"That must be Sister Agnes," Francina declared.

They gave her a minute to settle in and then approached the nurses' station again. The same one who had warned them about the end of visiting hours looked at them sternly.

"We'd like to see Sister Agnes, please," said Hercules.

"She's busy, and visiting hours have ended."

Francina noticed that the new arrival had appeared from her office, mug in hand, probably on her way to boil the kettle in the nurses' station.

"But we have to see Sister Agnes," Francina said loudly.

"Come back at three o'clock," the nurse repeated.

"But it's important." Francina noticed that the newcomer was listening. "It's to do with our daughter."

She moved closer to them. "Can I help you with something?"

"I told them to come back when visiting hours started again," explained the nurse.

"Would you like to step into my office?" Sister Agnes asked Francina and Hercules.

"Thank you, Sister," said Francina. She was tempted to give the junior nurse a look of triumph, but stopped herself.

Sister Agnes's office was a windowless square space lined with books. Francina and Hercules sat down across from her desk, and launched into an explanation of their search.

Sister Agnes nodded as she listened. When Francina was satisfied that she had clearly conveyed the risk of losing Zukisa if Lucy wasn't found, she sat back in her chair and waited.

Sister Agnes was in no rush to speak, and Francina wondered if all the nodding was just her manner, and she didn't remember Lucy, after all. She didn't consult the computer on her desk to jog her memory. Perhaps she was considering the ethical implications of divulging information about a patient. The clerk had said that Sister Agnes was nice, and to Francina, "nice" meant willing to disregard red tape when someone was in need.

Sister Agnes got up and asked Hercules to help her move

a stack of journals out of the way so the door could close. Then she sat back down at her desk.

"I wish you had come here two months ago," she said.

Francina gasped. "She died?"

The woman reached across the table and placed her hand over Francina's. "No, she didn't. She was seriously injured, but God showed her His mercy."

Sister Agnes explained that when the time had come for Lucy to be discharged, nobody came to collect her. "She couldn't walk on her own. We couldn't possibly just put her out on the street."

"She had a boyfriend," offered Francina.

Sister Agnes shook her head. "We never saw him once while she was here."

It turned out the kind soul had arranged for a church charity that cared for women at risk to collect her.

"Bethany House is not far from here," she added. "I can't tell you if she's still there or not, but someone at the hostel might be able to help you."

"God bless you, Sister," said Francina. She stood up, and Sister Agnes allowed herself to be hugged. Hercules shook her hand.

"I hope you find her," she said, opening her office door. "Now where's my mug? I was about to make tea."

The nurse at the front desk looked at them suspiciously when they came out, but didn't say a word.

"What a nice woman," Francina whispered to Hercules as they navigated their way out of the hospital.

Bethany House, Francina discovered as Hercules followed the route he had plotted on his map, was close to where

Monica used to work as a radio journalist. Melville was a fashionable area, but on the outskirts, where they found Bethany House, the homes had not been renovated and some even looked ready for demolition. Hercules parked on the busy street and rang the doorbell alongside the security gate in the perimeter wall.

A young woman opened the front door of the house and shouted, "Yes?"

Hercules raised his voice. "We're looking for Lucy."

"Who?"

"Lucy?"

The young woman disappeared, and Francina and Hercules heard the door slam. A short while later, the door opened again and the same young woman walked down the garden path toward them. She unlocked the security gate and locked it again behind them when they'd entered.

"You can wait inside," she told them.

As they followed her to the house, Francina glimpsed a tattoo on the back of her neck. The young woman told them to take a seat in the living room. Francina and Hercules chose a worn beige couch, sinking down so deeply that Francina wondered if she'd ever be able to get up. The other furniture was in no better condition and the curtains were almost worn through, but there was a shine on the battered coffee table and the lemony smell of wood polish. The place was clean and well cared for.

Hercules stood up when he heard the door open. The woman who entered was thinner than in the photograph, her hair was covered by a scarf and she leaned heavily on a cane, but there was no mistaking that she was Lucy.

The worried look on her face indicated that she had no

idea who Hercules and Francina were or why they wanted to see her.

Francina quickly explained their connection to Zukisa.

"You've seen my mother?" asked Lucy. Instead of the smile of relief Francina had expected, she seemed even more fearful.

Francina nodded.

"What did she tell you?"

Francina knew exactly what Lucy didn't want to hear, and felt relieved. Shame was the natural response of someone needing forgiveness. If Lucy felt shame, then Francina and Hercules might succeed in getting her to return to Cape Town.

Francina evaded the question. "Your mother misses you. Your children miss you."

"My mother said that?"

Francina could not lie and tell her that her mother had used those exact words, but she knew it to be true. How could a mother be separated from her daughter and not miss her?

"Your children need you," she told Lucy.

Zukisa's cousin sat down heavily in a threadbare armchair. "No, they don't. I'm not a good mother. I've done some bad things—"

"Shhh," said Francina, cutting her off midsentence. "That's all in the past now."

"I haven't had a drink since I came here from the hospital. I've been working in the kitchen and thinking about my life."

Francina realized then that it had not been God's plan for them to help Lucy dry out. He had already taken care of that. She offered up a silent prayer of thanks.

"Your life is in Cape Town with your children," Francina said gently.

Fly Away Home

"I can't face my mother after what I've done."

"Your mother and children will forgive you."

Lucy buried her face in her hands and began to cry.

Francina got up and put a hand on her trembling shoulder. Seeing Lucy in this state, she decided not to tell her that her mother was ill.

"We can take you home," said Hercules quietly.

Francina knew that Lucy had heard him because her shoulders stopped trembling. She did not uncover her face, but Francina sensed this was the pivotal moment in which she could decide to grant her her heart's desire—unwittingly, of course—or dash her hopes forever. Francina felt a twinge of guilt for thinking of herself when the future of Lucy's three children was also at stake, but it was not a sin for a mother to want to be with her daughter at all costs.

Lucy lifted her head. "Fundiswa won't even know me," she said.

Francina's stomach lurched. She and Hercules were going to get their daughter back!

"A child knows her mother," she said in as calm a voice as she could manage. What she really wanted to say was, "Hurry and get your things so we can leave now."

"Are you sure it's no problem to take me all the way to Cape Town?"

"Of course not," said Francina. "We're going home, too."

"What were you doing in Johannesburg?" asked Lucy.

She didn't realize that the two of them had traveled all the way to Johannesburg to find her. Perhaps it would be preferable, Francina thought, if Lucy remained oblivious of this fact. She had agreed to come back with them; this was all that was important, and anything they said now might undo the progress they had made.

Hercules, however, had other ideas. "We came to find you," he said. "That's how important you are to your family."

Francina watched Lucy try to digest this new information. "My mother is ill, isn't she?" she asked at last.

He nodded.

Francina worried that Lucy might start crying again, but her eyes were dry, her voice calm.

"Then I must go immediately." She stood up. "I'll tell the director I'm leaving, and get my things. I don't have much, just a toothbrush and some toiletries. I'll leave the clothes that were donated to me."

Francina and Hercules watched her go, and both let out a sigh of relief.

"Let's bring all the potatoes and onions inside," said Francina. "I told you we'd find a place for them."

They hurried to the car and carried the bags back into the house. Lucy was waiting for them in the hallway.

"Just what we need," she said, looking at the bags. "Someone dropped off a crate of carrots and celery this morning, so now we can make vegetable soup. The girls love it."

Seeing Lucy smile, Francina was struck by her resemblance to Fundiswa, who had spent more than four of her five years apart from her mother.

From Johannesburg to Kimberley, a distance of two hundred and ninety miles, Lucy sat in silence, which she broke only to say thank-you whenever Francina passed her a bottle of water or offered her a butterscotch drop. But as they entered the flat, dry landscape of the Karoo, Lucy began to talk about her early years as a mother, when the boys were babies, and about how their father had never been a constant presence in their lives.

As the temperature rose, they all rolled down their windows, and the smell of dried herbs filled the car.

"Wild rosemary," said Lucy. "It's wonderful with Karoo lamb."

"You're a cook?" asked Francina.

"I used to love cooking," said Lucy. "My favorite part was inventing something wonderful with the ingredients I had. I never used recipe books."

Francina's mind began to tick furiously. If Mama Dlamini was offered a permanent position as head chef at the golf resort, her café would need a replacement cook. Lucy's boys would be far better off growing up in Lady Helen than in that dangerous neighborhood of Cape Town. And Zukisa could be near to her aunt. Francina felt a flutter of excitement as the plans formed in her head. But, as Hercules would say, first things first. Let Lucy and her family become reacquainted with each other before Francina had them moving to a new town.

❧ *Chapter Twelve* ❧

While Francina was away, Mandla sat every afternoon in Monica's office, doing his homework without protest, or staring silently out of the window—both very out of character for him. He was missing his brother.

Emergencies at the hospital kept Zak busy, so he'd not been able to go to Cape Town to convince Jacqueline not to take Yolanda to Australia, but he'd told Monica he planned to go this evening. Since he'd be back late, Monica decided to take Mandla to Mama Dlamini's Eating Establishment for dinner.

The queen of the café was nowhere to be seen.

"Is Mama in the kitchen?" Mandla asked Anna, the waitress.

Monica had secured a full-time job for Anna at the café so that she wouldn't have to rely on her usual source of income, which was illegal abalone picking.

Anna shook her head. "No, she's not here. Your gogo is

cooking," she told Mandla, referring to Francina's mother-in-law.

"Gogo!" Mandla leaped out of his chair and, without waiting for permission from Monica or Anna, went into the kitchen.

A minute later he came out, dragging Mrs. Shabalala by the hand.

"Hi, Monica," she said.

"Hello. What a surprise. Why are you working here?"

Monica noticed that for an instant Francina's mother-in-law evaded her gaze. "Mama Dlamini has other work to do," Mrs. Shabalala said eventually.

"Oh." It was a reasonable excuse, but Monica could not shake the feeling that something was amiss. Mrs. Shabalala seemed uncomfortable, and glad for the distraction of Mandla's questions about the day's specials.

Eventually, Mandla decided on baked haddock with mushroom risotto, a combination of two of the evening specials, and he accompanied Mrs. Shabalala back to the kitchen to watch her work.

When the food arrived, it was clear that he had distracted her because the risotto was like porridge, the haddock dry and Monica's calamari fried to a crisp. But Mandla did not seem to notice, and Monica didn't say a word.

Later that evening, when Mandla was asleep and Monica had just stepped out of a relaxing hot bath, she heard Zak's car in the driveway and braced herself to bear the brunt of his frustration with Jacqueline. But when he came through the door, she saw his triumphant grin and knew that she had been correct to suggest he talk to his ex-wife.

"She's decided not to go until Yolanda starts university in a year's time," he said. "Then it will be up to Yolanda to decide where she'd like to study—in South Africa or Australia."

"That's wonderful news," said Monica. She was a little suspicious that Jacqueline would suddenly change major plans so quickly. Still, Zak could be highly convincing when he tried. Many people who had donated large sums of money to the hospital could attest to that.

She wondered briefly if she should voice her uncertainties, and then decided against it. She and Zak had another year with Yolanda, and hopefully the girl would decide not to leave at the end of it.

He put his arms around Monica. "You were right to suggest I talk to Jacqueline. Sorry I was such a jerk about it."

She nuzzled her head against his chest. "That's okay." She wondered if he'd choose this moment to talk about the child they were desperate to have together.

"Did Sipho e-mail today?"

Monica nodded. "He went to watch Connor's football practice today."

"Are you sure you're talking about our Sipho?"

"Unbelievable, isn't it?"

Sipho's mother, Ella, had encouraged him to play soccer when he was a small child, but he had never been interested in sports. Sipho was in the same class as the son of his host family now, but because Sipho had skipped a couple of grades he was two years younger.

"He also said that Connor gets a lot of attention from girls." Monica had reread that part of his e-mail, but Sipho had not revealed his opinion of Connor's popularity. Sipho himself had only ever mentioned a girl if he was working on a school project with her, and then it had only been to explain her role or lament her tardiness in meeting deadlines.

"Connor is seventeen. I wished I had attention from girls at that age," said Zak, laughing.

"Don't try and tell me you didn't," teased Monica.

"You should have seen how thick my glasses were. Like milk bottles."

"I still would have fancied you."

Zak planted a kiss on her lips. "Keep telling me that, okay?"

With the mood between them light and their emotional intimacy restored, this would be the perfect time to broach the delicate subject of whether or not to try another round of fertility drugs. But perhaps because she didn't want to destroy their mood, or perhaps because she herself didn't want to face making a decision, Monica could not bring it up. She wondered if he would.

"Have you eaten?" she asked.

He hadn't, but fortunately, she had some leftover chicken from the night before, which she reheated.

They didn't usually eat in front of the television—much as Zak tried to convince her otherwise—but tonight she brought his plate through to the living room. He was watching the news.

A crime reporter was interviewing a member of parliament about the government's decision to no longer publish crime statistics.

"What a farce," said Zak.

Monica was glad that her beat as the *Herald*'s editor and reporter no longer covered national political issues, which she found very wearing.

As one talking head replaced another on TV, Monica

found herself growing increasingly upset with Zak for not broaching the subject of her fertility treatment. She knew it was irrational. She had served him his food in front of the television; she had waived her chance to bring it up earlier when he'd kissed her. But she couldn't help herself.

The news ended and she picked his empty plate up off the floor with an exaggerated sigh.

When he came into the kitchen to make tea, he found her washing the dishes and crying quietly.

"Sweetheart," he said, his voice full of concern. "This is not about me leaving my plate on the floor, is it?" He turned her so that she was facing him. "It's about us not having a baby."

"I can't make all the decisions on my own," she said, sniffing. "It's hard."

"I don't want you to make decisions on your own. But you haven't mentioned it for ages. I was starting to think that you'd given up on the idea."

"Why would I give up on having a baby?" Monica buried her face in the drying cloth.

"Let's talk about this," said Zak. "Tomorrow when you're not so upset."

He put his arms around her and for an instant, as she breathed in the faded scent of the cologne that he'd put on that morning, she allowed herself to believe that everything would work out, just as Dudu kept telling her it would.

The next evening, as Mandla was preparing for bed, Monica and Zak talked and decided they would try one more round of fertility treatments.

❧ Chapter Thirteen ❧

Fundiswa, who had no memory of her mother, welcomed Lucy with enthusiasm. The little girl was simply happy for the attention, but the boys, especially Xoli, punished Lucy by staying out more and treating her to silence whenever they were home. For a few days after her daughter's return, Zukisa's aunt was able to sit up in bed and eat with a normal appetite.

Francina and Hercules were delighted to have Zukisa home, and promised to drive her to Cape Town every weekend to check on her aunt. Happiness reigned again at Jabulani Dressmakers.

With almost surreal timing, the spring wildflowers appeared the day after Francina's return, clothing the usually severe koppies in flamenco skirts of orange, white, yellow and purple. Every inch of open space in town, from the grassy medians to the park at the end of Main Street, was covered with colorful vygies, violets, gladioli and daisies. The first tour bus arrived that very afternoon.

The flowers marked not only Francina's triumphant return, but also the return of a daily routine that Monica had never grown accustomed to, though it was her fifth round of fertility treatment. In the past, Sipho had watched, enthralled, when she'd given herself the hormone shots in the belly, but Mandla ran out of the room when it was time for her injections. If Zak was home, he'd sit with her and tease that if she ever wanted to change careers there would be a job for her at the hospital.

The shots were not so bad. It hurt while she was administering them, and sometimes a bruise appeared on her belly the next day, but the anxiety was far worse. As she discarded each syringe in the safety canister that Ivy, the nurse, had given her, Monica knew that she was one day closer to the time of waiting. That awful two-week stretch as she waited to take the pregnancy test always felt like two months. At work she often felt light-headed, and once she had to rush to the bathroom to be sick. But the side effects of the shots were nothing compared to the stress of waiting.

On the day the wait began, Anna, the waitress from Mama Dlamini's Eating Establishment, came to see her at the office with news that provided a pleasant diversion. Four years ago, Monica had learned that a gang of foreigners was poaching abalone off the coast of Lady Helen. The tip-off came from Anna and three of her friends, whose own poaching—on a much more minor scale—was threatened by the gang's presence. After the police in Lady Helen arrested the gang members, Monica had warned the women not to continue their illegal early-morning activity or they, too, would be apprehended. She had found them jobs: one cleaning in the newspaper office; two with her friend Kitty, who ran a local inn; and one—Anna—at Mama Dlamini's Eating Establishment. At first the women had been reluctant to accept these jobs, since taking a mere seven abalone a day had earned them enough from the chef at the golf resort north of town to put food on their tables. But Monica had managed to persuade them of the very real possibility of arrest and a large fine.

Six months later, she had helped them form a limited corporation and to apply for a commercial abalone picking license. These were notoriously difficult to get, and, according to the word among fishermen, went only to government cronies. For three years in a row the ladies' application had been turned down, but this year it had been approved. Now, as licensed abalone pickers, they would be able to pick more than the daily four allotted to recreational pickers. And they would be able to sell their catch, something recreational pickers were forbidden to do.

"What about your jobs?" Monica asked as Anna stood to leave. She hoped the women wouldn't consider quitting their employment for the more lucrative world of abalone picking.

"We're old-fashioned," said Anna. "We'll go back to the way we did it for years—getting up before dawn, wading into the shallow water to look under the rocks, and not taking more than seven to sell to the restaurant at the golf resort."

Monica wondered if she was imagining that Anna seemed uncomfortable when she mentioned the resort.

"It only takes an hour or two each morning," continued Anna. "We'll all be at our jobs on time."

Monica was relieved to hear that nothing would change.

Anna paused at the door. "Thank you, Monica. You made this possible."

The irony of Anna's gratitude did not escape Monica. She had been the one who'd stopped the women from doing what they'd done for years. In a way, it was only right that she was helping them start again. Something else did not escape Monica's attention: the slight bump under Anna's dress. The woman was pregnant again.

As her footsteps grew fainter down the hall, Monica found herself growing more and more upset. She threw a pile of junk mail into the recycling bin with such vigor that the tub tipped over. It wasn't fair. Anna already had two children. The youngest was not even two years old! Why did God allow Anna to have babies so easily, while Monica had to struggle and suffer like this? She looked out the window and saw Anna walking back up Main Street toward the café. Life wasn't fair. God wasn't fair. Monica slumped in her chair, sobbing.

"What's the matter?" asked Dudu, coming in with a cup of tea. She set it down on the desk and put her arm around her boss.

Monica couldn't answer her.

"Oh, honey," cooed Dudu. "Those nasty hormone shots are just making you feel bad. Have a sip of nice, strong tea."

Monica stopped crying and sniffed.

"It'll happen, don't worry." Dudu righted the recycling bin and picked up the junk mail and used envelopes from the floor.

Dudu meant well, but in truth, it might *never* happen. The world was full of childless women who had given up their quest. And the majority had probably also been told not to worry, that it would happen in good time.

"I'm going to go back to work now," said Dudu. "But I'll check on you in a while."

Monica nodded.

After she had left, Monica tried to get started on a story she had been meaning to write for weeks about the discovery of a new species of jellyfish a few miles up the coast. But she couldn't concentrate.

And this was only the first day of waiting.

Mandla continued to mope around in the absence of his brother. Although Sipho had usually spent every afternoon in his bedroom doing his homework, it had been enough for Mandla to know that he could go in at any time—to ask his brother a question, to enjoy the reaction he got from rankling him, or just lie on his bed and study the posters of wildlife that had hung on Sipho's walls since he was a young child.

Mandla was glad to have Francina and Zukisa back, but ever since their return, Zukisa seemed older to him, more distant and far too prim for a fourteen-year-old. In short, she was no longer any fun, and fun was something he felt was lacking in his life. He was marking off the days on his calendar until the family's departure for the United States.

The return of the migratory birds to the lagoon north of town piqued his interest briefly, but even that didn't seem as enjoyable without Sipho's wild enthusiasm. This annual event, the official start of spring, always brought out exuberance in Sipho. He'd run around whooping with joy and punching the air with excitement. Mandla notified his brother by e-mail that the whimbrels had returned first this year, and that the seagulls had resisted relinquishing the lagoon they'd controlled all winter long.

Reading between the lines of Sipho's reply, Monica knew that he was feeling homesick and out of place.

✦ *Chapter Fourteen* ✦

On the day the waiting was to end, Monica woke early but couldn't find the energy to drag herself out of bed. The last four times she had gone to the doctor's office for a blood test to check if she was pregnant, she had sprung out of bed and been ready before Zak. Today, though, she remembered too clearly the grief she had felt all four times when Dr. Jansen had told them the treatment had failed. Disappointment could wear down even the most ardent optimist.

Zak got up first, and when he came out of the shower, she was still in bed.

"Come on, sleepyhead," he said. Zak, it seemed, was determined to keep the tone light this morning.

Mandla protested when they dropped him off at school.

"Why can't I come? I did last time," he said.

Monica reminded him that he'd recently missed a few hours of school when they'd taken his brother to the airport.

"It's not fair. Everybody goes somewhere, but I'm stuck in boring old school."

Monica knew this was a reference to his brother's stay in the United States.

"Mandla, sweetie, your chance will come," she told him.

"It better," he warned. He kissed her on the cheek before getting out, but did not say anything more about her visit to Cape Town.

Monica was not disappointed; a word of sweet reassurance from Mandla might have brought on the tears that were so close today.

When they walked into Dr. Jansen's waiting room, there were so many couples there the only chairs Monica and Zak could find together were next to a blaring television.

She glanced at the women around her. Most appeared to be in their late thirties, early forties, but there were at least three who were much younger.

Zak's beeper went off and he excused himself to make a call outside. Monica was happy to have him with her when she took the blood test and heard the news from Dr. Jansen, but she felt badly that he'd had to leave the hospital at Lady Helen without a doctor.

"Everything under control?" she asked when he returned and sat down beside her.

He nodded. "But I really should be back by noon."

Fifteen minutes later, the receptionist called Monica's name and led her to a small room where a phlebotomist took her blood sample. Since Dr. Jansen had his own laboratory for reading blood tests on the premises, the results would

be available within forty minutes. Monica returned to the
waiting room.

A new soap opera had begun, but chairs were now readily
available away from the television, so Monica and Zak could
watch the minutes tick by in relative peace.

Zak, also an optimist by nature, did not offer any words
of encouragement, as he had in the past, and Monica
wondered if he was less sure this time.

After ten minutes, Monica's thoughts turned to Sipho and
Mandla. What did they really think of her quest to have a
child of her own? They both professed excitement, and
Mandla, especially, had been devastated when the last result
had been negative. But did the boys ever wonder if they were
not enough for Monica? She hoped not. Before she had
embarked on this journey—and before she'd known how
arduous it would be—she had explained that when two
people married it was natural for them to want to have a
baby together, because a baby symbolized the love they
shared. Mandla, who was too young when his father died to
remember him, had nodded sagely, but Sipho had said that
sometimes that love didn't last long enough to see the baby
start school. Sipho and Mandla's father had become unfaithful to Ella when the family had returned to South Africa from
their exile in Zambia. Themba had milked his own status as
a returning freedom fighter in every bar and nightclub in Johannesburg, and then he'd passed the spoils of this celebration on to his wife, in the form of the HIV virus.

"Monica Niemand."

Ivy was calling her back. Lost in her memories of Ella, she
found the minutes had slipped by, and now Monica wished
she was still watching the clock, preparing, with every move

of the minute hand, to hear the news she had traveled to Cape Town to receive. She did not want to leave the waiting room and go through the double doors.

"Dr. Jansen will be with you shortly," said Ivy, ushering them into his empty office.

Once again, her tone did not offer Monica an inkling of the results of the test. Ivy had missed her calling in life; she should have been on the stage. Once again, Monica studied the photographs of Dr. Jansen's smiling children. Zak squeezed her hand and leaned over to give her a quick kiss before the specialist arrived.

"I love you," he whispered.

Monica was too choked up to reply.

"Good morning, Monica, Zak." Dr. Jansen closed the door behind him and eased himself into his leather executive chair on the other side of the desk. He placed Monica's file on the desktop in front of him, but did not open it. She knew why. He had checked the results of the blood test before walking into his office.

Monica realized that neither she nor Zak had returned the doctor's greeting. She searched Dr. Jansen's eyes for a clue to what he was about to say, but he was, as always, composed and difficult to read.

"Monica, Zak, the news is not good."

Monica burst into tears. Zak pushed his chair closer to hers and put an arm around her shoulder. She knew the doctor wanted to add something, but she didn't care. She had heard all she needed to. Sobbing, she buried her face in Zak's shoulder. He brushed her hair out of her eyes and took a tissue from the box offered by Dr. Jansen. Monica wiped her eyes, but she couldn't stop crying.

"Do you want to try again?" said Dr. Jansen.

Monica's breath came in sharp shudders.

"Think it over."

Monica heard Zak thanking him.

The doctor stood up. "I'm so sorry, Monica, Zak. Take as long as you need in here." He rested his hand lightly on Zak's shoulder and then quietly closed the door as he left.

Zak put his other arm around Monica and held her tightly. He didn't say anything and she was glad. No words could comfort her.

She pulled away. "We'd better leave so you can get back to the hospital." Her voice sounded thick. She saw that her mascara had run all over Zak's shirt. Once more, she found herself wishing that Dr. Jansen had a rear escape route for patients who had received crushing news.

Zak wiped her eyes with another tissue and brushed the hair from her face. As his gaze met hers, she felt that she would start sobbing all over again, but she couldn't. There were sick people waiting for her husband in Lady Helen.

Ivy put an arm around her waist as they came out of Dr. Jansen's office. "I'll give you a call," she whispered.

Monica could not bring herself to respond.

She could feel the eyes of every woman in the waiting room on her, and knew that they, too, were probably wishing Dr. Jansen had a rear entrance for his failures.

Outside, the morning had warmed. Two joggers wearing T-shirts and shorts passed on the sidewalk.

"Spring is definitely here," said Zak.

Monica said nothing.

Not even the riotous display of color that greeted them as they reached the top of the koppie outside Lady Helen lifted

Monica's spirits. Zak stopped the car so they could get out and enjoy the view, but she told him to drive on. He had done his best to console her on the journey home from Cape Town, but nothing he said gave her comfort, or even a reason to reply, and eventually he, too, had settled into silence. She knew that she was being selfish—Zak had wanted this pregnancy as much as she had—but the fact that he already had a biological child made her feel entitled to nurse her own grief. It wasn't a mature reaction, she knew, or a healthy one, but she no longer felt in charge of her own emotions.

Zak returned to the hospital and, although it was lunchtime, Monica went home and to bed without bothering to call Dudu to explain that she wasn't coming into the office. The receptionist knew where she had gone this morning and would put two and two together. With birds singing the joys of spring outside her drawn curtains, Monica drifted into a heavy sleep.

She awoke to hear Mandla's voice in the house and, after a short silence, Francina's. There was a quiet knock at her bedroom door. They had noticed her car in the carport.

"Monica? Are you okay?" Francina's voice was full of concern.

Monica did not trust herself to answer. Her friend tried the door and opened it a crack.

"It didn't work, Francina." She burst into fresh tears.

"Oh, Monica, I'm sorry." Francina sat down on the bed and took her hand.

Monica realized that Mandla was at the door, and held out her arms to him. He came to her. He did not cry, but she could feel the tension in his body.

Francina stroked his back. "Go and eat your lunch, baby," she told him. "And tell Zukisa to stop watching television."

He hesitated in the doorway for a moment and then slowly walked back down the hall.

Monica took the tissue Francina offered, dried her tears and then blew her nose.

"I'll bring you something to eat," said Francina. "I bet you didn't even have breakfast."

A short while later, Mandla pushed open Monica's bedroom door. She had brushed her hair and was sitting on the bed, and when she patted the space next to her, he came to sit down.

"How come everyone else has babies and you can't?"

"Not everyone can have their own children. Francina didn't."

"But she didn't have a husband. You do."

Monica knew he was being petulant because he was disappointed, but his words stung.

"I know, sweetie."

He gave her a withering look. "God's not fair."

"Don't say that," said Monica, but her tone did not match the admonition of her words, because she had started to think this herself.

Mandla got up to answer a gentle knock at the bedroom door. Francina had returned with a tray bearing dainty little crustless sandwiches and a cup of strong tea.

"You've got to eat," she told Monica sternly. "And when the children have finished their homework, you'll come with us for a walk to see if there are any wildflowers left."

From her tone Monica knew that it would be senseless to argue.

"Come, Mandla, time for your lunch, too."

When Monica was alone again, she opened the curtains

and sat down at her dressing table to eat her lunch. She found she was hungry, and by the time she had finished she was feeling stronger.

She called Dudu to let her know that she wouldn't be coming in that afternoon. The woman didn't need to ask about the result of the pregnancy test.

Francina was right to force Monica to take a walk that afternoon. There was a breeze coming in from the ocean, and although she couldn't see any flowers on the koppies from here, it felt good to be out in the fresh air. They waved to Peg, whose dairy farm they had chosen to walk through to gain access to the koppies. Peg didn't mind; in fact, none of the other farmers and homeowners whose properties ran up to the base of the koppies minded the townsfolk taking shortcuts across their land.

The two women left Mandla watching Peg clean the milking machine, and with Zukisa, walked behind the barn to the fields where half of Peg's herd was grazing.

"Perhaps it wasn't a good idea to come here," said Monica, eyeing the large cow closest to her.

"Nonsense," said Francina, whose father had raised cattle his whole life. "They won't hurt you. Walk faster and we'll be out of the field and on the koppie."

With her eyes on the ground, searching not for flowers but for cowpats, Monica picked up the pace and climbed over the stile at the end of Peg's property. A short way up the side of the hill, Francina sat down on a flat rock and motioned for Monica to join her. Zukisa, who had only taken her nose out of the novel she was reading when Francina had warned her of a step up or down, came to a stop close by.

Monica guessed what was coming. More advice not to worry.

"I want to tell you something before you find out from someone else," said Francina.

Monica was both surprised and relieved to discover she was wrong.

"Mama Dlamini is moonlighting as a chef at the golf resort." Her friend folded her hands in her lap and sighed.

"I thought something was going on when I went to the café the other day and your mother-in-law was cooking. Mama Dlamini is working for Mr. Yang?"

"I know, I know. I was as shocked as you are now when my mother-in-law told me."

"After everything that happened." Monica shook her head.

"If they like her, she'll get a permanent appointment. That's a big deal for a woman with no official training."

"But there are so many hotels up the coast, or even in Cape Town. How can she forget that Mr. Yang tried to destroy Sandpiper Drift?"

Francina sighed again. "Opportunities like this one don't come looking for a woman like Mama Dlamini. I can't defend her. All I can tell you is that she was once a girl in a village, with no prospects except for becoming a maid."

"Is your mother-in-law going to work at the café permanently?"

"I hope not. Jabulani Dressmakers needs her. If Mama Dlamini decides to hire a permanent replacement, I have just the person for her."

Monica listened as Francina revealed her plan to move Zukisa's sick aunt, Lucy, and her three children to Lady Helen so that Lucy could become the new cook at Mama Dlamini's Eating Establishment.

"How will she take care of her sick mother if she's busy at the café?" asked Monica.

While Lucy worked the lunch shift, Francina would check on the aunt, before collecting Mandla, Zukisa and Lucy's boys from school. And Lucy's daughter would just have to go to the café with her. In the evenings, Zukisa could get the little girl ready for bed and make sure the boys did their homework. The café was not open late unless there was a concert in the amphitheater, so Lucy would be home by eight to put her children to bed.

"My mother-in-law has volunteered to do the breakfast shift," said Francina. "She doesn't start work at my shop until I leave to pick up the children from school."

"How can Mama Dlamini look that man in the eye?" asked Monica, and Francina shrugged.

Zukisa had wandered off a little, still reading her book. "Careful you don't trip over a rock," Francina called to her. "Why don't you stop reading and take a look at the view?"

Zukisa looked up briefly and then went back to her book.

"Ah, children," said Francina. "They take beauty like this for granted." She waved her hand toward the glint of the ocean in the distance.

"Except Sipho," Monica reminded her.

"That boy is not a child, never has been," said Francina. "What's his latest news?"

Monica told Francina her suspicions that Sipho was intimidated by the confidence of his new friends in Houston. "There's a big difference between fifteen and seventeen. I hope he doesn't do anything silly."

"If there's anyone who won't be led by the nose like an old donkey, it's Sipho," said Francina. "He knows his own mind, just like his mother did. Oh, Monica, I'm sorry, I shouldn't have said that."

"Ella was his mother. You're right."

"But today of all days. Me and my big mouth."

Monica found herself using the words she had dreaded hearing from Francina. "It'll be okay."

"I meant to take your mind off your disappointment by telling you about Mama Dlamini."

"You did." Monica stood up. "Shall we go and find Mandla before he gets into mischief?"

They found him helping Peg put fresh hay in the milking stalls.

"Don't tell me he helped you muck those out," Monica said to her.

Peg nodded.

"And I can't even get him to clean his room."

Mandla wanted to pick up one more load of hay with the pitchfork before leaving. Afterward he washed his hands with a garden hose and dried them on his jeans.

"All that work made me hungry," he announced.

Zukisa rolled her eyes. "You're always hungry."

"That's because I move around and don't have a book in my face all the time."

"That's what we get when our children spend so much time together," said Francina. "They start to fight like brother and sister."

Monica told Francina to go home, since she would not be returning to the office that afternoon. Zukisa's eyes brightened at the suggestion and for the first time Monica wondered if the girl saw this daily arrangement as a chore.

At the entrance to Peg's farm, Monica and Mandla waved goodbye to Francina and Zukisa and started toward home.

"Are you going to keep trying to have a baby again?" asked Mandla.

The brief interlude of respite was over. Monica felt grief settling over her like fog off the ocean.

"I don't know."

"You always tell me not to give up."

How could she explain that sometimes giving up might be the best option?

Arriving home, Monica stared at the contents of the fridge, trying to think of something to make for dinner. Eventually, she closed the door without taking anything out. There were leftovers from last night's roast pork. Sandwiches would have to suffice tonight.

That night she left the dirty dishes in the sink, went to bed early and lay awake listening to the sounds of Mandla and Zak talking. When Zak was in charge of the bedtime ritual, he always allowed the boy to stay up late.

When Zak finally slipped into bed beside her, she pretended to be asleep. She was unsure why, but felt herself withdrawing from her family. It was selfish and futile but she couldn't stop herself.

Please help me, God, she prayed silently. She had doubted Him lately, even accused Him of being unfair, but she knew that she was losing her way and needed His help.

⚓ *Chapter Fifteen* ⚓

Mandla was already dressed when Monica awoke the next morning, and he'd attempted to make his own sandwiches for school. Peanut butter was smeared across the cupboard where she kept his lunch box.

"I overslept. Why didn't you wake me?" she asked.

"I tried but you groaned and rolled over. I'm already late for school. Maybe it's better if I just stay at home."

"No, I'll take you now and explain to your teacher that it's my fault."

Sighing, Mandla went to brush his teeth, and Monica pulled on some clothes and scraped her hair into a ponytail. She'd come back and shower before going to work.

Dudu was not at her desk when Monica arrived at the office, more than an hour late. She was relieved to sit down at her desk without answering any questions.

She could hear the receptionist singing in the tiny galley kitchen, where she was presumably making a cup of tea. Monica took out a blank sheet of paper. It was time to start planning the next issue. She sat for a few minutes, pen in hand, thinking of events coming up in Lady Helen. Nothing seemed exciting enough to warrant a story. On her computer, she found a list of topics that she added to whenever a new idea came to her, but although these possibilities had excited her when she'd thought of them, they now seemed better suited for a newsletter than the town paper.

Dudu walked past her open door and stopped in surprise. "I didn't hear you come in."

"I overslept."

"Are you okay?"

Monica nodded.

"If you want to talk, you know where to find me. Do you want some tea?"

Monica shook her head. Dudu had come to the correct conclusion—that Monica's absence from work yesterday afternoon was confirmation that her fertility treatment had been unsuccessful.

The next day Monica overslept again, but this time Mandla was more persistent in his attempts to rouse her.

"Either I go to school on time or I don't go at all," he said.

Even in her sleepy state Monica realized that he was losing patience with her.

That day at work she tried again to think of story ideas, and jotted down a few weak ones, but by lunchtime she was ready to leave, and took her sandwiches to the park, where she sat on a bench next to the statue of the town's founder,

Lady Helen Gray. The warm sun on her face felt comforting and before long Monica dozed. When she awoke, it was past two o'clock and she had a crick in her neck from sleeping sitting up.

Dudu said nothing when Monica walked into the office, but clearly wanted to talk. She kept walking by Monica's open door, ostensibly to fetch new ink cartridges or reams of paper from the stationery storage room, all of which could have been collected in one trip. But Monica did not want to talk. Zak had tried, too, after Mandla had gone to bed the night before. Talking was futile. Either Monica must throw herself into one more attempt at getting pregnant, or she had to give up the idea of ever having a child of her own.

By the end of the week, when it was time to turn copy in to Dudu to be laid out for the next issue, Monica had completed only two stories.

Dudu read them quickly and said, "I thought we did a piece on Justice's new job last month." Justice was the son of Gift and David, the couple from whom Monica had bought her house and with whom she now shared a close friendship. Gift was one of Lady Helen's most successful artists. Justice had been a Rhodes Scholar at Oxford University in England and had recently been promoted from his lowly clerk's position at the African Bank to deputy director for Southern Africa.

"Did we?" asked Monica.

Dudu nodded.

"I forgot."

"Do you have any other stories you're working on?" asked Dudu.

"No, that's it." Monica could not remember how she had spent the past few days.

"We don't have enough copy for a whole issue."

Monica nodded.

"Monica, do you want to talk to me now?"

She feigned ignorance. "About what?"

"Let me make us a nice cup of tea and we'll have a chat," said Dudu.

"You're very sweet, but I just can't. Not yet."

"You don't have to talk to me, but you must talk to someone. We don't have a newspaper to bring out next week. The other day I had to beg the electricity company not to turn off our power because you forgot to pay the bill."

"I did? I'm sorry, Dudu. What would I do without you?"

"I have a few ideas for stories. If you want, I'll write them this weekend. Do you think you can give me at least two more by Monday?"

Monica promised she would. "Thanks, Dudu."

"The *Lady Helen Herald* has to come out. People in this town depend on it."

Monica's good friend Kitty called that evening to ask if the family wanted to come for lunch at the inn on Sunday, but Monica declined, claiming other plans.

"We don't have any plans," said Mandla, who had over-heard the conversation.

Monica said the first thing that came into her mind. "There's lots of work to do around the house, you know. Spring cleaning."

"But Mom—"

"It has to be done, Mandla."

She knew that he was disappointed and confused by her response. He loved going to Kitty's inn, the first place they had lived when they'd arrived in Lady Helen. Plus Kitty's four-year-old daughter, Catherine, adored him. Monica knew she was being selfish, but she wasn't in the mood to see Kitty with her two children, especially her youngest, one-year-old Jimmy. Kitty, the onetime fashion model and entrepreneur, always acted as though she was surprised to find herself with a family, as though her husband and babies had appeared in a puff of smoke with no effort at all. At first, Monica had found it mildly amusing, but now she found it painful. "Just look at me," Kitty would say. "And to think that not long ago I was partying until dawn with the jet set in Milan."

The next day, Saturday, Monica tried to appease Mandla by taking him and Yolanda to lunch at Mama Dlamini's Eating Establishment. Zak had to be at the hospital for an hour or two. Mandla always acted as though the café were his own private club, and would leave the table to greet friends and neighbors. Today was no exception; he had spied Francina, Hercules and Zukisa in a booth.

Yolanda ordered Mama Dlamini's speciality: snoek done West Coast style over an open fire, served with lemon juice and homemade apricot jam.

"I'm not sure if Mrs. Shabalala is up to cooking that," said Monica.

Yolanda shrugged. "I'll try it anyway."

When the food arrived, Monica tasted Yolanda's snoek and found it surprisingly good—up to Mama Dlamini's standards, even.

"I should apologize to Mrs. Shabalala," she said.

"Francina told me she's not here," said Mandla. "Mama Dlamini is cooking today." He pointed at the door to the kitchen. "There she is."

Mama Dlamini wiped her hands on her apron and began to greet her patrons, as always.

"Mmm…I'm in the mood for a chocolate milk shake," said Mandla. Mama Dlamini always gave her "two favorite boys" a milk shake on the house.

"Who's my best boy?" Mama Dlamini called out to Mandla. She came over and pinched his cheeks. Sipho hated that and had been grateful when she'd stopped doing it to him, the day he turned fifteen.

"We haven't seen you for a while," said Monica.

"Yes, yes, I've been busy," replied Mama Dlamini vaguely. "How about a milk shake, you two?"

"Yes, please," said Mandla and Yolanda in unison.

"Busy with what?" asked Monica.

Mama Dlamini's eyes followed Anna as the waitress moved about the café. "Business stuff."

"What business stuff?" persisted Monica.

Mama Dlamini studied her face. "If there's something you want to ask, just ask it, Monica."

Monica knew that this was not the time to confront Mama Dlamini about her divided loyalties, but she had started it and now she'd finish it.

"How can you work for Mr. Yang? Have you forgotten that he tried to bulldoze Sandpiper Drift? How do you think Daphne, Miemps and Reginald would feel if they knew you were cooking for the man who tried to destroy their home?"

"That's their business, not yours, Monica." Mama Dlamini's tone was curt.

"Have you told them? No, you haven't. It's because you're ashamed, aren't you?" Monica noticed Francina and Hercules staring at her.

Mama Dlamini raised her voice. "Who are you to tell me what I should and shouldn't be ashamed of? I shouldn't have to remind you, Monica, of the differences between you and me." She wagged a finger in Monica's face. "My daddy didn't send me to university. The only way I would have gone to university is if I'd got a job cleaning classrooms."

"What's that got to do with—?"

"You've had opportunities I could only dream of."

"But—"

Mama Dlamini did not give her a chance to finish. "If you think that I'm going to say no when someone offers me a chance to prove myself in a world-class restaurant, then you're a foolish woman."

"Well, I just think Mr. Yang should ask forgiveness of the people he has wronged," said Monica, her tone defensive.

"Enough, ladies," interrupted Francina, stressing the word *ladies* as if to remind both women that they were behaving badly.

"I'll go and make the milk shakes," mumbled Mama Dlamini, and disappeared into the kitchen.

Francina sat down at Monica's table. "How are you, Yolanda?" she asked, as though nothing had happened.

The girl looked nervously at Monica before speaking. "Okay, I suppose."

"And you, Mandla? What are your plans for the weekend?"

Mandla glared at Monica. "Spring cleaning."

Anna arrived with the milk shakes. While the youngsters were unwrapping their straws and arguing over which glass had the most whipped cream on top, Francina put her hand on Monica's arm and dropped her voice. "What were you thinking, Monica? Why argue with Mama Dlamini here, at lunchtime, in front of all her customers?"

Monica sighed. "I know, I know, I was wrong."

"You and I both know that this is not just about Mama Dlamini working at the golf resort. You're upset with your life. You're angry, you're disappointed. But you can't take it out on other people. Mandla tells me you don't get up on time in the morning, you forget to make him lunch for school, you don't sign his homework. You have to pull yourself together."

Monica knew Francina was right, but what she advised was easier said than done.

⊸ *Chapter Sixteen* ⊸

Monica had expected a call from Miemps, but she wasn't prepared to see her elderly friend walking up her garden path with a tin of freshly baked scones. The grapevine in Lady Helen was speedy and it would have taken less than twenty-four hours for everyone in town to know of Monica's altercation with Mama Dlamini. Monica readied herself to commiserate with her friend for the shocking lack of loyalty from Lady Helen's best-loved cook.

But Miemps had come to talk about something more important than Mama Dlamini's defection. Miemps's son-in-law, Silas, had taken her daughter, Daphne, and their little boy, Victor, to Zimbabwe in the middle of the night, without Miemps or her husband's knowledge. Miemps thrust a scribbled note in front of Monica. It read, *I knew you'd beg me not to go, but I have to. My husband is worried about his parents and sister. Don't worry about us. We'll be fine. Your daughter, Daphne.*

Monica tried to reassure Miemps that as visitors in Zimbabwe Silas and Daphne and their son would be safe. It was natural, Monica added on a more lighthearted note, for Daphne to be eager to meet her parents-in-law after more than four years of marriage.

"What if Silas decides to stay, to get involved in politics again?" asked Miemps. "Last time, the authorities let him out of prison. This time they might not."

Monica assured her that Silas knew he was making more of a contribution to democracy in his country through the newsletters he smuggled in from South Africa than he would as an out-of-work journalist living in Zimbabwe. "The people there have come to rely on him for news." Monica heard in her own words echoes of Dudu's speech to her about the *Lady Helen Herald.*

"I just wanted to fill you in on the news and give you these," said Miemps, holding out the scones. "I baked two batches to try and cheer up Reginald. He hasn't been outside in the glorious spring weather the whole day."

"Have you told him about Mama Dlamini?" asked Monica. It would be impossible for Miemps not to have heard.

She shook her head. "He doesn't need more to fret over. And I don't, either. As far as I'm concerned Mama Dlamini can do what she wants, and good luck to her. I'm too worried about my daughter and grandson to think about her."

Miemps's words were cavalier, but Monica sensed the hurt underneath. She wished that her own comment to Mama Dlamini about Mr. Yang asking forgiveness would come true. But he was a man who saw only the bottom line on a spread-sheet. Ostriches would take flight with the migratory birds before Mr. Yang came knocking on Miemps's door to apologize.

* * *

Ten days later, Miemps returned to Monica's house with a letter she'd received from Daphne and more scones. Mandla took a seat on the arm of Monica's chair as she read it aloud. Monica had always believed that children should not be shielded from the realities of life, and this included the situation in their neighboring country. Mandla was old enough to understand that even the most glorious dreams for the future could be perverted by the greed and self-destructive vanity of those in power.

"*My dearest Mother and Father,*" read Monica. "*My husband's parents and sister have made me feel very welcome. They are happy to see that Silas finally has a family after the disappointments he has suffered in his life. But, of course, they are sad that the distance between us is so great. His mother cried when she first saw Victor. She says he looks just like Silas did as a boy. Victor was shy at first, but he is more comfortable with them now. Every day he asks when we are going to see you and Gramps again. My sister-in-law is a friendly woman, but sometimes her temper is short. Mine would be, too, if I had to stand in a line for six hours to buy bread.*

"*Silas was shocked to see how thin everyone has grown. On the night we arrived, his mother served us stew and the family ate as though no one had seen meat in months. I felt guilty eating my share, but my mother-in-law would have been insulted if I hadn't cleaned my plate. The electricity is often off for days at a time and then it's necessary to cook outside over an open fire.*

"*We haven't been to the capital yet to see Silas's ex-colleagues because there is no petrol available for his father's car. As soon as the local filling station gets some, there will be a line a mile long. Silas really wants to go to Harare, so he says he'll wait in* line. *I worry about him. It's fine to write about the country from the safety of South Africa, but I don't think he should get involved here. I told him so, but he said he just wants to go to Harare to meet the distributors of his newsletters. Sometimes I wonder if he's withholding the truth from me because he doesn't want me to worry.*

"*There is a truth that I do not wish to withhold from you, my dear parents, but it is too risky to put in a letter. I will tell you all about it when we get back from our two-week trip.*

"*Your loving daughter,*

"*Daphne.*"

"You can't tell me not to worry now," said Miemps, folding the letter.

"What does Reginald say about it?" asked Monica.

She shook her head wildly. "I read him the letter and left out the last part."

Monica wished that Daphne had been less of a dutiful daughter and done the same. Miemps wouldn't be able to sleep until her daughter and grandchild returned in three days.

"At least you know Silas hasn't decided to stay in Zimbabwe. Daphne says she's coming home."

"I hope Daphne and Victor stay behind with Silas's parents when he goes to the capital to see his colleagues," said Miemps. "I thought our family was finished with political business for good."

"You were active in the struggle against apartheid?" asked Monica.

"Not me! Or Reginald. Only Daphne. She's been arrested three times for taking part in protest marches."

Monica was not surprised. Daphne had been the first to climb up on her roof to begin the protest sit-in when Mr.

Yang's bulldozers had arrived to knock down Sandpiper Drift. Daphne had been the first to throw her shoes at Mr. Yang when he'd arrived to order the women of the neighborhood down from their roofs so the bulldozers could get busy. Daphne and Silas were even more suited to each other than Monica had previously thought. And now that she knew of her past, she was not so sure Daphne would not become involved with Silas's political cause.

Zak walked into the living room, greeted Miemps and helped himself to one of the scones.

"When's my most senior nurse coming back?" he asked her.

Miemps glanced at Monica. "In three days." Then she added quietly, "I hope." But Zak didn't hear because he was busy helping himself to another scone.

"These are delicious, Miemps."

"I'll make you some more then. I've got to keep my hands busy." She stood up to go.

"I'll walk you out," said Monica.

"Give my regards to Reginald," said Zak.

At the front door, Monica told Miemps to call if she heard anything further from Daphne. Monica watched her elderly friend walk back down the road, and although the cake tin Miemps carried was now empty, Monica wished she had been able to lighten her friend's load.

Daphne did not arrive home on the day she was expected, and Miemps called Monica in a panic. Monica listed all of the reasons why Daphne might have been delayed: car trouble, little Victor had an upset stomach from strange food, a long line at the border. But Miemps believed that something terrible had happened and would not be consoled.

Monica did not admit it to her friend, but she was just as worried. Daphne had never missed a day of work at the hospital, and for her to miss one without an explanation to Zak meant that something serious had happened.

The next day a telegram arrived for Zak from Daphne, apologizing for being absent from work. The only explanation she gave was "trouble at the border."

Monica searched the news headlines but could find nothing about the border post being shut down. Zak was the one who came up with the most plausible explanation— Silas had tried to smuggle his parents into South Africa and had been caught. Monica showed the telegram to Miemps, and Miemps reached the same conclusion.

"Daphne and Victor are South African citizens by birth. Silas is a naturalized citizen by marriage. Why would they have trouble at the border unless they tried to do something illegal?" said Miemps.

There were no reports on the wire service of South Africans being arrested for smuggling illegal immigrants into South Africa. Miemps told Reginald that Daphne had phoned to say they'd decided to stay an extra few days because Victor was having such a good time.

A day passed with no word from Daphne, and a dream Miemps had had about Silas floating on the Limpopo River became a waking fear.

"He's going to bring his parents and sister over on a boat," she told Monica.

"But that would be crazy after all the rain up there," said Monica. As soon as the words were out of her mouth, she knew she'd made an error. She tried covering it up. "But someone will have to drive the car over the border and that will be Daphne, since she's the only South African by birth among them."

Miemps sighed. The stress had taken its toll on her the past few days. She no longer looked a decade younger than her sixty-five years. "Reginald is growing suspicious," she said, "because I've been baking day and night."

"Zak said the staff and patients went wild for the cakes you sent to the hospital."

"It's difficult keeping all this worry to myself. I have to do something," explained Miemps.

Monica wondered how Silas would manage to hide his parents and sister in Lady Helen if he succeeded in smuggling them out of Zimbabwe.

Shortly after midnight, Daphne, Silas and Victor returned to Lady Helen without Silas's parents and sister.

The next morning, Miemps told Monica what had happened. After hearing that immigration officials at the Beit Bridge crossing were open to bribery, Silas had loaded his family into the back of their car with Victor, locked up the house and set out for what they thought was a one-way trip to South Africa. As they'd waited in the line of cars to cross the bridge, they'd noticed immigration officials confiscating travel documents, even South African passports held by Zimbabweans. Another driver waiting in line explained that this was a crackdown ordered by the South African government, which had discovered that corrupt immigration officials had been selling fake passports to desperate Zimbabweans.

Silas and Daphne watched as shocked men and women

turned their vehicles around, or, if they were traveling in minibus taxis, unloaded their suitcases from the roof, and then walked away from the border post, back into the country they were so desperate to leave. Another driver told Silas that, farther upstream, local entrepreneurs would ferry people across the Limpopo River in rickety rowboats for a fee. Returning to their villages in Zimbabwe was not an option; their families would starve without the money they earned in South Africa.

Daphne was terrified that the immigration officials would accuse Silas of having false papers if he offered a bribe for his family's crossing, and so, agreeing that it was too dangerous, Silas had turned the car around with a heavy heart and driven his parents and sister home.

Silas promised them that he would work from within South Africa to get them a visa to join him, and in the meantime he would continue sending money. Filled with sadness and not a small measure of fear, Silas and Daphne had approached the border crossing again.

Though Silas did not try anything illegal this time, the official who checked his documents declared them fake. Daphne was so incensed that she got out of the car and began a tirade against the man for daring to prevent her husband from coming into the country where he had legal residence. The official was so shocked that he immediately backed down and let them pass.

"He's lucky she didn't throw her shoes at him," Monica told Miemps.

But Miemps did not see the humor. "They could have refused to allow Silas to cross, and then Daphne would have stayed with him."

Monica thought of Silas's parents and sister, who had packed their most precious possessions into tiny suitcases that would fit in the trunk of Silas's car, then left their home, not knowing how long it would be before they saw it again, only to return a few hours later without having made it across the border.

The leaders of South Africa were no strangers to the struggle against oppression and suffering. Monica prayed that they would now take up the challenge to alleviate the suffering of their neighbors to the north.

❧ Chapter Seventeen ❧

Mandla's suitcase had been packed for two weeks when the final day of school came and the December summer holidays began. Monica had worried that his head might be too full of excitement about their trip to the United States to concentrate on his end-of-year exams, but his report card showed otherwise.

His enthusiasm was tempered by regret at leaving his grandparents behind. They'd arrived from Italy at the beginning of the summer, as they always did, and were happily settled into the Old Garage. They understood that the family had to leave to visit Sipho, but Mandla did not feel that it was right, and suggested that they make the trip, too.

"There are only two places I go, son," said Monica's father. "Italy and South Africa. The rest of the world can get on without me."

Mandla had traveled on airplanes before to visit his grandparents in Italy, but the passengers sitting near them would have been forgiven for thinking this was his first time. He played with the personal television screen, flipping it in and out of its place in the armrest; he pushed the buttons for the air-conditioning and lights and twice the flight attendant came to check why he had called for assistance. And this was before the airplane had even taken off.

"Sit still," Monica told him after he'd tried the window shade for the fifteenth time.

"He's excited about seeing his brother again," said Zak.

"And the land where movies are made," added Mandla. "Sipho wouldn't even know if he was standing in the middle of the street where a movie was filmed."

"I don't think they make many movies in Houston," Monica told him.

Mandla was not listening. He had stood up to peer over the headrest at the passenger sitting in front of him. "I'm going to America," he announced loudly.

"Me, too," replied the man.

"Sit down," Monica told him again. "You'll have plenty of time for socializing after takeoff. It's a two-hour flight to Johannesburg and then eighteen hours to Washington." She hoped that the people sitting near them were the talkative type.

Nine hours into their international flight, the airplane refueled in the Cape Verde islands, off the northwest coast of Africa. Monica wished that they could get out and stretch their legs as passengers used to be able to do in the past, but security concerns now meant that they had to wait on board the airplane.

Nine hours and five full-length movies later, Mandla

couldn't wait to get out of the airplane, and was irritated to learn that they had to board another flight to get to Houston.

He fell asleep with his head on Monica's lap just before landing in Houston, and was not pleased to be awakened to put on his seat belt and bring his seat back to the upright position.

Sipho's host parents had offered to meet them at the airport, but Zak said that they would make their own way to the hotel.

"Why's Sipho not at the airport?" asked Mandla.

Monica and Zak looked at each other. Perhaps it had not been a good idea to turn down Sipho's host mother's polite offer, even if it had been to spare her a long drive.

Mandla fell asleep again in the taxi on the way to the hotel and did not wake up when Zak carried him to their room and put him to bed. It was only lunchtime in Texas, but in South Africa it was evening, and he had only slept for five hours the previous night on the flight. Sipho was due to arrive at their hotel at three, after he finished school for the day, but at this rate Mandla wouldn't be awake to see his brother.

Zak and Monica stretched out on either side of him on the bed, and the next thing Monica knew, the telephone was ringing, and she was fumbling on the wrong side of the bed to answer it. After ten rings, Zak got to it. Sipho was in the lobby of the hotel.

Monica had meant to shower and change before meeting his host mother, but now there was no time. She ran her fingers through her hair and left Zak with Mandla, who had not even changed positions in his sleep, and went down to the lobby.

Sipho's eyes lit up as she stepped out of the elevator, but he did not, as she'd hoped, hurry over to meet her. He was with another boy, almost two heads taller, with the broad shoulders of a natural athlete. This had to be Connor. The blond woman next to him was just as tall, and dressed in sweatpants and sneakers, as though she had just come from the gym.

"Sipho," said Monica, with her arms outstretched. She refrained from calling him sweetie in front of his host family.

He hugged her back, but when she wanted to hold on a few seconds longer, he pulled away.

"Mom, this is Connor and my host mother, Nancy." There was a new confidence in his voice, and for a moment Monica felt a twinge of jealousy at his easy use of a word she had waited so long to hear him use with her.

As they shook hands, Monica noticed that Nancy was wearing a diamond-studded gold bracelet, which was an unusual accessory to wear while jogging or working out at the gym. Perhaps this was just how she normally dressed.

"He's been counting the days," Nancy said.

Her Texan accent did not seem as pronounced now as it had on the telephone.

Connor slapped Sipho on the back and Sipho laughed. It was a new laugh, one Monica had never heard before, that seemed to come from deep in his chest.

"We'd like to invite you to our house for a barbecue tonight," said Nancy, "but since we've never taken such a long flight ourselves, we don't know if you're up to it."

Monica smiled at her in appreciation for her thoughtfulness. "I don't think Mandla, my other son, is going to wake up until it's morning time in South Africa." She looked at her watch. "Which means midnight Houston time."

"Oh, dear, you'd better all get your sleep then. What about you, Sipho?"

"I'll stay awake," Monica told him.

Sipho and Connor exchanged looks. Monica wondered why there was any doubt that Sipho would spend the rest of the afternoon and evening with them. She had even re-quested a roll-away bed so he could sleep over.

"Connor has a game tonight," explained Nancy.

"It's up to you, Sipho," said Monica. "If you want to watch football, that's fine. Maybe we can meet afterward."

"Games usually end pretty late," said Connor, who up until now had not said anything except a polite hello.

"I'm sorry, Mom, I—"

"He promised us, Mrs. Niemand," said Connor. "It's the opening game of the season."

"I didn't know that it would be on the night you arrived," explained Sipho.

"Oh, okay," said Monica, feeling disappointed, but not wishing to embarrass Sipho in front of his friend. "Then we'll see you tomorrow after school."

"The guys are all going bowling, since it's the last day of school before the Christmas holidays," said Connor.

Monica was beginning to be irritated by this boy's assured manner. She and her family had just traveled thousands of miles to see Sipho, and Connor presumed Sipho would choose a get-together with school friends who he saw every day over a reunion with his family.

"Do you want to go bowling?" Monica asked Sipho.

He looked at Connor. "Is it okay if I miss it this time?" he asked.

Monica was shocked at the submissive tone of her son's voice. Sipho had never enjoyed group activities with his class-mates in Lady Helen, and Monica had even had to push him to invite boys to their house to help celebrate his birthdays.

"I suppose you have no choice," said Connor.

Monica sensed the young man was perfectly aware his remark was callous, but did not care.

"Do you want to come up to the room to say a quick hello to your dad?" she asked Sipho. "He couldn't leave Mandla asleep alone."

Sipho looked at Nancy to check if it was all right.

"Go ahead," she said. "Connor and I will grab a soda at the coffee shop over there."

In the elevator, on the ride up to their floor, Sipho asked about their flight, and Monica told them how difficult it had been for Mandla to be confined for so long.

Just before the elevator doors opened, he said, "I'm glad you came, Mom."

Monica had to bite her tongue not to reply, "Well, then why are you choosing football over us?" The instinct she had developed over the years as a mother told her that this would be more harmful than helpful.

"I'm glad to see you've settled in and made friends," she said pointedly.

"They're Connor's friends, but they like me. They think I'm cool, being African and all."

"I see."

She unlocked the hotel room door, and Zak came to greet Sipho with a big bear hug.

"We missed you," he said, not letting go. "Your mother hasn't stopped worrying about you, and your brother has been counting down the days from the minute you left."

Sipho walked to the bed where Mandla lay sprawled across the sheets.

"He's absolutely wiped out from the trip," said Zak,

coming to stand behind Sipho and resting his hand on his shoulder. "Sit down and relax. I'm feeling better after my snooze. How about you, Monica?"

"Sipho can't stay. He's going to a football game," said Monica, trying to keep her voice as neutral as possible.

Zak's eyes widened. "Is that so? Who's playing?"

"It's the opening match of the season. My school's playing last year's champs."

"Interesting," said Zak. He had tried to involve Sipho in soccer, cricket and rugby, just as Sipho's mother, Ella, once had, but he, too, had been unsuccessful. Sipho had even refused to watch their national team play others on television. "Maybe while we're here, I can come with you to a game. Not tonight, though. I don't think I'm physically capable of setting foot out of this hotel."

Monica wondered if Zak was genuinely not hurt by this development or if he had simply decided that it would be better to involve himself in Sipho's new interest rather than alienate him by questioning it.

"I'd better go. They're waiting for me in the lobby," said Sipho.

"That's quite an American accent you have there," said Zak, smiling and squeezing his shoulder.

"I don't have an accent," he declared. "Do I, Mom?"

"A little bit," said Monica. She thought Sipho looked pleased to be informed of this fact.

"I'll come down with you again," she said.

"It's okay. You're tired. I'll find my way."

Monica took him into her arms and gave him the long, enthusiastic hug she'd wanted to give him earlier in the lobby. Eventually he pulled away, but instead of being irritated as she thought he might be, he was smiling. "I'll see you tomorrow, Mom. Tell Mandla I was here."

After they'd watched him walk down the hall and disappear into an elevator, Monica turned to Zak and burst into tears.

"It's normal. He's growing up," said Zak softly. "A girl he's interested in is probably going to the game."

"A girl? He's ditching his family for a girl? He's never been interested in girls." If Zak thought he was making Monica feel better, he was wrong.

"He's not ditching us, Monica. Anyway, we need to sleep."

Monica went into the bathroom and closed the door on him. Why did he insist on making this less than it was? In the shower she went over the conversation in the lobby, but that only upset her more. She gave up trying to find her nightgown in the suitcase she was too tired to unpack and settled on a T-shirt to sleep in. Mandla had not left much space for either her or Zak in the bed, but she slipped in beside him and drifted off to sleep while Zak flipped through the television channels.

Chapter Eighteen

As Monica had predicted, Mandla woke at midnight, ready to start a new day. After waking Zak to show Mandla how to operate the television, she went back to sleep.

She awoke at five to find Mandla sleeping with his head on her shoulder. He looked younger than his eight years, and for a moment Monica thought of the first time Ella had brought him to her house, as a chubby toddler. He'd charmed Francina, who at that time was still working as Monica's full-time housekeeper. Hopefully, he'd be able to sleep until at least seven, and then stay awake all day. She had heard that jet lag was far worse after the return journey to South Africa.

Trying not to wake Mandla, she shifted his head onto a pillow and slipped out of bed. Through a chink in the curtains she saw that the sky was turning pink. The sun would soon be up. They were not staying downtown, but there were a number of high-rises surrounding the hotel. Sipho's host family lived somewhere to the northwest. It still hurt that he'd chosen his new friends over his family.

By eight o'clock they had eaten breakfast and were ready to start the day. Mandla wanted to go to the shopping mall across the street.

"You can see malls at home," said Monica.

"Not in Lady Helen," replied Mandla.

"Thank goodness," said Zak.

But Mandla didn't think it was funny. "We never go to a mall when we're in Cape Town."

He relented when Monica told him about the full-size dinosaur skeletons at the Museum of Natural Science.

Since they would be leaving to visit a theme park in Los Angeles in two days, there was no point renting a car in Houston, and so Zak called a taxi to meet them downstairs.

As expected, Mandla was enthralled by the dinosaur collection at the museum, and the day passed without any more whining from him. But by three o'clock, he was exhausted and wanted to sleep. It was past his bedtime in South Africa.

Sipho had not said what time he'd be coming, so Monica decided that it would be best to return to the hotel, put Mandla to bed for a nap, and wait for Sipho to call.

At four, Monica woke with a start at a knock on the door. Zak had fallen asleep, too. She looked through the peephole and saw Sipho outside.

"Come in," she said. "We all fell asleep. This jet lag is something else."

He smelled of an unfamiliar fabric softener, and he was wearing new sneakers.

He noticed her looking. "My host mother bought them."

Sipho never wore sneakers unless he was going on a long walk or a climb up the koppies.

Zak was awake now. He gave Sipho a hug. "It's good to see you," he said.

"How you doing, Dad?"

"Listen to that. You're sounding like a real American."

"I am not. Do you have any bottled water?" He had started to say water the American way, and then switched to his old accent and said it the way South Africans did: *wartuh.*

Mandla did not want to wake up, but if he was to adjust to the time difference he was going to have to try and stay awake till a normal bedtime. Finally, he heard Sipho's voice among those trying to rouse him, and opened his eyes.

"What took you so long?" he asked his big brother. "I've been waiting for two days to see you."

"I was here yesterday but you were fast asleep, dozy head."

"You should have come to the museum with us. There was a skeleton of a Tyrannosaurus rex."

"I've been to that museum before."

"Did Connor take you?" asked Monica.

Sipho shook his head. "We went on a class trip. Connor doesn't go to museums."

Monica wondered how Sipho could have chosen to go to a football game with a boy with whom he had nothing in common over spending time with his family. He had never been influenced by peer pressure before, but something was different about Sipho in this new country.

Mandla announced that he was starving after his nap, and Sipho explained that since many Americans ate dinner early there would be many restaurants open at this time.

They chose an Indian establishment two blocks from the hotel. Mandla was excited when the waiter gave him a hot towel so he could eat with his hands. Halfway through their meal, Sipho showed Mandla a tiny portable music player that his host mother had bought him. Mandla put on the earphones.

"What's this?" he asked.

Sipho named a band Monica had never heard of.

"They're from Seattle," added Sipho. "Connor's going to get us tickets when they come to Houston."

Sipho listening to rock music? Monica looked at Zak to see if this was hard for him to register, as well. But he was mopping up the sauce of his murgh makhani with the last of the naan bread and seemed oblivious to the monumental change in his adopted son.

As they walked back to the hotel, Monica tried to eavesdrop on the conversation between the boys, who were walking in front.

She heard something about a party, and then Mandla asked if there would be girls there, to which Sipho replied that there would. Monica did not have to strain to catch Mandla's loud response of disgust.

How could this change in Sipho have happened so quickly? Zak would say it was long overdue, but Monica was not ready for it and found it shocking.

Sipho had brought with him an overnight bag, and settled into the roll-away bed, while Mandla climbed in again between Zak and Monica.

Although Monica was pleased to have Sipho back, she couldn't help hoping that the old Sipho would reappear once he was away from Connor.

* * *

Monica's hope became more fervent the next day at Sipho's host family's barbecue, where she watched Sipho interacting with Connor. Surprisingly, Sipho did most of the talking. Connor laughed often. Monica could only imagine the adolescent hilarity.

Connor's family lived in a neighborhood with lots of trees, and houses and gardens far larger than any in Lady Helen. The public high school was within walking distance, a fact Monica had been pleased to learn, because she didn't want Sipho in a car driven by a sixteen- or seventeen-year-old. In South Africa, young people had to be eighteen to drive.

Connor lived in a sprawling ranch house from the sixties that had been recently renovated. Monica and Zak's whole house would fit in the open-plan living room and eat-in kitchen. It was expensively furnished and everything matched perfectly, including the artwork on the walls. The artists Monica knew in Lady Helen would have been appalled. To them, art should be the focus of a room, not an accent piece like a throw pillow.

Monica wished Sipho would stop being so uncharacteristically talkative so she could relax. Nancy was a charming hostess and went out of her way to make them feel at home. Mandla did everything Monica should have done; he complimented Nancy on her home and garden and told her the bruschetta was delicious.

"How did you know what these hors d'oeuvres were?" Nancy asked. "Connor would call them sandwiches."

Mandla told her that he had been to Italy and that his grandfather was teaching him Italian.

"Is that so?" Nancy was impressed.

There was a large heated saltwater pool in the backyard. Nancy gave Mandla one of Connor's old bathing suits and he was soon splashing around on his own. Monica was glad she'd brought a jacket so that she could sit outside to keep an eye on him. Sipho and Connor stood with Zak and Bill, Nancy's husband, at the barbecue.

"It's been wonderful for Connor to have company," said Nancy, sitting down beside Monica on the wrought-iron patio furniture. "It's not easy being an only child. It wasn't our choice. We tried to have another, but no luck."

Monica was shocked at the easy way with which Nancy had shared this personal information. She could not imagine telling a stranger about her own fight against infertility. She was at a loss how to reply to Nancy's confidence, but the need quickly disappeared.

"I wanted to adopt, but Bill was against it. You're lucky you have a supportive husband."

"Zak and I hadn't yet met when I adopted the boys," said Monica.

"I didn't know that. Sipho doesn't talk about the past very much."

Monica was happy to hear that Sipho hadn't succumbed to this family's easy familiarity. "He's a private sort of boy," she said.

Nancy nodded. "I hear you've been trying to have another baby."

Monica froze, her glass of sparkling mineral water pressed to her lips. How could Sipho have told his host mother that? She didn't know which urge was strongest, to cry or to march Sipho inside for a talk. Nancy was waiting for her answer.

"Yes," she croaked, and then took a sip of her water.

"You poor thing. I know what it's like. Bill and I did all

the treatments, tried three different doctors. It just wasn't meant to be. You should join a support group. It helped to be able to cry on the shoulders of women who were going through the same heartache. Men just don't understand."

Monica wished that Bill would announce that the hamburgers were ready, so she could politely withdraw from this conversation.

Nancy leaned forward and placed her hand over Monica's. "The only way you can cope is if you open up to others."

Monica could have clapped in appreciation when Bill walked up carrying a plate of cooked hamburgers and asked Nancy where she wanted them.

"On the dining room table," she said.

Monica escaped to get Mandla out of the pool, and while he dressed, she found a place at the dinner table between Zak and Bill. Nancy told Connor he and Sipho could take their dinner into the family room so they could watch television while they were eating. Monica would have preferred them to remain at the table and take part in the conversation, but, of course, the boys jumped at Nancy's suggestion. Mandla was offered the same option but chose to remain with the adults, and Bill moved one seat along to allow Mandla to sit next to Monica.

After dessert and coffee, Mandla fell asleep at the table and Monica said they ought to leave.

"You can put him on my bed," Nancy told Zak.

"Let them head back to the hotel if they want," said Bill testily. "I'll get my keys and drive you."

Nancy looked disappointed, but Monica was relieved that the evening had come to an end.

Sipho went upstairs and collected the bag he had packed.

"Enjoy yourself," Connor told him.

Monica detected sarcasm in the boy's voice. Sipho had expressed enthusiasm for this trip to the theme park when she'd spoken to him about it on the phone from South Africa. Did Connor think he was too mature for this type of fun?

That night in the hotel room, Monica asked Sipho about the atmosphere in his host family's house.

"Connor's parents each have their own bedroom. And everybody eats dinner and watches TV in their own room," said Sipho.

"But Nancy and Bill get on okay in front of you boys?"

Sipho nodded.

At least she didn't have to worry about Sipho witnessing emotional or even physical abuse. A cold-war situation was unhealthy, but Sipho wouldn't be upset by it.

Monica knew that she was being hypocritical. Her own relationship with her husband wasn't as it should be, and this was her fault. If she would stop bottling up her emotions and open up to Zak, things might return to normal, but she was too wrapped up in her own disappointment and misery to do what was sensible. Nancy had said men couldn't understand what infertile women went through, but Monica had first been attracted to Zak because he was not like most men she had known. Zak hadn't changed; she had. And if things were to be normal between them again, she would have to stop being so insular and let him in.

✎ Chapter Nineteen ✎

Mandla stepped out of the airplane into the crisp California air, his arms spread wide as though he were a dignitary arriving to cheers and banners.

"Now we'll see where movies are made," he said.

In the rental car on the way to their hotel, he identified a number of locations where movies had been filmed. Monica had no idea whether he was correct or not, but she was pleased to see him excited.

Sipho wore a black T-shirt with the name of a rock band she had never heard of, given to him by Connor. As soon as he'd climbed into the rental car, he'd put on a pair of sunglasses, another gift from Connor.

Zak was not used to driving on the right-hand side of the road, but the rental car had automatic transmission, so at least he didn't have to remember to change gears with his right hand instead of his left. And most of the trip was on the freeway, which also made it easier. The hotel, only a short distance from the theme park, provided a shuttle service for guests, but they planned to use the rental car to drive up Highway 1 as far as Monterey, where Sipho wanted to visit the famous aquarium.

Halfway to the hotel, they stopped at a sprawling mall for Mandla to use the bathroom.

"You can use one there," said Monica, pointing to a coffee shop that was nearly deserted.

Monica asked for directions to the bathroom from a young man wrapping silverware behind the counter.

"The restroom is for customers only," he told Monica, not looking up. "Buy something and you can use it."

"My son will only be a minute," she replied.

"Order something and he can use it."

"I've got to go," whined Mandla.

"You go," Monica told him. "I'll buy a coffee from this gentleman." She did not bother to disguise her sarcastic tone.

When Mandla came out of the restroom Monica was still waiting for her coffee to be poured.

"I've paid three dollars fifty, so we might as well wait," she told him.

Zak and Sipho had wandered next door to look at the computers in the window of an electronics store.

"Three dollars fifty to use the bathroom!" exclaimed Mandla. "How many rand is that?"

"About twenty-five."

"We can get five milk shakes at Mama Dlamini's for twenty-five rand." He turned to the man who was putting a lid on Monica's coffee. "How can you stop a little boy from using the bathroom—I mean restroom?"

Monica touched his shoulder. "It's okay," she murmured.

Mandla shrugged her hand off. "No, it's not."

The man looked at Mandla with a bemused smile.

"Everybody told me Americans were friendly, but you're not."

The man's smile slid from his face. "Listen, brat. Store policy is store policy. Now clear out of here."

"Don't call me a brat," said Mandla, raising his voice.

Monica noticed a customer behind them, listening intently. "Shh, let's go now," she said. "I don't need his coffee."

Mandla turned his back on the man behind the counter and addressed the handful of customers in the shop. "You should all find somewhere else to buy your coffee. This man is rude—and his bathroom is dirty."

Some of the customers grinned, others commented quietly to each other.

"Excuse me," said the man who had been waiting behind them. He spoke directly to Mandla. "I was impressed with what I just saw." He handed him a card. "Give me a call. I think I can find you work." And then he turned and walked out of the shop, apparently taking Mandla's advice to buy his coffee elsewhere.

Mandla stuffed the card in his pocket and ran out to tell Sipho what had happened with the store manager. Monica met Zak's eye as Mandla related the story. He, too, seemed surprised at how upset Mandla was. She wondered if the atmosphere at home over the past few months had done Mandla more damage than she'd realized, and if his outburst today was an emotional release.

Sipho told Mandla that an American would have simply

ignored the manager and used the restroom without buying a thing.

"He wouldn't have you arrested," said Sipho. "Now Mom paid for a coffee she didn't get."

Mandla looked crestfallen.

"There's no harm done. Let's forget all about this and go to our hotel," said Monica.

After they'd checked into the hotel, Mandla was eager to set off for the theme park. Monica agreed, and told him to put on a long-sleeved shirt, since it was not as warm in California as in Texas.

Mandla disappeared into the bathroom and came out wearing a sweatshirt bought at the botanical gardens in Cape Town. "Mom, what's a talent agent?" he asked.

Monica told him that it was someone who searched for people to be in movies.

Mandla shrieked with excitement. "I'm going to be in a movie."

"What are you talking about?" asked Sipho.

"That man who gave me his card in the coffee shop is a talent agent." He handed the card to Sipho.

"We could go to an Internet café and check him out," suggested Sipho.

But Mandla wanted Monica to call him right away. "Please, Mom, before he forgets about me and I lose my chance."

Monica looked at the card. She had never heard of the man or his agency. She told Mandla that Sipho was right; they would have to do some investigating before calling him.

"Let's go to the theme park now," she said.

Mandla was quiet on the shuttle ride to the park's entrance and answered in monosyllables if Monica asked him a question. If Zak spoke to him, however, he was his usual self. He was punishing her for not doing as he wished, she knew. Perhaps for a lot more.

While they were at the park, Mandla forgot to sulk and Monica felt more lighthearted than she had in years. The look of gratitude on Zak's face at seeing her enjoying herself was almost enough to make her cry. She was the center of the family, and over the past few months she had let them all down.

When they returned to the hotel room that night, Sipho flopped onto the bed next to Zak to watch the television news, and Mandla said he was going to take a shower.

Ten minutes later, he emerged from the bathroom, still dressed in the clothes he had worn to the park, and beaming.

"I woke him up, but he wasn't angry. He wants to see me tomorrow," he said triumphantly.

"Who does?" asked Monica. "Oh, no. Tell me you didn't phone that talent agent, Mandla."

"This could be my big chance. And if it were up to you, I'd miss it."

"But Mandla, we're going back to South Africa soon. Is there any point?" She sat down next to Zak with a sigh. "Did you hear this?" she asked him over the noise of the television. "Mandla's got an appointment with a talent agent tomorrow."

Zak looked away from the screen. "Mandla, you should have let us check him out first. That man could be a scam artist. He might tell you that, before he gets you work, you have to do a course that costs thousands."

"We were supposed to go to the other park tomorrow," moaned Sipho.

Monica saw that Mandla was close to rushing back into

the bathroom in tears. "I suppose we can delay it an hour or two." She looked at Zak, and he shrugged. "Okay, Mandla," she said, "we'll go and see what this man is about."

Mandla did lock himself in the bathroom again, but this time to shower in preparation for his big meeting the following day.

Mandla was up at seven the next morning and made more noise than usual as he dressed, presumably so that the others would get up, too. They were expected at the talent agent's office at ten, but with Mandla so excited there was no point in trying to continue to sleep.

Monica came out of the shower to find Mandla describing to a yawning Sipho how he planned to divide his time between South Africa and Hollywood. He was not amused when Sipho asked where he would attend school.

Monica wanted to tell him not to get his hopes up, and then decided that he would misinterpret that as an expression of no confidence.

Zak found the correct high-rise office building in downtown Los Angeles with an hour to spare. "It's going to cost us a fortune in parking," he grumbled, and then gave Mandla a playful squeeze at the back of the neck. "We'll take it out of your movie star earnings."

Mandla laughed, but he clearly thought that was quite feasible. Monica prayed that if the man was going to let him down, he would do so gently.

The talent agency was on the tenth floor, and Monica was surprised to learn that it was a large company with offices in Europe and Japan. A receptionist led them to a waiting room with replicas of designer leather chairs from the nineteen thirties. Although early, they did not have to wait more than five minutes to see the talent scout.

Monica didn't remember much about him except that he had a beard, but he greeted her as though they'd all had coffee together that day and become friends. Zak, as he always did in the presence of effusive personalities, retreated into his shell. The talent scout asked if they would like to accompany Mandla into his office. Only Monica took him up on his offer, and the scowl Mandla gave her indicated that he would have preferred to go on his own, but she would not allow that.

For half an hour, the talent agent asked Mandla questions about his life and ignored Monica completely. She did not mind. It was interesting to hear Mandla describe their home. She had never before realized that he was bothered by Lady Helen's distance from a big city. He was always keen to accompany her to Cape Town whenever she needed to go there, but he had never expressed any dissatisfaction with small-town life. Perhaps she had overlooked the signs.

Although the talent agent was probably as old as Monica's father, his hip black clothing and rectangular glasses belonged to a younger generation. The walls of his office were lined with posters of films that, judging from the fashions and styling, went back to the seventies. Many had never made it to South African screens, perhaps due to strict censorship by the apartheid government.

The man saw her studying the posters. "I represent all those stars," he said.

"Did you hear that?" Mandla asked Monica, wide-eyed.

"Your son could be on a poster like these."

Mandla almost jumped out of his seat.

"Mrs. Niemand. I'd like to send him on an audition tomorrow."

Mandla gave a little yelp of excitement.

"It's only for a bit part, but it will be the start he needs."

Mandla really did jump out of his seat this time. "Oh, Mom, please say I can do it! Please say I can do it!"

They had planned to drive the rental car up to Monterey tomorrow to visit the aquarium Sipho was so keen to see. Monica asked the talent scout to write down the details, and said she'd discuss it with her husband. Mandla glared at her, but he perked up in order to charm the talent scout on their way out.

"Thank you, I'll give the audition my best shot," he told the man. It was obvious that Mandla intended to go to the audition, whatever it took.

As was to be expected, Sipho was upset that they were even contemplating postponing the trip to Monterey. Monica told him that it would only be by one day.

"But what if Mandla gets the part? He can't stay here for months to be in a movie. It's ridiculous even going."

If they hadn't been in the car on the way to the next theme park, Mandla would have stalked into the bathroom and slammed the door, but all he could do was turn his head away and study the passing buildings.

Monica and Zak did not have a chance to discuss the matter any further until both boys were on a ride together at the theme park.

"There was no point in driving him to this meeting if we didn't intend to let him take the next step," said Zak.

Sipho's disappointment, when they broke the news to him, was understandable.

"We can go to Monterey the day after Christmas," said Monica.

Sipho did not respond.

Dinner that evening at an Italian restaurant was not the fun occasion it should have been for a family on vacation together. Sipho sulked, Mandla accused him of being selfish, and Monica felt too weary to deal with either of them. For a while on this trip, she had started to feel herself again, but now she wanted to go to bed and not get up for days. Only Zak, it seemed, was unaffected by the emotions running high around him. After trying to engage the boys in conversation and failing, he concentrated on the signed celebrity photographs on the walls and enjoyed his meal in silence.

Then a group of carolers entered the restaurant and captured everyone's attention. Monica's heart ached. On any other occasion, Mandla would have been the first to join in with the singing, Sipho would have looked on with good-natured patience and Zak would have applauded the loudest. She needed to do something to pull her family together. But what?

Chapter Twenty

The next morning, Christmas Eve, Mandla had forgotten about being angry with Sipho because he was excited about going to a movie studio.

"Are we there yet?" he asked for the tenth time, while Zak negotiated the heavy traffic between their hotel near the theme park and the area where most of the movie studios were located.

Mandla had changed his clothing four times before settling on jeans and a T-shirt with an African print on the front, "to distinguish himself from the American boys," he'd said.

Monica had told him not to be nervous, just to be himself, but Mandla couldn't sit still, even with his seat belt on.

A security guard at the gate to the studio checked Mandla's name on a list.

"You see that, Sipho? My name is on his list."

Sipho, who had been lectured not to ruin his brother's day, gave a polite smile.

The family was not allowed to accompany Mandla into the studio, but were shown to a small lounge, to wait with the families of other young hopefuls.

"Great way to spend Christmas Eve," muttered Sipho, looking at the television, which was set to a soap opera channel.

Monica watched the child actors' younger siblings playing with a basket of grubby toys in the corner. Her attention was particularly caught by a little girl of about eighteen months. The child had blond hair, an infectious laugh, and didn't mind when her older brother pushed her away from the car he was pretending to drive. Each time, she laughed, as though he were playing a game with her. Monica could not keep her eyes off the little girl and hardly noticed Sipho's groans of impatience. When Zak and Sipho announced that they were going to take a walk, Monica elected to remain in the lounge. The little girl had found a new game: switching the television on and off. Her mother tried to stop her, but the only way she could do that was by restraining the girl on her lap.

The mother noticed Monica's interest. "One day they're babies and the next they're into everything," she said, smiling ruefully.

Monica nodded. She had not known Sipho as a baby, and Mandla had been about the same age as this little girl when she'd first met him. Feeling melancholy, she got up and put her head out the door to see if she could spot Zak and Sipho.

The road outside was deserted. She was wondering whether to sit back down or take a stroll when she saw Mandla sauntering toward her, whistling. His audition must have gone well.

He pulled her outside and closed the door to the waiting room behind her.

"I got the part," he said in a theatrical whisper. "It's a secret because they're still auditioning the other boys on the schedule for today."

Monica went to hug him but he put up his hand. "No, someone will see," he said.

She was proud of him but dreaded the answer to the question she had to ask. "When will they need you?"

"Filming begins in six days and will take two weeks." He looked at her defiantly.

"I see." There was no point in discussing it here, especially within earshot of one of the parents whose son would be given the part when Mandla told the director he couldn't take it. "I wonder where Zak and Sipho have gone."

"I'll find them," said Mandla, and walked off as though he knew the lot as well as his own back garden.

Monica grabbed him by the hand. "I think it's best if we wait for them here. I don't want you getting lost, too."

"Oh, Mom, the director showed me around already. I have to report to studio A at eight o'clock in six days."

Zak and Sipho rounded the corner, and Mandla ran to tell them his news. Monica could see from their faces that they felt as trapped as she had.

In the car on the way back to the hotel, Sipho said what was on everybody's mind. "But Mandla, you're returning to South Africa in a week."

He folded his arms. "Mom can change the tickets. Can't you, Mom?"

She told him they could be changed for a fee, but that there were other considerations, such as Zak's job, her job.

"Dudu was doing all your work, anyway," Mandla said sulkily.

"Mandla! Apologize to your mother," said Zak.

"It's true. Everyone says so. And I'm always late for school because Mom doesn't want to get up in the morning."

He was angry, but Monica could hear that he was also about to cry.

"I'm sorry, Mandla. I've been having a rough time," she said.

"Does that mean we can stay for the filming then?"

Monica put her head in her hands and waited for Zak to say something.

"Your mother and I will discuss this," he stated.

A car behind beeped at them. Zak looked in the rearview mirror. "What's his problem?"

"I think you're going too slowly, Dad," said Sipho.

"I'm driving at the speed limit."

"Nobody else is," Sipho explained.

For the rest of the ride, nobody spoke. Zak concentrated on the traffic and the others were lost in their own thoughts.

At the hotel, Zak sent the boys upstairs to the room and he and Monica pretended to look in the window of the gift shop so they could have a few moments to talk privately.

"It's up to you," Zak told her. "But I can't stay on here."

Mandla looked up expectantly when they entered the hotel room.

"And?" he said.

Monica sat down on the bed next to him. "I'm sorry, sweetie, but we have to go home. Maybe you can try for a part in a movie in Cape Town."

Mandla rose to his feet. "How many of those do they

make? Mom, this is Hollywood. If a newspaper here offered you a job you wouldn't turn it down."

"Yes, I would," she said quietly.

"You just want to be mean," he shouted. He stormed to the bathroom and locked the door behind him.

Monica looked at her husband helplessly.

"He'll get over it," said Zak.

"No, he won't," said Sipho.

"I have to go home to relieve the locum," Zak murmured. "But I don't mind going on my own if you want to stay."

"And after this movie? What if there's another—and this time with a bigger part that requires him to stay longer? If we allow this to start—"

"One step at a time, Monica."

"That's easy for you to say. You're the one going home."

"Monica, I can't stay away from the hospital any longer."

"And, of course, the newspaper is not a real job." Monica's voice dripped sarcasm.

"Monica, calm down."

"I am calm," she shouted at him.

Zak looked at Sipho, who took his cue to excuse himself to visit the hotel's heated pool.

Monica watched her son leave and then turned on Zak. "You're supposed to be helping me make a difficult decision, not washing your hands of it."

"Monica—"

"That's what you always do. Let me do the worrying all by myself."

Zak's voice was icy. "You're not talking about Mandla and the movie anymore. Are you?"

"Why? Do you have a guilty conscience?"

"Monica, I have been there for you every step of the way with this whole baby business."

"Yes, but in silence." She knew Mandla would be listening to every word from inside the locked bathroom, but she could not help herself.

"That's unfair."

"I'll tell you about unfair," she shouted.

"Keep your voice down," snapped Zak. "Just listen to yourself, Monica. You're not being rational. Mandla's right. You have been neglecting him."

"How dare you?" she screamed. "What do you know? You're not a full-time parent."

Zak stared at her in disbelief. She had gone too far.

"I'm going to ignore that vicious comment," he said icily. "Because I know you're not yourself. You need help, Monica. We need help. This obsession about having a baby is destroying us all."

"That's easy for you to say. You already have a child of your own."

They heard the lock turn on the bathroom door.

Mandla's face was deadpan. "Let's go for a walk, Dad," he said in a small voice.

Zak picked up his wallet. "Good idea."

Mandla refused to look at Monica.

As soon as they'd closed the door, she burst into tears. Mandla would never forget what he had heard. All along he had been enthusiastic about her having a baby, but now that he had heard her refer to a baby as a child of her own, he would think that he was not enough for her. What had she done?

* * *

Late in the afternoon, Monica got up from the bed and went to the bathroom to wash her face. Her eyes were swollen from crying and her skin was blotchy. She had fallen asleep, only to be woken by a knock from a hotel employee wanting to know if they had enough filter coffee. After that, Monica had put the Do Not Disturb sign on the door, but she couldn't fall asleep again.

As she dried her face, she heard a key in the door. Zak and the boys had returned. She looked at her miserable expression in the mirror. How difficult would it be to agree to stay on in this country for two more weeks? If Mandla could choose any gift for Christmas, she knew it would be to appear in the movie, so why not make this her Christmas gift to him?

She opened the bathroom door.

"It's Christmas Eve," said Zak, as though she might have forgotten.

She did not meet his gaze.

"Let's go to a movie down the street and then have a look at the Christmas decorations in the store windows," suggested Sipho, the only one who had not been party to Monica's earlier outburst.

She shook her head. "I think we should go to church tonight."

Zak nodded. It was as though he, too, realized that the only way this family would find peace on Christmas Eve was in the presence of God.

The clerk on duty at the front desk gave them directions to two nearby churches. After calling both, they learned that only one had a Christmas Eve service.

Their choice of a restaurant was also made easy. The only one within walking distance that could offer them a table at a time that would enable them to make the Christmas service was a Chinese buffet—not exactly what Monica would have chosen for the occasion, but the boys were excited.

As soon as the waiter had served them their drinks, Monica turned to Mandla and made her announcement. "Okay, Mandla, we can stay for two more weeks."

He almost fell off his chair in his rush to hug her.

"Oh, thank you, Mom. Thank you, thank you, thank you. You'll see. It won't be a waste. One day I'll be famous and I'll buy you anything you want."

She smiled back at him. "I want you to be happy."

"I am now," he shouted. "Dad, are you going to stay, too?"

Monica knew she should have discussed her decision with Zak before announcing it to Mandla, but she didn't feel like being mature. This was petulant of her, and potentially destructive, but she believed that he had betrayed her; she wanted a baby and he was telling her to give up the idea.

She was surprised to see Zak smiling at her as though everything had been sorted out. For the sake of the boys, she smiled back at him. Their problems hadn't been solved, but there was no need to ruin Christmas for her family.

The Christmas service was exactly what their family needed. Though they didn't recognize any of the Christmas hymns, the boys joined in as best they could, and when the reverend prompted the congregation to greet their neighbors, Mandla charmed the family in the pew behind by wishing them a merry Christmas in Sotho, Zulu and Afrikaans.

"He's adorable," the mother told Monica.

This sort of remark would usually have prompted Sipho to roll his eyes, but he, too, was caught up in the joyful atmosphere of the Christmas service.

Afterward, when they returned to the hotel, Monica and Zak gave the boys their gifts.

"What's this?" said Mandla, affecting surprise. "You've already given me mine. I get to stay to be in the movie." But he wasted no time in tearing off the wrapping and then assembling the mini telescope that Zak had picked out while Monica distracted Mandla at the museum in Houston.

"I'm not sure you'll see much in this city with all the light and smog," said Zak. "But it will be useful back in Lady Helen."

Sipho was equally pleased with his illustrated guide to the national and state parks in the United States.

Zak handed Monica a small brown paper bag. "Sorry it's not gift wrapped," he said.

Inside she found a beautiful pair of earrings of silver and turquoise.

"The woman assured me that they were made by members of the Apache tribe in southern New Mexico," he explained.

"You bought them this afternoon?"

Zak nodded.

Monica felt tears come to her eyes. After all the vicious things she had said to him, he had gone out and bought her this gift.

"Thank you," she said, kissing him lightly on the lips. Their eyes locked and a message of understanding passed between them. Their relationship needed mending, but it was built on solid ground and would survive.

Her gift to him seemed dull in comparison.

"Thanks," he said, holding up the sweatshirt she'd bought at the theme park.

She hoped that when he wore it back in Lady Helen, he would remember only the good times they'd had on this trip.

After their late night, they all slept in the next morning. They found a pancake place that was open for breakfast, and then joined other tourists who were without their families for Christmas on the beach. A few eager children entered the cold water up to their waists, but everyone else was content to enjoy the bright winter sunshine on the warm sand. Before long, Mandla had collected a group of children and engaged them in a sand-castle building contest. Even Sipho, who would normally have stayed away from the action and read a book, joined in.

Monica wondered if her parents had enjoyed their Christmas meal at Abalone House. Kitty and Francina had fought over who would host them for Christmas with Monica away, and in the end, Mirinda and Paolo Brunetti had agreed to spend Christmas with Kitty, and the day after, Boxing Day, with Francina. Monica had called her parents the night before and caught them on their way to the early-morning church service. They missed the boys and were upset to learn that Monica would be staying on in the United States.

After Zak had judged the sand-castle contest—and declared a talented team of brothers from India the winners—he suggested to Mandla and Sipho that they join a soccer match some older boys had started. Sipho agreed reluctantly and Monica watched the three males in her life tearing after the ball, falling on the sand and sharing high fives with strangers they would never see again.

It was not a traditional Christmas, but Monica had a feeling it would be one she would remember for many years to come.

⤜ Chapter Twenty-One ⤛

On the first day of filming, Monica, Zak and Sipho all accompanied Mandla to the studio. The night before, Zak had tried to talk to Monica alone, but she'd become angry when he kept saying that she was depressed and needed help.

"If you think that a bottle of pills is going to help me, then you're wrong," she'd said.

"I meant you need to talk to someone," said Zak. "You don't talk to me about it. It's not healthy."

She could only shake her head at him; she knew that if she said anything she might start crying.

The director of the film, a young man with a meager goatee and artfully ripped jeans, allowed the family to stay on the set, as long as they turned off their cell phones and didn't utter a word.

They watched Mandla listen to the director's instructions, and then he must have cracked a joke because the director tipped his head back and howled with laughter. Monica knew Sipho was probably itching to comment about his brother's confidence, but they had all promised to be silent.

Mandla took one last look at the script he had been studying for three days, and threw it aside on a couch as though he'd never again need it. Sipho rolled his eyes. Mandla went to stand on a cross marked on the wooden floor with duct tape, and lifted his arms while the wardrobe lady fussed around him, untucking and then partially tucking his crisp white shirt into his gray flannel pants. Mandla was playing the part of the friend of the main character at a private boarding school. Of course, he wished he had the leading role, and Monica saw him sizing up Steven, the petite blond boy who had been given it.

The director shouted, "Action," and Mandla underwent a transformation. His posture changed, his eyes showed the pain he was supposed to convey, and his voice dropped to a whisper. He *was* the boy who had been wrongfully accused of stealing the main character's watch.

"You don't belong here," sneered the main boy.

A tear trickled down Mandla's cheek and he wiped it away with the sleeve of his shirt. This was not in the script, Monica knew. A minute ago, Mandla had been joking with the director. Now he was crying real tears. She had known that he had talent, but she hadn't realized how much. The director, she noticed, couldn't take his eyes off Mandla, and the assistant director had to nudge him in the ribs to yell "Cut," when Steven fluffed his lines. The director walked across to Mandla and put his hand on his shoulder. Monica watched Mandla smile coyly, presumably in response to words of praise. She noticed, too, Steven watching with a look of malice on his face. Life, as it so often did, was imitating art in this cavernous movie studio.

When the director gave the order to break for lunch, Mandla asked Monica if he might skip lunch with the family in order to eat with the director and his crew.

"Your dad's going home tomorrow," she said.

"That's okay. Go ahead, Mandla," said Zak. "We'll have dinner together tonight."

"Um, actually, I've been invited to the opening party tonight."

Out of habit, Monica looked at Zak for support. Even he appeared doubtful, and he was usually the more lenient parent.

"I don't think so," said Monica. "It'll be an adult party. They'll be drinking."

"But I want to meet everyone," whined Mandla.

"You'll meet them over the course of the next two weeks. No, Mandla, you can't go." She had given in to his wish to stay in the United States to make the film; she was not going to give in to this.

"Please, Mom."

"No, Mandla. You're a child, not an adult. But you may go to lunch with the cast after I speak to the director."

"Ah, Mom. It's just sandwiches in the next room."

"Are you sure?"

He nodded.

"Well, okay, but I'm going to walk past and check up on you."

True to her word, she did peer in the open door and was relieved to see all the child actors sitting at a long table together. At the next table, there were a few parents, caretakers and Steven's tutor. Steven would be filming for two months and would then go to Singapore to take part in an action film. Mandla was too caught up in telling a funny story to notice Steven glaring at him.

"Let's go in," Monica said to Zak and Sipho. "The other parents are eating lunch here."

Sipho groaned, but he followed dutifully. Monica sat at the end of the trestle table next to a lady who was picking at her salad.

"Which one is yours?" asked the woman.

Monica pointed at Mandla, who again had tears rolling down his cheeks, this time from laughing. The other children, except Steven, were screeching with laughter, too.

"I see," said the lady, but it was clear from her tone she was confused.

Monica noticed her looking at Sipho, then Zak, and then searching for a wedding ring on Zak's finger. Monica could have satisfied her curiosity by explaining that she had adopted the boys, but it really wasn't any of her business.

"Mine is playing the lead," said the lady, responding to the question Monica should have asked but didn't.

"I see," said Monica, borrowing her phrase.

"This is his third film. Did you see him in *A House of Angels?*"

Monica replied that the movie had not yet been released in South Africa.

"Is that where you're from?" asked the lady.

"Yes," said Monica.

"What part of L.A. do you live in now?"

"We live in South Africa."

Her attitude warmed a little after that, perhaps because she sensed that Mandla could not be a threat to her son's career if he lived so far away.

"My father-in-law and some friends went hunting in South Africa," said the lady.

Monica wondered if Sipho had heard.

"The lion's head he brought back is in his den. Hideous thing. A photograph would have been enough."

"What a brave man your father-in-law is," said Sipho, shifting his chair closer. "The workers at the game farm probably killed a buck, hung it in a tree and then built a hide close by for the big game hunters from America."

"I don't know how they did it," said the lady. Her frown told Monica that she was not sure how to interpret Sipho's comment.

"That's how they all do it, but I bet that's not the way he'd tell the story. Oh, no, he'll tell you he stalked it for days on foot and took aim from two hundred meters away."

Monica put her hand on Sipho's leg to try to get him to stop.

"And after the kill, I bet your father-in-law tipped the workers at the game farm five dollars each, because five dollars goes a long way in Africa, you know."

By now the sarcasm in his voice was discernible not only to Monica.

"You don't know what you're talking about," said the lady.

Monica caught Sipho's eye and glared hard at him.

"I'll be outside," he said, pushing his sandwich away.

"He hates hunting," Monica explained to the woman when Sipho had left. She knew she ought to apologize, but in a perverse way she felt as though Sipho were avenging Mandla for the treatment he was about to suffer at the hands of the young star of the movie.

"That's no excuse for his rudeness," said Zak. "I'll make him apologize to you."

Now it was Zak's turn to be the object of Monica's glare. How dare he undermine her in front of this lady? Let him try. The only way he would get Sipho back in here to apologize was if he threatened him in some way, and that was not Zak's style.

Zak left and, as Monica had predicted, returned alone to the table. "He's sorry," Zak said rather lamely.

"Thanks," said the lady.

The children were being ushered out of the lunchroom and back into the studio. Monica caught Mandla's eye. He winked at her.

"Is this his first movie?" asked the lady.

Monica nodded.

"He has talent. It's a shame you're going back to South Africa." Monica could tell that she didn't mean a word of it.

Mandla had less chance to show the range of his emotions in the afternoon session, since he was part of a group scene and didn't have a line of his own. At three o'clock, the director called for a break so Steven could look over his lines again. He could not make it through a scene without a mistake. If this were a play, Monica knew that Mandla would happily prompt him from the wings. Mandla, of course, knew his own and everybody else's lines. Steven's mother looked mortified, so it was a good thing that Mandla did not have the opportunity to offer his help; his older brother had caused enough upset for one day.

Sipho had not returned to the studio after his outburst in the lunchroom, and Zak had found him sitting on an upturned crate reading a discarded detective novel. He'd refused to accompany Zak back to the studio.

At the end of the day, Mandla climbed into the car with

a smile on his face. "I think I like this business," he said. "And next time I'm going to go to the party."

"There's not going to be a next time," muttered Sipho. He was still reading the detective novel.

"Yes, there will be. The director told me at lunch."

"You're going home to South Africa and these Hollywood people are going to forget all about you," said his brother.

"Sipho!" scolded Monica. She had had enough of his hostile attitude. Even if he was correct in his assumption, he should not treat his brother this way. What was happening to him? What was happening to all of them?

Dinner that night was subdued. Mandla was still upset about Sipho's comment, and Sipho was disgusted that his brother even wanted to be a part of the business where people like that "morally vacuous woman" and her son were allowed to succeed. Monica was secretly relieved to see a glimpse of the old Sipho. The new one, who spoke of girls and rock bands, unnerved her far more. A couple of times Zak squeezed her knee under the table, but she pretended not to notice.

That night in bed, he put his arm around her. "I wish you would talk to me," he whispered.

"Shh, the boys are not asleep yet," she said.

A short while later, she heard Zak's breathing become regular and knew that she had lost her chance. Tomorrow he would fly off and return to his familiar world in Lady Helen. If she hadn't been feeling lonely for months already she might have feared being left alone.

Zak took a taxi to the airport the next day after giving Monica a lesson in driving the rental car on the right-hand side of the road. Ten years of driving in Johannesburg had prepared her for the impatient and unforgiving drivers of Los Angeles.

Two more days remained before Sipho had to return to Houston to start school, but, for him, the time couldn't pass quickly enough. While Monica watched Mandla in the film studio that afternoon, Sipho sat outside listening to music or talking to Connor and other friends on the cell phone Connor's mother had given him. Twice Monica did what she had told herself years ago that she would never do when her children were teenagers: she eavesdropped on Sipho's conversation. Afterward she regretted it, not because she thought it was morally wrong, but because what she had heard disturbed her. Sipho was another boy entirely when he spoke to Connor. In fact, he was not a boy at all but a young man, and what upset her the most was that he was a cynical young man.

The following morning, just before five, the telephone rang in the hotel room. Only Zak and Monica's mother knew the number, but neither would call at this time except in case of an emergency.

"Monica, it's Zak." He sounded agitated.

Her heart started to pound in her chest.

"She's gone, Monica."

"Who?"

"Yolanda. That woman took her to Australia while I was in the United States."

Monica sat up in bed. "But Yolanda would never agree to go."

"Well, she's not here." His voice cracked. "She left me, Monica."

"I'm sure she didn't do it willingly," she said softly.

There was a sniff on the other end of the receiver. Was Zak crying?

"Did you contact her school?" she asked gently.

"There's nobody there now because it's still summer holidays. I called the principal at home and she said Yolanda's mother never said a word about taking Yolanda out of school."

"Have you phoned Jacqueline's office?"

"I just got back from the airport."

"I'm sorry, Zak. I wish I was there to help you. See if Jacqueline's colleagues or friends know anything."

"Okay," he said in a small voice. "I'll let you know what happens."

"Call anytime. Zak?"

"Yes?"

"Nothing. Good luck."

That afternoon at the film studio, Monica waited five minutes after Sipho had ended another call with Connor, and then pulled up a chair beside him. She would have preferred to watch Mandla in the scene where he had most of his lines, but this was more important.

"Are you sure you want to go back?" she asked Sipho.

His eyebrows lifted.

"You could come home with Mandla and me. Your principal, Mr. D., would welcome you with open arms."

"I'm supposed to stay four and a half more months."

Monica sighed. "Sipho, there's no easy way to say this. You've changed. This place has changed you."

"The only thing that's changed is I'm having fun," snapped Sipho.

Monica was taken aback. "You have fun in Lady Helen."

"Mom, there are only ten boys in my class. None of them share my interests."

"But neither does Connor. You hate sports."

Sipho flipped his cell phone open and then closed it again. "It's different here."

"That's what I'm worried about. Come home. We miss you. Your brother misses you."

"Maybe you should worry about getting him on the plane with you."

"Why? Has he said something to you?"

Sipho shook his head. "Just look at him, Mom. He loves this. He loves it here."

Since the boys were young Monica had feared that Mandla would one day want to wander off and explore the world. If she had foreseen that it would happen when he was eight, she might not have had a minute's peace. Although she couldn't bring herself to open up to Zak, she decided that she had to be honest with Sipho.

"You're growing up too fast here."

He shook his head.

When she'd first moved to Lady Helen and the principal of Green Block School had allowed Sipho to jump ahead two classes, she had wondered if the day would come when she'd regret it. Today was that day.

"You're only fifteen. Connor's seventeen. That's a big difference when you're a teenager."

Sipho stood up. "Mom, Connor and his friends accept me. They think I'm cool because I'm different."

"And you've proved you can fit in, so now you can come home."

Sipho put a hand on her shoulder and she put her own hand over his. "I have to complete this year, Mom, or it will all have been a waste of time. I need this to get into medical school."

"You can do something else back in Lady Helen to prove yourself."

"I can't give up something I've started. Don't worry about me, Mom. I'll be fine. Mandla is not the only actor in the family." He withdrew his hand. "Are you still coming to Houston for a couple of days before you fly home?"

She nodded.

"I'm not the one you need to worry about, Mom." He gave her a meaningful look.

He meant Mandla, Yolanda and Zak, but also herself. Sipho, with his big serious eyes, had always seen more than he let on.

Zak called that evening to tell her that if Jacqueline's colleagues or friends knew where she was they weren't sharing the information.

"I know she's gone to Australia and taken Yolanda," he said flatly.

Monica wished there wasn't an ocean between them so that she could wrap her arms around her husband.

"I've put a call in to the police, but I was told to wait another twenty-four hours before filing a missing person report."

She heard the desolation in his voice and her eyes filled with tears.

"What about the South African embassy in Australia?"

Zak had not tried this avenue and his attitude brightened after he gave it some thought.

"Call them, sweetheart, and then please try and get some sleep."

He started to protest.

"You're no use to your patients in this state."

"You're right."

After Zak had hung up, Monica woke her mother in Lady Helen to ask her to keep an eye on Zak. Mirinda promised she would.

The next morning, after Monica had said goodbye to Sipho at the airport, she arrived at the studio to find Mandla in tears.

"What's wrong?" she asked, hugging him.

"Steven says they're going to have to put subtitles on the screen when I talk because nobody will understand my accent." Mandla burst into fresh tears.

"He said this to your face?"

"No," sniffed Mandla. "I heard him telling the other kids in the break room. They all laughed." He threw his arms around Monica's neck, sobbing.

"Come now, sweetie, don't cry," she said, stroking his back. "I'm going to have a word with his mother and make him apologize."

Mandla pulled away from her. "No, please don't do that. He won't mean it even if he says he's sorry."

Her son had a point.

"Do you know why he's saying mean things about you?"

Mandla shook his head.

"Because he's jealous of you."

"Of me? He's been in two other movies."

"That may be true, but it's obvious to anyone with eyes that you have natural talent. The director loves you. And this makes Steven feel threatened."

"He shouldn't be threatened by me. We'd never be up for the same roles."

Monica caught her breath. Mandla was only eight years old and yet he had already grasped how the world worked. She wished it were not true, but it was.

"In South Africa you could have any role you wanted."

He nodded. "But it's not Hollywood."

"Come on. Dry your eyes. We don't want Steven to see that he's upset you."

Mandla took the tissue she offered and blew his nose.

"Has Sipho gone?"

Monica nodded.

"He's changed since he's been here, hasn't he?"

"I think that deep down he's still our old Sipho." She hoped that this was true.

That afternoon during filming, Mandla pronounced a few of his meager lines with an American accent. It was slight enough to escape the director's attention, but not Monica's, and her heart ached for her little boy who wanted so badly to fit in.

Zak filed a missing person report and the South African embassy in Australia agreed to contact the local police in Sydney, since that was where Jacqueline had originally intended to live before Zak had put a stop to her move. And then the waiting began. The embassy promised to call Zak weekly with updates, but it was not enough for him, and so he phoned the embassy every day.

On the day Mandla finished filming his part in the movie, the director hosted a small party for him. Steven and his friends did not attend, but all the adult actors were there, along with the entire crew. The celebration consisted of nothing more than soda, chips, a chocolate cake and balloons, but Mandla was thrilled to be the center of attention.

Before Mandla cut his cake the director made a toast. "To Mandla's future in the film business. I have a feeling we're going to be seeing a lot of him."

Everybody cheered and Mandla looked as though he might burst with pride.

After the cake had been eaten and people started to leave for the evening, the director took Monica aside. Mandla hovered close by, listening.

"I meant what I said. Mandla has a great future ahead of him."

"Thank you," said Monica.

"He needs some work."

"Work?"

"Acting lessons, of course. A new, more hip hairstyle. And his accent was perfect for this movie where he played an outsider, but if he wants to get more roles he'll need a voice coach to get rid of his South African accent."

Later, Monica would think of a number of suitable replies, but at this moment she was speechless.

"If you want any recommendations, call my assistant," said the director. He put out his hand. "It's been a pleasure having your son on this film. He has incredible presence."

Monica shook his hand and was relieved when his assistant drew him away because she didn't trust herself to speak. How dare this man say Mandla had to get rid of his South African accent? Mandla's accent was part of who he was, not something to be discarded like old clothes. And what was wrong with his natural hair? It suited him. He had never worn his hair any other way. Did the man want Mandla to start growing dreadlocks? All of a sudden, she longed to be on a flight back home with both her boys beside her. This country wanted to suck in her family and spit it out changed and new. There was only one place for her and her boys and that was Lady Helen.

That evening, as she packed their bags, muttering under her breath about the "cheek of the man," Mandla asked her what she planned to do.

"Visit Sipho for a couple of days and then go home, of course," she told him.

"But what about me?"

"What about you?"

"The director said I have a great future. He meant here."

"Ouch!" Monica caught her finger in the lock of her suitcase. "It's out of the question, Mandla. You belong at home with your family." Her words had come out sharper than she'd intended.

"Sipho's staying here," said Mandla sulkily.

"Only for four more months, and he's older than you."

Mandla threw a pile of his clothes into his suitcase. "It's not fair. I'm the one who should be here. This place is wasted on Sipho. He's not talented."

"Mandla! How can you say such a thing about your brother?" Monica noticed that her finger was bleeding.

"There aren't any big movies being filmed in South Africa."

"Yes, there are. The South African film industry is growing. And foreign production houses are always going there to make movies, especially in Cape Town. They hire local people."

"As extras. I don't want to be a face in the crowd. The director said I had talent."

"Mandla, we cannot all move here. It's a ludicrous idea. When you're a grown-up, you can come back and try again."

"That'll take forever," yelled Mandla. "And they will have forgotten about me by then." He stormed off to the bathroom.

"Don't you lock yourself in there again!" shouted Monica.

But it was too late. She heard the lock turn. Sighing, she tidied the pile of clothes he had thrown into the suitcase, and began to pack the rest of his things.

An hour later, he came out of the bathroom, but he would not speak to her unless it was to answer a question in monosyllables. Monica was starting to regret ever having helped Sipho submit his application to be a foreign exchange student.

Parenting was the toughest job in the world. Just when Monica thought she had the hang of it, new challenges were thrown at her, and she found herself floundering like an absolute beginner.

Chapter Twenty-Two

Sipho, at least, was smiling when he met them at the Houston airport the next morning with Nancy and Connor. It wasn't long though before Monica realized that part of his happiness could be attributed to a wildly successful party the boys had thrown at Connor's house the night before. Monica hoped that Nancy and Bill had provided proper supervision, but she would not embarrass Sipho by asking about it in front of Connor.

Nancy insisted that Monica and Mandla stay at her house, and since their extended sojourn in Los Angeles had run up quite a credit-card bill, Monica accepted gratefully. Staying close by would also give her the opportunity to see how Sipho lived his day-to-day life.

"You've come in time to hear Sipho talk to the student body tomorrow," Connor told her in the SUV on the drive home from the airport. "What's your topic, Sipho? I hope it's not lame."

Sipho grinned, but refused to tell him. "Wait until tomorrow," he said.

"You better make it funny or everyone will fall asleep," said Connor.

"They won't fall asleep," replied Sipho. He caught Monica's eye and smiled.

There were three exchange students at Sipho's school, and each of them had been asked to give a fifteen minute presentation about their home country.

The first student, a girl from Colombia, started her presentation the following morning by asking the audience to forgive her faulty English. She then got everyone laughing by listing the errors she had made while learning the language. She had brought slides to show the Colombian countryside and cities. As she started to talk about the turbulent politics of the country, Monica noticed a lot of fidgeting and whispering in the audience. Connor was correct; the students wanted the speaker to make them laugh. She began to feel so nervous for Sipho that she had to wipe her sweaty palms on her skirt. Never in his fifteen years had she known him to make a crowd laugh.

It was his turn next. As he went to stand behind the podium, she could feel her heart racing in her chest. His voice cracked when he greeted the audience, and she covered her face with her hands. He cleared his throat.

"I feel very privileged to have been given this opportunity to study abroad."

She heard a few giggles and thought of the film director's advice to Mandla to lose his accent.

"I want to thank you all for welcoming me to your

school." His demeanor was more formal than that of the school principal who had introduced him.

Monica knew that he would have to change gears now or face losing his audience.

"Today I want to talk to you about the children in my home country, South Africa—those less privileged than you and me."

Beside Monica, Mandla shifted in his seat. Sipho turned on the laptop he had set up on the podium, and a photograph of a little African girl appeared on the screen. He explained to the students how more than a million children in South Africa had lost one or both parents to AIDS and the number of orphans was growing faster than anyone cared to admit. He changed the slide to show a little girl holding a cup of water to her mother's chapped lips. Ailing parents, he said, were being cared for by their young children. Some households were now headed by children as young as ten years old.

"I am one of the lucky ones," said Sipho, looking at the row of chairs where the parents, including Monica, sat. "I was adopted by a good woman."

Monica felt her stomach flip. In all their years together, Sipho had never mentioned that he was grateful to her for taking him in, and she had never expected it of him. The agreement she had made with the boys' mother to adopt them had come naturally—they had not even thought to put it in writing before Ella died.

Flipping through slides that showed children involved in a variety of household tasks, including collecting firewood, Sipho described to the students the daily struggle of these AIDS orphans, whose schooling had to take a backseat to the grinding task of eking out a living. Monica noticed a few girls near her wiping their eyes. There was not a sound in the packed auditorium.

Monica had never seen Sipho so in command of himself and his listeners before. His words were eloquent, measured and heartfelt, his gestures large enough for the whole auditorium to see, but still natural. He was his mother, Ella, all over again, but with a subtle difference: she had filled the room with her larger-than-life personality. Sipho filled it with the quiet intensity of his words. The result, though, was the same: people took note. Monica saw many students writing in notebooks when Sipho listed the ways in which they could help.

When he finished, there was silence, and then a boy in the front row stood up and began to clap. Soon the entire student body was giving Sipho a standing ovation.

After the presentation by the third student, who struggled to gain the audience's attention with his account of daily life in Japan, the students swarmed around Sipho to ask questions. Even Connor, Monica noticed, had a question. She wanted to tell Sipho how proud she was of him, but didn't want to intrude. After ten minutes, Sipho left the group to come to her. If the other students hadn't been watching she would have taken him into her arms and probably shed a tear or two, but she behaved as any parent of a high school student should: with restraint.

"You were fantastic," she told him.

"Thanks. Did you like the slides? A nongovernmental organization in South Africa e-mailed them to me."

"The slides were great, but you were…you were your mother up there on that stage."

Sipho gave a pinched smile. "I felt her watching me. Is that crazy?"

Monica shook her head. "Not at all."

"I meant what I said about being lucky."

Monica felt a sob catch in her throat. "No, sweetie, I'm the lucky one."

He stepped forward and put his arms around her shoulders. "I love you, Mom."

"I love you, too, Sipho."

He pulled away shyly and pinched Mandla's cheek. "I'd better go back to the students so I can get them to donate money to AIDS charities while they're all fired up. You know what it's like with teenagers."

He had returned to being the Sipho she knew, older and wiser than his years. She was going to miss him over the next four months.

Mandla barely spoke to her on the flight home to Cape Town. He slept little and watched all the films available. With time, he would get over his disappointment and realize that it was impossible for him to live in the United States at this point in his life. Until then, Monica would have to endure his censorious silence.

As the airplane approached the airport in Cape Town, Mandla looked out the window and caught his breath.

"Look, Mom," he said, for an instant forgetting to be sullen.

Monica leaned over to view the city many called the most beautiful in the world. The sky was the same color that Hercules always painted it in his landscapes—the one Francina called artificial. Frothy white waves fringed Cape Point, the rocky peninsula some mistakenly called the most southern tip of the African continent. Table Mountain was not covered by its usual beautiful white tablecloth, and

Monica imagined tourists at the top marveling at the clear view of the bay below and the houses crafted into the rocky cliffs overlooking the ocean.

"It's good to be home," she said, and instantly she regretted her words because, predictably, they reminded Mandla of where he would rather be.

He retreated into his shell again, and although the flight crew had turned off the in-flight entertainment system, he stared at the gray screen as though it might come to li at any moment.

✎ Chapter Twenty-Three ✎

Zak had sent Mirinda and Paolo to pick up Monica and Mandla from the airport because he had to go to the main police station in Cape Town to make a statement—his fifth so far.

"So how's my little movie star?" asked his grandmother, hugging Mandla.

"Fine," he said.

"Fine? You go on holiday, land a role in a movie and you're just fine?"

Mandla shrugged. "I probably will never be in another one as long as I live." He spotted his suitcase on the baggage carousel and tried to lift it off, but it was too heavy for him and he had to jog alongside it until his grandfather lent him a hand.

Monica took advantage of his distraction to explain to her mother why Mandla was not happy to be back in South Africa.

"Ah, that explains his sour face," said Mirinda. "Come

here, little man." She grabbed hold of his hand. "You don't want to stay in America and start saying 'toe-may-toe and ketchup.'"

Mandla shook his hand free. He did not find the matter amusing.

"Too many young kids here are putting on American accents to be cool. Haven't you heard them, Paolo?" Mirinda did not wait for her husband's reply. "I don't know what this 'cool' is, anyway. When I was a child we didn't have time to worry what our hair looked like or if we had the right clothes. We were happy if we had shoes on our feet."

Mandla rolled his eyes. "But you wanted more. That's why you left your little town to go to Johannesburg to become a model. Can we go now? I'm tired."

"Ooh, Monica, you've brought back a grumpy little man," said Mirinda.

Monica smiled but did not say a word for fear of upsetting Mandla further. All she wanted was a long soak in a hot tub and then her own bed.

In the car on the way home, Mirinda told Monica that she had taken a plate of food to Zak every night, but had often found it untouched the next day.

"We've hardly seen him," said Paolo. "I wish I could do something to help."

Mirinda told Monica that Francina, Hercules and Zukisa had been visiting Zukisa's aunt every weekend and her condition was unchanged. Lucy had settled into a life of domesticity she had not known for years, but the family was short of money and she would soon have to look for work. The older boy, Xoli, had started to be more civil to his mother, and Francina hoped that eventually he would start spending more time at home. Lucy's daughter, Fundiswa, never left her side, not even when she took a shower.

Zak's car was in the driveway when they arrived home, and Mirinda thought it better if she and Paolo didn't accept Monica's offer to come in for a cup of tea.

"You've got lots to talk about," she said, giving her daughter a serious look.

Zak came to the door and Monica was shocked at his appearance. He hadn't shaved for days, there were dark rings around his eyes and he had lost weight. She kissed him hello.

"Have they found her?" she asked.

He gave a weary smile. "Yes. They just told me when I was in Cape Town."

"That's fantastic. What happens next?"

He told her that the Sydney police had taken Jacqueline into custody for questioning, but she would be released in twenty-four hours unless he laid a formal charge of kidnapping against her.

"So what are you going to do?" Monica sank onto the sofa.

"I'm leaving for the airport now. I was just packing."

"Is there anything I can do?"

He shook his head. "I'm sorry I have to rush off like this."

"Don't be sorry. I just hope you'll be able to get some sleep on the flight."

"When I get back we'll have a long talk, okay?"

She knew what he meant, but she did not know if she was ready for it.

Zak had planned to drive himself to the airport, but Monica would not allow it in the state he was in.

"I'll ask Oscar if he can do it," she said, and went off to phone their family friend.

Oscar said he was free for the afternoon and that it would be a pleasure to help out. "Yolanda belongs in Lady Helen, not Sydney, Australia," he said.

Monica knew that Zak would not have told Oscar—or anyone else—what had happened, but it was impossible to keep a secret in Lady Helen, where the grapevine was so short.

After Zak left, Monica lay down on her bed to rest her eyes for a minute before unpacking. The next thing she knew the doorbell was ringing and it was dark outside. Francina had come to welcome Monica and Mandla back, with a pot of lamb stew and a small covered dish of steaming hot rice.

Mandla emerged from his bedroom, rubbing his eyes. "What's that smell?" he asked.

"Aha, I thought my good South African food would catch your attention," said Francina. "It's better than American hot dogs and hamburgers, isn't it?" She kissed Mandla hello.

"We also ate Indian and Thai and Mexican food there," he said.

"Oh, well, lah-dee-dah, aren't we sophisticated?" said Francina, serving the stew and rice onto plates. "Take one bite of this and tell me you'd rather have a taco."

Mandla did not comment but cleaned his plate and asked for more, which Francina gave him with a broad smile on her face.

"Tomorrow I'm bringing you good old African pap and gravy," she said. "It's more delicious than any fancy foreign food."

After Francina had left, Mandla took a bath, but he was refreshed after his long nap and couldn't think of going to bed at the normal time even though he had school the next day. It would take at least a week for him to get back into his normal routine. He went into the living room and Monica heard the television flick on. She was washing the dinner dishes when she heard Mandla give a scream.

"What is it?" she shouted, rushing into the living room.

"Look." He pointed at the screen.

An American movie was on and there was no mistaking the identity of the boy getting into the car with his father. It was Steven.

Mandla turned up the volume. Steven spoke with a Southern drawl.

"He's good with accents," said Monica.

"That's not put on. That's how he used to speak. He's from Alabama."

"But he didn't sound like that when we met him."

Mandla gave Monica a look of impatience. "He had a voice coach to help him get rid of it."

"Oh," said Monica. So it wasn't only Mandla who had an accent that needed to be eliminated. She thought of her mother, who, after moving to Johannesburg, had worked hard to remove from her speech all traces of her small-town upbringing in the Karoo desert.

"Are you going to watch the movie?" asked Monica.

Mandla's frown reinforced her realization—too late—that this was a stupid question.

"You need your sleep. School starts tomorrow."

"I'm not tired yet."

Although it was bedtime in South Africa, Mandla's body was on United States time, where it was early afternoon. Perhaps the movie would relax him and he'd be able to fall asleep. She told him that she was going to take a bath and would check on him afterward.

"Don't you want to watch Steven?" he asked.

"He's not as good as you," she replied, and again she realized she had said the wrong thing.

"Yes, but he's the one with a career in movies, I'm not."

"Mandla, I told you I'd take you to any audition you wanted to go to."

"Yes, in Cape Town."

She was too tired to go over this again with him.

"I'll see you in a bit," she said. He looked so small and frail sitting there in the blue light of the television that she wanted to put her hand on his soft cheek, but he would shrug her off and she was not in a state to take rejection.

After her bath she found him fast asleep on the sofa, with Steven's movie still playing on the television. She switched it off and scooped him into her arms to carry him to bed. He stirred when she put his head on the pillow, but then turned over and went back to sleep. She leaned down and kissed him on the cheek. Her little boy was disappointed with his lot in life at the moment and there was nothing she could do about it. Hopefully school would take his mind off it.

She looked at her watch. Zak had been flying for three hours now and would only arrive when she was waking tomorrow morning. What could Jacqueline have told Yolanda to make her leave her father in South Africa?

Monica lay down on the bed and heard an owl call outside. A warm summer breeze drifted in through the open window. She had planned to go through all the mail Zak had not touched, but before long she fell into an exhausted sleep.

* * *

The next morning Mandla shook her awake.

"You turned the alarm clock off again and went back to sleep," he moaned. "I can't be late on the first day of the year."

Monica dragged herself out of bed. "Why are you wearing the sneakers I bought you in Houston?"

"Because they're cool," said Mandla, pronouncing cool with a decidedly American accent.

"Cool they may be, but they're not part of your school uniform. Go and put your school shoes on now."

Mandla stalked off, muttering about "boring old South Africa."

After dropping him at school, Monica went straight to the office and if she hadn't been carrying a gift bag she was sure Dudu would have jumped into her arms.

"Was it that bad?" asked Monica.

"Oh, Monica, I'm so tired. I was fiddling with the stories until midnight and then still had to do the layout. If Gift comes in here waving this issue at me, I'll scream."

"When was she here?"

"Last week and the week before that. I know there are mistakes in the stories. I know they're not all newsworthy. I'm not a journalist."

"Dudu, I'm sorry. Here, I bought you something to say thanks." Monica handed her the gift bag. "Mandla picked these out."

The bag contained a bottle of perfume for Dudu and a pair of American jeans for each of her three children.

"They'll love these. Thank you."

Monica knew that she owed Dudu for more than taking the reins of the newspaper while she was in the United

States. For months, Dudu had been covering for Monica while she moped around. A bottle of perfume would never be enough to repay her.

Monica sat down at her desk to sort through a pile of mail. Dudu had warned her that the letters to the editor might upset her, but she was not prepared for the accusations some of them contained. *If you're letting things slide here because you're going back to your glamorous job in television, then you'd better come clean with your readers,* an anonymous individual had written. Another said that the word in town was that Monica had gone to Johannesburg to audition for a position as a talk-show host on TV. If these people only knew the truth about her exit from the world of television reporting, they might not be so suspicious. She had filled in at the news program *In-Depth* for a reporter who'd gone on maternity leave, and when the woman had decided not to come back, the producers had given her permanent job to someone they thought more suitable than Monica.

She picked up the issues of the *Lady Helen Herald* that Dudu had written and began to scan them from front to back. Dudu's grammar could not be faulted, but her stories read more like school essays than news or feature stories. Someone with less loyalty than Dudu might have refused to take on duties she had neither been hired for nor felt confident doing.

When Dudu came into her office midmorning with a cup of tea, Monica jumped up and gave her a hug.

"What's this for?" she asked.

"I think you know," replied Monica. "And I want you to take a few days off, at least until it's time to lay out the next issue."

"But the telephone starts ringing at eight-thirty sharp."

"I'll be here on time from now on."

Nothing had changed in Monica's personal life, but she could not continue to take advantage of her coworker. Under duress, Dudu went home to nap.

That afternoon Zak called Monica with good news. Jacqueline had agreed to hand over Yolanda's passport to him, if he promised not to press charges.

"And what have you decided to do?" asked Monica.

"She's the mother of my child. I can't send her to prison." His voice was flat. Zak was beyond tired.

He said that Yolanda would be crushed if her mother decided to stay in Australia without her. It would seem that she had chosen her husband over her own daughter. Knowing Jacqueline's history of weakness when faced with temptation, Monica feared that Yolanda would have to make the difficult choice between remaining with her in Australia or returning to South Africa with her father.

"So how did Jacqueline get Yolanda to go in the first place?"

Jacqueline wasn't saying, but Zak was about to go to Yolanda's new school to pick her up, and would find out firsthand.

"Monica, what if Yolanda doesn't want to come home with me?"

"That won't happen," she said softly. She hoped that she was right.

That night Monica and Mandla ate dinner in front of the television. Her rule against doing so seemed suddenly futile.

"Those jeans you have on are dirty, and so is that T-shirt," she told him.

Besides supervising Mandla's homework, laundry was one of the things she ought to be doing tonight instead of watching a mindless game show on television.

"You always tell me to change out of my school uniform when I get home," whined Mandla.

"Yes, but you have clean clothes in your closet."

"I like these," he said. "My other clothes are lame."

He had picked out the jeans and T-shirt at a mall in Los Angeles. She didn't have the energy to argue with him.

Later, when she went into his room to kiss him goodnight, she found him singing and dancing in front of the full-length mirror on the inside door of his closet.

"Don't stop," she said.

He slumped back on his bed. "What's the use? I'm going to be stuck in this dump forever."

Six months ago a comment like this would have made her cry, but she was tired of crying.

She tried putting an arm around his shoulders, but he shrugged her off. "When you're older you'll realize that I made the right decision," she told him.

He screwed up his mouth.

Monica wished she could help him get past his disappointment and frustration, but she didn't know how, not without going against what she believed to be right. She prayed for strength to be able to stand firmly behind her decision.

✦ Chapter Twenty-Four ✦

Monica did not hear from Zak for another twenty-four hours, and when she considered calling him, she realized he had never given her a contact number. She had intended to throw herself into her work, but now all she did was stare at the telephone on her desk or out the window at the activity on Main Street.

Just before she was about to leave for the day, Zak called sounding completely different.

"Jacqueline, her husband and Yolanda are all coming back," he said triumphantly. "I had a talk with Jacqueline's husband."

"You did?" Monica could only guess how difficult it must have been for Zak to face, for the first time, the man who'd stolen his wife from him.

"I reminded him that he'd never have any time alone with Jacqueline because I would be unable to take Yolanda at weekends."

Monica thought it implausible that the man had not thought of that before leaving South Africa with his step-daughter, but she kept her doubts to herself.

"Jacqueline told Yolanda that you and I had gone to the United States to look for new jobs. She felt hurt and abandoned."

"I thought it would be something like that," said Monica. "Jacqueline is…" The unfinished sentence hung in the air. She had never criticized Jacqueline to Zak, although she had often been sorely tempted, but a long-distance telephone call was not the place to start. "So when are you coming back?"

"Yolanda and I are flying back tomorrow. Jacqueline and her husband have to stay behind to tie up some loose ends, and will return in a month."

It was a credible excuse, but Monica had a nagging feeling that Zak, and, even worse, that Yolanda were being deceived. There was no point in suggesting this to Zak. What could he do?

After saying goodbye to him and locking the office, Monica bought some curried fish from Mama Dlamini's Eating Establishment and went home to pick up Mandla for a picnic on the beach.

He was watching a movie on television when she arrived. Francina motioned for Monica to accompany her to the kitchen.

"That boy doesn't want to do his homework," she said. "All he does is sit on the couch and watch TV. It's not healthy."

"I know," replied Monica. "I'm taking him to the beach now for dinner and a long walk. He needs fresh air."

"I'm sorry to tell you, but I don't like the way he's been

talking to Zukisa. He used to pester her to play with him. Now he bites her head off whenever she speaks to him."

"He's angry with me for ruining his movie career."

"Well, you'd better tell him to leave Zukisa out of it. If she refuses to come here, then I won't come, either."

"I'm sorry. I'll have a word with him." Monica had never considered the possibility that Francina might one day refuse to watch Mandla after school. "Zak arrives the day after tomorrow and then we'll try and get this family back to normal."

"Is Yolanda coming with him?"

Monica nodded. "Her mother will follow in a month."

The look on Francina's face only reinforced Monica's own doubts. Poor Yolanda *would* be crushed if she and Francina were right.

Zak and Yolanda arrived home, and after a day of rest, Yolanda was ready to begin at Green Block School, which she had attended before her parents' divorce. She'd gone there as well for a brief period when she had come to live full-time in Lady Helen because she wasn't getting along with her mother's new husband. As soon as Jacqueline returned from Australia the old custody arrangement would go back into operation, with Yolanda spending weekdays in Cape Town and weekends in Lady Helen with her father.

Monica thought Mandla would be pleased to have company while his brother was away, but he didn't show it. On the surface, Monica and Zak's relationship appeared amiably reestablished, but the argument in Los Angeles remained undiscussed. Zak had said that they'd talk as soon as he returned from Australia, but Monica didn't have the courage to reopen the conversation after the horrible accusations she'd made. Zak didn't seem keen to rehash those heated words, either. Some evenings, as the two of them sat in front of the television after the children had gone to bed, Monica would look at him and wonder how they could have drifted so far apart. The atmosphere wasn't unpleasant; no harsh words were spoken. But something had gone from their marriage. Monica felt it and wondered if Zak did, too.

Two weeks after Zak and Yolanda returned from Australia, Zak arrived unexpectedly at Monica's office during lunch.

"Jacqueline is the most selfish person I know," he said, sitting down on her desk.

"What has she done?" Monica thought she knew what the answer would be but prayed she was wrong.

"She says she can't come back now because she has to stay close to her doctor."

"Her doctor?"

Zak sighed. "I didn't want to tell you, Monica, but she's pregnant."

Jacqueline pregnant? It was impossible. Yolanda hadn't said a word about it.

He read her thoughts. "Yolanda doesn't know."

Monica felt herself grow cold. "Was it planned?"

Zak shook his head.

Monica was stunned. Jacqueline, at age forty and already a mother of a seventeen-year-old, was pregnant without even trying, while Monica, who was younger, was trying desperately to conceive. In the past, when Monica learned about a friend's pregnancy, she had grieved, alone in her car or in the bathroom, but now she was so angry she felt like hurling a paperweight through the window. It was not fair. No one deserved a baby more than she did. Jacqueline, who had deceived first her husband and then her daughter, was being rewarded with a precious baby, when Monica, after years of raising her late friend Ella's children as her own, could not conceive, no matter what she tried. Where was the justice in that?

"She says she's having some bleeding and her doctor doesn't want her to travel."

"But as soon as the spotting stops, she'll come?"

Zak nodded.

"I don't believe it. That woman is going to make every excuse under the sun not to return here."

"I know you're upset. But we have room for Yolanda. She won't be any trouble."

Monica pushed her chair out so forcefully it slammed against the filing cabinet. "Is that why you think I'm upset? Because Yolanda will be living with us now? Don't you know me at all?"

"I just thought—"

"Well, you thought wrong. I'm upset because Jacqueline didn't even want another baby. And don't try and tell me I'm wrong."

"It was a surprise," Zak conceded.

"I'm sick of hearing about people's little surprises."

He got up and walked around to her side of the desk. "Your situation is not related to Jacqueline's. Try to put this into perspective."

Monica jumped out of her chair. "That's a telling comment. 'Your situation,' huh? Why not say *our* situation, Zak? It all boils down to the same thing. You have your child and don't need another one."

His face went white. "Don't start this again, Monica."

"We didn't end it, so I can't be starting it again, can I?"

"Monica, I wish you would realize that I am not the enemy here. There is no enemy." There was disappointment in his eyes as he looked at her. "I have to get back to work and think about how I am going to break it to Yolanda that her mother is not coming back to South Africa to be with her."

"You're just going to leave me then?"

"I'm ready to talk when you can be calm and rational, Monica."

He shut the door behind him as he left.

"Run away, you always do," she shouted, and then hurled her paperweight at the door. The wood did not splinter, but the missile left a definite dent.

Monica was grateful that Dudu, who must have heard the noise, had the good sense to stay away until her temper cooled.

It was not fair. God was not fair. Monica had been as obedient to Him as she could be and He refused to reward her with the gift He had given millions of women all over the world.

She had to get out of her office. In a few minutes, Dudu would come in offering solace, but also wanting an explanation.

Normally, on such a hot day, Monica would have worn a hat, but today she did not care if her skin turned red and peeled. She needed to be on the beach, where nobody would be able to distinguish the weeping of a person from the cry of a seagull.

A line of palm trees formed a natural break between the grassy park and the start of the beach, and it was there she left her shoes. The beach was deserted by people at this time of the day, when the sun was directly overhead. Even the gulls had gone in search of shade and the leftovers behind Mama Dlamini's Eating Establishment.

The sand was hot beneath Monica's feet. She ran quickly to the water's edge. And then she kept running, up the beach toward the golfing resort north of town. On and on she ran, the seawater soaking the hem of her pants, her lungs straining for oxygen, sweat dripping down her face. When her muscles ached and she felt she could not take another breath, she stopped and walked slowly into the water. Knee-deep, she flung herself forward and landed with a belly flop in the cold Atlantic Ocean. Then she turned onto her back and floated, letting the petite waves of low tide break over her. There was not a cloud in the sky. She felt the sun burning her face and arms, but it was not unpleasant with the rest of her body chilled by the water. Anyone walking by now might think she had gone crazy, and perhaps, for this moment, she had. Her life was in disarray. One son was halfway across the world, the other resented her because he was not; she and her husband were fighting bitterly; the newspaper had suffered under her neglect; she was losing her best friend, Kitty, because she could not bear to look at the baby in her arms; and lastly, she had stopped believing that God truly loved her. She could no longer go on like this. The time had come to deal with the crises in her life.

Floating in the water, Monica didn't have a solution come to her like a bolt of lightning, but it was a comfort to have taken stock of her life and to know that action was the next step. When her fingers grew numb from the cold and she could no longer feel the back of her scalp, she stood up and waded out of the ocean. For five minutes, she sat on a boulder, wringing water from her clothes and hair, and then she began the long walk back to where she'd left her shoes in the park.

She was grateful not to meet anyone on the way to her office.

"What on earth happened to you?" asked Dudu.

Facing Dudu, Monica had decided, was the first step toward fixing her life.

"Jacqueline is pregnant and I'm not," she said, and burst into tears.

"Oh, Monica, I'm sorry," said Dudu, taking her by the hand. "Let's get you dry before you catch cold. I have a spare set of clothing here in case I have to do any dirty work."

"Do I give you dirty work?" Monica laughed in spite of her tears.

"That's better," said Dudu. "Here's a towel. Now go into the bathroom, dry yourself off and I'll bring you the clothes. We're almost the same size."

Monica allowed herself to be pushed in the direction of the bathroom. As she removed her wet clothing, she had to laugh again; Dudu was at least three sizes bigger than she was.

When she came out, dressed in Dudu's old cotton skirt—held up with the help of a safety pin—and a matching blouse that gaped at the armholes, Monica accepted the cup of hot rooibos tea that Dudu offered, and sat down to talk about the moment when Zak had broken the news of Jacqueline's pregnancy.

"I should be more worried for Yolanda," she added.

Dudu put a hand on her arm. "You do not need to feel guilty for reacting the way you did. This longing to have a baby is as natural as breathing, walking and talking."

"But what if it can't *be*?"

"I have a friend who went through the same thing. She and her husband almost split up over it."

"Did she ever have a baby?"

Dudu shook her head. "But she saved her marriage."

"What did she do?"

Dudu told Monica that her friend had attended a support group in Cape Town for women struggling with infertility. Dudu offered to find out the details if Monica was interested. Monica looked at her wet clothing, hanging up to dry in front of an open window.

"Okay, give your friend a call," she said.

When she went home that afternoon, an hour earlier than usual, Mandla wanted to know why she was dressed like a fisherwoman.

"My clothes got wet," she said, and he nodded because this was something that happened to him all the time—or had before he'd started wearing American blue jeans and taking obsessive care of them.

Francina raised her eyebrows. "Is everything all right?"

"It will be," said Monica, and she went off to change into her own clothes.

When Zak got home from work, he did not notice that she was wearing a different outfit than the one he'd seen her in at lunchtime. He put his arm around her waist as she stood at the stove, stirring the fish soup, and asked if she was okay.

The intimacy that had been absent between them for so long made her too emotional to speak, so she merely nodded.

"I'm sorry," he said.

"No, *I'm* sorry."

He put his fingers to her lips to stop her from speaking further, but she pushed his hand away.

"You were right. I need help. And I'm going to find it."

❧ Chapter Twenty-Five ❧

An hour inland from Cape Town, surrounded by vineyard-covered hills, the small university town of Stellenbosch was filled with buses bringing tourists to taste the country's famous wines and picnic on the grounds of gabled farm-houses.

Monica was already late for the workshop. She couldn't find a parking spot near the hotel, an old converted pump house, but she wasn't distressed. What was fifteen minutes, anyway, when she was going to be here for the whole day and night? She had expected to attend a meeting that might last one or two hours at the most. Then she'd learned that this was a two-day conference and she'd have to stay overnight. At least it was in a beautiful location, she told herself, finally finding a parking spot. If she grew bored with the workshop agenda, she could take a walk around town. It had been more than two years since she'd visited Stellenbosch.

A lady with long gray hair and sandals greeted Monica at the door to the conference room, presenting her with a box of tissues.

She shook her head. "I won't need those," she said.

"Yes, you will," the lady replied.

As she held out the box, Monica was tempted to turn around and leave. Instead, she took a few tissues.

"You've missed the introductions," said the lady.

Monica mumbled her regret but, in truth, she was relieved, because now she could slip in anonymously.

"Shirley will give you some time to introduce yourself, though."

"Oh, that's good," said Monica, forcing a smile.

"Go on in, then," said the lady. "You don't want to miss any more." She opened one of the double doors into the conference room.

Twenty heads turned in Monica's direction. She gave a small smile and a wave.

"Welcome," said the woman at the front of the room. Monica presumed she was Shirley. "There's space on the left." She indicated an empty seat in the second row.

Monica walked down the outside aisle and sat.

"Would you like to introduce yourself?" asked Shirley, smiling warmly.

Monica wished she had the courage to say no. But her trip here would be a waste if she did not participate fully.

Shirley had shoulder-length gray hair and a surprisingly unlined face. Monica wondered if she was one of the childless, or merely a sympathizer. "You can stand up or stay seated," the woman said. "We're casual here."

Here goes, thought Monica, getting to her feet. "My name

is Monica. I live in Lady Helen, although I'm originally from Johannesburg. I'm a newspaper editor."

"And you're here because?" prompted Shirley.

"My husband and I have been trying for a few years to have a baby."

There were nods of sympathy from the women in the chairs, most of whom looked to be in their late thirties or early forties. But some of whom, Monica was surprised to note, were younger than she was.

Shirley thanked her and Monica sat down.

"After this weekend, some of you will continue to try to have a baby, but others will be able to let go and follow different paths. Either way, I hope that this time we have together will fill you with the strength to make the right decision for yourself, and the strength to see it through."

Monica noticed a few women dab their eyes with tissues.

Then Shirley announced that it was time to break into groups of four. Monica was put with two of the younger-looking women and one who appeared to be in her early forties. They were directed to an adjoining room, while the other groups were also assigned private meeting spaces. Shirley, it appeared, was going to lead Monica's group. When she handed around more tissues, Monica began to feel nervous.

Shirley suggested each of the women introduce herself again. "This time I want you to tell us more about what motivated you to come to this conference." She pointed at one of the younger women to go first.

"Hi, I'm Anelle," she said. The tiny blonde had the fairest skin Monica had ever seen. "I live in Stellenbosch, so at least I didn't have to fight with the tour buses to get here." She gave a little laugh. "I live on my in-laws' wine farm, which my husband runs."

"You'll have to give us a tour later," said Shirley.

"With pleasure," said Anelle. "Our farm is not as big as some other nearby wineries, but I think it has the best views." She laughed again. "I'm from Johannesburg, where I had no view. Views are important to me."

Shirley pressed Anelle to tell the group why she had come to the workshop.

"My husband and I have had more fertility treatments than I can count, but now our doctor says we will not be able to conceive." Anelle began to cry. "He thinks that both my husband and I are infertile because of the pesticides used for the grape crop, which have been contaminating our drinking water for many years." She blew her nose into a tissue. "At first, my husband refused to consider adoption. I was devastated that he could be so stubborn. I almost left him, but my mother persuaded me to stay. Now he says he'll adopt, but only if the child is of—" she gave a sheepish smile "—of our own race."

The one black woman in the group nodded, out of contempt or agreement, Monica could not tell.

"And how do you feel about that?" Shirley asked Anelle.

"I want a child, any child. I'm tired of waiting. But the lady at the adoption organization said we may have to wait years for a white child."

"Are you worried what might happen to your marriage in that time?"

Anelle nodded.

Shirley thanked her for sharing and then turned to the older woman in the group. "What about you, Jo? Why did you come here?"

Jo said that she and her husband had never sought fertility treatment, believing that if it was God's will for them to conceive, they would. Recently, at age forty-two, she had paid a secret visit to a fertility doctor and had been told that her ovarian reserve was depleted. She'd left it too late.

"All developments in the field of fertility treatment came about through the grace of God," she said. "And I did not even think to go to a doctor to find out what was wrong with me till I was past childbearing age." The worst, she said, was not knowing if her problem had been treatable or not.

Anelle was still crying and now Jo, too, began to cry. Shirley handed around more tissues.

"And what do you hope to gain from this workshop?" asked Shirley.

Jo looked at each one of them. "I don't know. I suppose I just needed to feel that I wasn't alone."

Anelle reached across and squeezed Jo's hand. Monica was thankful that Shirley chose the other younger woman to go next.

"My name is Kholeka. I'm originally from Port Elizabeth, but now I work in a bank in Cape Town." She looked at each of the women in the group. "I have a son. He's twelve. His father and I did not marry. Now I am married to a wonderful man. I have been to the doctor. He says there's no reason why I cannot have another child and that maybe my husband has the problem. But my husband refuses to come with me to the doctor. He says there's nothing wrong with him and he's not going to have a doctor checking his private business." She began to cry. "I have to choose between my husband and having a baby."

"Count yourself blessed because you already have a child," said Anelle.

Jo nodded emphatically.

"That's the problem," said Kholeka. "People think that because you already have one child you won't suffer when you can't have another. I love my husband and I want us to have a child together."

Shirley asked Kholeka what she hoped to gain from the workshop.

She attempted a smile. "I'd like it if someone could think of a way to change my husband's mind." Then she grew serious. "I need to know how to switch this part of myself off, this part that makes me long to hold a baby in my arms again. I was hoping someone would be able to tell me how to do that."

This was exactly what Monica had hoped to gain from the workshop.

"And now you, Monica," said Shirley.

"My story is like Kholeka's, I suppose. My husband and I have tried without success to have a baby, and the strain on me, on my family, is too much." She looked at Anelle. "I have two adopted boys. They are the sons of a good friend who died of AIDS." She saw the question in Anelle's eyes. "Their mother, Ella Nkhoma, was a returned exile."

As Monica had expected, Anelle looked surprised.

"I want to have a baby, not because I need a child that looks like me, but because my husband and I want a new life to come from our love. It's as Kholeka says—there's a part of you that yearns to hold a baby, and it's hard to switch that off."

"Is that what you wish to gain from this workshop?" asked Shirley. "To be able to get past that yearning?"

Monica looked at the women who had each shared her intimate details with the group. She saw the anguish in their eyes and, without knowing why, she began to sob.

"My life is a mess. My marriage is falling apart. I can't do anything except think about the baby I won't have."

Shirley offered her another tissue, which she took gratefully. Kholeka patted her gently on the back.

"Ladies, you have just taken an important first step," said Shirley. "You have opened up to strangers and shared your pain. This is the first step toward surrender. For years, you have tried to control your bodies, without success. At this workshop, we are going to teach you to surrender yourselves, as though you had adopted or stopped trying to conceive—even if this is not the case. And to do this we are going to concentrate on our minds and our bodies."

Monica imagined the scornful look on Zak's face if he were here at this moment. In the absence of any published research to confirm a treatment's legitimacy, to him such treatment was a waste of time and money. Still, he had said he would support her in getting the help she needed, and coming to this workshop had been her choice.

A short while later, tea was served in the courtyard of the hotel, next to the original sluice that had once provided irrigation for all of Stellenbosch's crops. Anelle cornered Monica as she was helping herself to a plate of sliced guavas and pineapple.

"How did you get your husband to agree to adopting your late friend's boys?" she asked.

Monica wished that she could provide an easy solution to the younger woman's problem with her husband, but all she could do was tell the truth. "I wasn't married when I adopted them."

Anelle sighed. "But he's okay with it?"

Monica nodded. "It was never an issue. But, Anelle, you can't force your husband to do something he doesn't want to."

"But there are hardly any white babies to adopt."

Monica did not know how to console Anelle, and was grateful when Kholeka came to stand with them.

Kholeka sighed. "So here we are, three women desperate for a baby, and the country has more than a million orphans."

Anelle burst into tears.

"I'm sorry if I upset you," she said. "But it's the truth."

"It's complicated," said Anelle, sniffing.

"I know. If I told my husband I wanted to adopt a child, he'd say I'd lost my mind."

"Monica did it the right way," said Anelle. "She did it on her own."

"That was just the way things worked out," said Monica quietly. She did not like being held up as an example.

"But she still wants a child of her own," added Kholeka.

"I never had my boys as babies," said Monica. Why, she wondered, was she being defensive?

Jo had refilled her teacup and joined the discussion. "You're fortunate," she told Monica. "You've already been through the adoption process. My husband and I were told to be prepared to wait ages for our paperwork and background checks to be completed."

The sound of a bell announcing the next session interrupted their conversation. Monica quickly poured herself a cup of tea and took it to the classroom where a lesson on how to take care of your body by changing your diet was to be held.

The instructor, a tall, slim, middle-aged woman, started by saying that she was sure all of the attendees would never think of putting anything other than state-tested and regulated gas in their cars. Why then would they put junk in their bodies?

By the end of the session, Monica had realized that whether she decided to continue trying to conceive or whether she gave up, she had to take better care of herself, not in the way her mother would suggest by going for manicures and massages and buying designer clothes, but by watching what kind of food she ate. There would be no more preservatives and additives in her house. From now on, there would be less meat and more fruit and vegetables. The whole family would benefit.

At the end of the day, after a session on how to manage stress, one of the largest obstacles to conceiving, Monica asked the other ladies in her group to join her for dinner at the restaurant next to the hotel.

Anelle, Jo and Kholeka all accepted her invitation. Anelle wanted to know about Sipho and Mandla: what language they spoke to Monica, how she helped preserve their cultural identity, any problems they'd had at school with other children, whether they ever talked about their mother. Monica answered as best she could, all the while thinking that it was a pointless conversation if Anelle's husband wouldn't agree to adopt nonwhite children. Over dessert of fresh pears and ice cream, she came to a heart-sinking realization. Anelle planned to follow her example and do it alone.

"You're not going to leave your husband, are you?" Monica asked.

Anelle put down her spoon and looked her in the eye. "If you can do it by yourself, so can I."

Monica glanced at Kholeka, then at Jo for assistance. When neither reacted, Monica understood the depth of desperation in these three women. One was prepared to leave her husband so she could adopt children, and the others didn't see a problem with that. Monica knew Zak was right; she was depressed. But she had never considered anything as drastic as what Anelle proposed and Kholeka and Jo tacitly supported.

Anelle was prepared to give up her husband and the life she had known for years for what Monica already had. How could Monica have been so blind? She had what other women dreamed of: two adopted sons and a husband who loved her and her boys as much as he loved his own daughter. And yet Monica had taken her family for granted, and lately even neglected them. God had blessed her, and she had believed He didn't care about her. Tears filled her eyes.

"What did I say?" asked Anelle in a panicked voice.

"Thank you," said Monica.

"For what?"

"For making me realize what a fool I've been." She looked at Kholeka and then Jo. "You all have." Then she turned back to Anelle. "Don't leave your husband. You can work it out. The two of you should come to Lady Helen for a weekend. Spend time with my family. My son Sipho is still in the United States, but if anyone can bring your husband round, it will be my boy Mandla. He's quite the little actor."

Anelle looked uncertain. She had worked up the courage to tell strangers of a tentative plan she had probably been wrestling with for many months, but now Monica was advising her not to follow through on it.

Jo shrugged. "It's worth a try. You can still leave your husband later, if you feel you have to, Anelle."

"She won't have to," said Monica emphatically. "Mandla will make sure of that. Now, if you ladies will excuse me, I'm going to turn in for the night. Tomorrow I want to be on the road early so I can go to church with my family." She handed one of her business cards to each of them. "My family and I will be happy to welcome you to our home anytime you want to come to Lady Helen."

Anelle started to cry. "I'll miss you," she said.

Kholeka put an arm around Anelle's shoulder. "What did you learn today about how to manage stress?"

Anelle began to breathe deeply.

"That's right," said Kholeka. "In and out."

"I mean it about bringing your husband to see us, Anelle," said Monica. Then she looked at Kholeka and Jo. "Let's all stay in touch."

∝ Chapter Twenty-Six ∝

Zak, Yolanda and Mandla were having breakfast in the garden when Monica arrived home.

"What are you doing back so early?" asked Zak, rising to greet her.

"I didn't want to miss going to church with you," she responded, kissing him on the cheek. She felt guilty when she saw the surprise on his face. It had been so long since she'd been affectionate with him. "What's for breakfast?"

"French toast," said Mandla. "Yolanda made it."

"I'm sure it's delicious," Monica exclaimed.

Mandla looked at her quizzically. He was not used to seeing her so cheerful.

During breakfast, Monica felt Zak's eyes on her and knew that as soon as the meal was finished, he would corner her for a private talk. Their chance came when it was time to do the dishes and the children quickly disappeared.

"I think it might be time for us to have *the* talk," he said. "You seem ready."

To her surprise, Monica felt a sob catch in her throat. "Oh, Zak, I'm sorry for what I said to you in Los Angeles."

He put his arms around her. "I'm sorry, too, if I haven't been as supportive as you needed me to be."

"I know you want another baby as much as I do," cried Monica, burying her face in his chest.

"Are you ready to try again?" he asked softly.

She pulled away so that she could look at his face. "I think we've given it our best shot," she said quietly. "But if you want to continue trying, then I will go along with your wishes."

Zak wiped the tears from her cheeks, then sighed. "Are you sure you'd be okay about giving up now? I don't want you to regret it years down the line when it's too late."

"I'm blessed to have Sipho and Mandla and to be a stepmother to Yolanda."

"They're great children."

"I've finally decided what I should have known all along. The boys are all the babies I need." She began to cry again.

"Are you sure?"

She nodded. "I'll need some time to grieve, because it's the end of my dream of having a baby, but I know this is the right decision."

Zak handed her a tissue and she blew her nose. He took her face in his hands. "I've missed you, Monica—and I don't mean this weekend, I mean these past months." He kissed her gently.

"I love you," she said.

"I love you, too."

"Are the dishes done?" Mandla stood in the doorway to the kitchen.

"Strange how that happens, isn't it?" said Zak.

"I was going to help," said Mandla with a smile.

"We knew that, didn't we, Monica?"

She pinched Mandla's cheeks. "Of course we did."

That morning at church, with the cries of the migratory birds coming in through the open windows from the lagoon, Monica asked God to forgive her for losing faith in Him. Reverend van Tonder, although he could not have known it, chose the perfect scripture for her: the story of the prodigal son.

The family took a walk together on the beach after lunch. Monica did not tell Zak how she had flung herself into the ocean, fully clothed, after learning that Jacqueline was pregnant. She did not mention Jacqueline at all, not only because she didn't want to think about Zak's ex-wife having a baby, but because Monica didn't know if Zak had told Yolanda about it yet.

When Yolanda and Mandla went down to the water's edge, Monica asked him if he had.

"I didn't want to tell her in front of Mandla, so I was waiting till you got back."

"Have you spoken to Jacqueline again?"

Zak nodded. "I don't think she has any intention of coming back. She'll make all the excuses she can think of until the baby…" He paused to check the effect his words might be having.

"It's okay, Zak."

"And then it will be the end of Yolanda's school year and Jacqueline will try and persuade her to go to university in Australia."

"Do you want me to take Mandla for a walk?"

"Please." Zak sighed.

"There was something Ella used to call the 'Ella Nkhoma Shake and Bake,'" Monica told him. "It was her expression for trying to put a positive spin on something."

"I don't see how I could in this case. Jacqueline lied and now she's prepared to live without Yolanda for a while."

"Yes, but having Yolanda full-time has been a dream of *yours* since the divorce."

A smile appeared on Zak's face. "You're right. If I present it to her like that, the blow might not be as bad."

Mandla was always eager to go farther than usual on the beach, but he wanted to know why Yolanda and Zak weren't accompanying them on their walk. Monica told him what Yolanda was about to learn.

"Yolanda's mother is too old to have a baby," he said.

"Not really."

"Well, then why can't you have one?"

"Some people just can't." She stopped and took his hand. "But I have two wonderful boys. You and your brother are all I need."

He squinted at her in the bright sun. "Are you sure?"

"I'm sure."

He resumed walking, and for a second she was disappointed that he hadn't done something dramatic like throw his arms around her and tell her that he loved her. Then she noticed the tiny smile at the corners of his mouth and realized he hadn't pulled his hand away from her. She took this as a sign that at long last they had returned to normal.

At the golf resort, they stopped and sat down on the sand.

"Why is Mama Dlamini working here now?" Mandla thumbed in the direction of the hotel.

"I wish she wasn't, but Francina says it's a chance of a lifetime."

Mandla thought for a while. "Like I had in Hollywood."

So things were not quite yet normal between them.

"I'm sorry you were disappointed about not staying," she said.

He nodded. "Sipho wouldn't want to live there. He'd miss his birds and animals and snakes and whales." Mandla gave an exaggerated shiver. "So when can I go to Cape Town to audition for a movie?"

Monica told him that she would look into it first thing the next morning.

"And I suppose I'd better do what that director said—go for acting lessons."

"I'll find out about those, too. What about losing your South African accent?"

"I've been trying."

"So I've noticed."

"But it's too hard to keep up. And there's no point if I'm not moving to Hollywood."

Monica had to suppress a smile at the serious tone with which he said this, as though it had indeed been a possibility.

"I like the way you talk," she told him.

Mandla rested his head on her shoulder. "Of course you do. You're my mother."

Monica saw a dive boat bobbing on the water about two hundred yards offshore. It was probably James, her friend Kitty's husband, with a group of tourists.

"Is Yolanda going to stay with us for good?" asked Mandla.

"I hope so. But it won't be for good, because next year she'll be going away to university."

"Do you think I can go away to university? To America?"

"I suppose so. If we can afford it. Or maybe you'll win a scholarship."

"Don't forget to find out about the acting lessons tomorrow."

Monica assured him that she wouldn't forget. Ever since he was little, she had predicted that he would leave the nest first. Sipho had beaten him to it, but Sipho would return; when Mandla went, it would be for good.

Monica stood up and shook the sand from her skirt. She didn't want to think about that now, when she was just getting her family back on track.

"I hope Yolanda will be happy to stay with us," said Mandla.

"Me, too, Mandla. Me, too."

When they returned to the others, Yolanda was crying. Monica indicated to Zak that she and Mandla could turn around again and leave, but he put up his hand for her to stay. Monica went to Yolanda and laid her arm across her shoulders.

"Dad says he wants me to live with you," said Yolanda, sniffing.

"We both do," said Monica.

"My mom—" Yolanda began to cry again.

Monica pulled her closer. "Don't cry. It will all work out. You'll see."

Monica thought about how these words, which she had once despised hearing from well-meaning friends, had turned out to be true for her life. She had decided to give up her wish for a baby, yet had gained a daughter—at least until Yolanda went away to university. One mother had given her the boys, another had lent her Yolanda. Monica thought of Anelle, Kholeka and Jo, who were still at the workshop, and prayed that they, too, would be blessed with children, their own or those born to others.

After Mandla and Yolanda had gone to sleep that night, and Zak was in the living room, reading the latest issue of a medical journal, Monica went into the bathroom, gathered up her ovulation predictor kits, pregnancy tests, basal temperature thermometer and unused ovulation charts. She put them in a plastic shopping bag, which she set down next to the front door for Zak to take to the hospital the following day. Someone else might need them; she no longer did.

When she awoke the next morning, she told herself it was Monday, not day eight of her cycle. Never again would she count off days on her calendar unless it was to show Mandla how many there were till his birthday or Christmas, or until his grandparents arrived.

Shirley had told them at the workshop to look after their bodies, and today would be the start. From now on she would eat well, exercise more, breathe fresh air outdoors whenever she could, and control her anxiety. It was time for her to take back her life.

❧ Chapter Twenty-Seven ❧

Francina leaned against the kitchen counter, sipping her tea and watching Zukisa complete an essay for her English homework. Zukisa was a good student, not exceptional like Sipho, but among the best in her class. Unlike Sipho and Yolanda, she did not aspire to go to university, and Francina was secretly disappointed. She was touched that Zukisa wanted no more in life than to join her behind the counter at Jabulani Dressmakers, but Francina wanted her to attain what she had never been able to, a degree certificate with a fat gold medallion. In her attempts to persuade Zukisa, Francina had shown her exactly where the certificate would hang, on the wall in the shop next to the one she herself had obtained just three years ago, for completing high school.

Francina had not told Zukisa of her plan to bring the girl's family to Lady Helen, not for fear that it wouldn't be possible, but because Francina was not quite ready to see the joy on her daughter's face that such an announcement would bring. Even after all these years as Zukisa's adopted mother, and against her will, Francina still felt jealousy when she saw her daughter with her blood relatives.

Lucy had taken over her mother's job cleaning the cafeteria after the breakfast shift, and she had also been hired as the cook for the dinner shift, which was usually quiet because most of the dockworkers returned to their homes at the end of the day. While Lucy was away, Xoli was supposed to be in charge, but he often didn't come home until after his mother, and then would not reveal where he had been. This past weekend, Lucy had shared with Francina her suspicions about Xoli's involvement in a gang, which was why Francina had decided that now was the time to bring her plan to fruition. If she didn't, Xoli would be lost, just as his mother had once been.

The success of her plan depended on the cooking skills of Mama Dlamini. Her Zulu friend's apprenticeship at the golf resort was almost up, and if Mama Dlamini was offered a job as head chef, Lucy could take over from her at the café. Mama Dlamini knew nothing of this, but Francina would use all her skills as a negotiator to persuade her.

Hercules would be able to tell Mama Dlamini that it was difficult to escape Francina's persuasive skills, or what he called nagging. She had been on at him for a year to submit his name as a candidate for the mayoral election that was set to take place in a month. Only a week remained for him to register as a candidate.

"What are you plotting, Mother?" asked Zukisa. "I know that look on your face."

"Never mind. Have you completed your homework?"

She nodded. "Let's go downstairs and work on Gift's dress."

Gift had been invited to exhibit her work at a gallery in London, and she wanted something new to wear to the opening of the show.

Francina followed her daughter down the stairs to the shop, where the Closed sign hung on the door. Late summer sunlight streamed through the windows, giving the polished wooden floor a golden hue. Dinner was ready upstairs, but Francina and Zukisa were waiting for Hercules, who had gone to church to discuss the upcoming visit from a choir based in Mpumalanga Province.

"How am I going to get your father to run for mayor?" Francina asked as they sewed shimmering silver beads onto Gift's black chiffon dress.

"Oh, Mother, I think that is one plot you should give up. He'll never willingly submit his name."

Zukisa's words gave Francina an idea. Hercules was a man of honor; if *she* were to put in his name, he would never withdraw it. That was it! Just before the deadline, she would submit her husband's name as a candidate for mayor of Lady Helen. The town deserved him, and his integrity deserved recognition. Francina decided that this, too, would have to be a secret to keep from her daughter.

A week later, as Francina and Zukisa returned home from watching Mandla for the afternoon, Francina asked her daughter to go upstairs to their flat and peel the potatoes for dinner while she popped into the general store to buy some milk.

"There was plenty of milk this morning," said Zukisa.

"We need more because I want to make baked custard for dessert this evening."

Francina waited until Zukisa had gone inside before crossing the street and hurrying into the mayor's office. It was five-thirty. Only half an hour remained before the deadline expired for entries into the mayoral race.

"Hello," said Mayor Richard. "What can I do for you?"

"I want to register for the election," said Francina.

She tried not to look at Mayor Richard's naked calves as he got up from behind his desk to open a large ledger on the windowsill. At that moment, the telephone on his desk rang, and he hurried to answer it.

While he was talking to the caller, Francina filled in the entry form on behalf of Hercules. She didn't need him here to help her with any of the answers; as his wife, she knew all there was to know about him. Mayor Richard was still on the telephone when she reached the line where Hercules was supposed to provide his signature. Pushy she might be, but she was not a fraud, and so, using her most legible script, she wrote her own name on the line and put the letters *pp* next to it, as the secretary at Green Block School did when the principal, Mr. D., did not have time to sign his name.

Mayor Richard waved at her as she left, but did not interrupt his telephone conversation. Outside on the sidewalk, she gave a sigh of relief. It was done. Everything else would fall into place. There was not much time to campaign, but Hercules was so well-known in town there would be little need for it.

"You lucky people," she said under her breath as she watched shop and gallery owners close the doors and pull the blinds for the night. The merchants did not know it, but the leadership of Lady Helen was about to change for the better.

* * *

While Francina and her family ate dinner that night, the telephone rang, and Zukisa rose to answer it.

"It's for you, Dad," she told Hercules. "It's the mayor."

Francina felt the blood drain from her face.

"Are you okay?" her mother-in-law asked, as he hurried off to take the call.

"I'm fine," replied Francina, taking another bite of roast potato. She strained to catch Hercules's conversation, but could hear nothing. Then she noticed Zukisa observing her. "Eat up," she told her. "Your food is getting cold."

Her husband returned to the table. He did not look angry, so perhaps Mayor Richard had wanted to talk to him about some other business. Hercules sat down and spread his napkin on his lap.

"Congratulations, Francina," he said.

"For what?"

"I understand you're running for mayor."

Zukisa and Mrs. Shabalala broke into big smiles.

Francina dropped her fork onto her plate. "There must be some mistake," she said.

Hercules shook his head. "Mayor Richard said you signed your name on the dotted line of the entry form."

"Yes, but…" Francina trailed off in misery. How could she admit in front of her daughter and mother-in-law what she had done?

"I think you'll make a fantastic mayor," continued Hercules.

"Why didn't you tell us?" said Mrs. Shabalala. "I'll make some signs to put up around town."

Zukisa gave her mother a lingering, questioning look. "Tell me what to do and I'll do it." Her words were supportive, but her tone was just curt enough for Francina to notice. Her daughter was upset that she had not confided in her.

"There's been a mistake," said Francina, getting to her feet. "I'm not running for mayor." She rushed to the bathroom and locked herself in.

What had she done? She didn't have time to run for mayor, let alone be the mayor. And now Hercules was upset with her and Zukisa was disappointed in her. What an impetuous fool she had been. Tomorrow she'd tell Mayor Richard that there had been a mistake, and ask him to withdraw her name from the race. And now she would do what she did whenever she was upset: run a hot bath and climb in for a long soak.

When she emerged from the bathroom in her robe, Mrs. Shabalala and Zukisa had gone for a walk to the park, and Hercules was sitting on the couch in the living room, waiting for her.

"I'm sorry, Hercules," she said. "I shouldn't have put your name down without your permission."

"No, you shouldn't have. That's fraud."

"But I didn't forge your signature. I wrote mine very legibly."

"And that's why you're the candidate now and not me."

Francina sat down on the couch next to him. "Tomorrow I'll ask Mayor Richard to withdraw my name."

Hercules turned to look at her. "I think that would be your second mistake."

"What do you mean?"

"I meant what I said at dinner. You'd be a good mayor."

"Yes, but what about the shop and looking after Mandla and—"

"Yolanda's old enough to watch Mandla in the afternoon."

He was right about this, but not about her being a good mayor.

"And you told me yourself that Zukisa wants to take on more responsibility for designing dresses in the shop."

Francina began to sob.

"Why are you crying?" Hercules moved closer and put an arm around her shoulders.

"I'm scared."

"There's nothing to be frightened of. You've run Monica's household, you run ours, you run a shop. You can run a small town with your eyes shut."

Francina cried even more then because her husband was so sweet.

"Shh," he told her, drying her cheeks with the palm of his hand.

"I might be worrying for nothing," she said brightly. "Richard could get more votes than me."

"Possible, but not likely."

Hercules was not one for open displays of affection, but since his mother and Zukisa were out, Francina reached up and kissed him on the cheek.

"What's that for?" he asked.

"You know very well what it's for," she said.

They heard footsteps on the stairs leading up from the shop, and Hercules pulled away. Francina was not offended. It was his way, to remain discreet even in front of family.

"There are sixteen lampposts on Main Street," said Mrs. Shabalala. "Zukisa and I counted them. We can put a poster on every other one and a few down in the park, so we should probably make at least twelve."

"You'll have to tell us about your platform," said Zukisa.

Her tone was still reserved, but Francina could tell that she was being swept up by the excitement of tonight's developments.

"My platform?" asked Francina.

"The issue you think is most important," she explained. "What are you going to promise the residents of Lady Helen?"

Francina smiled. "Not to wear shorts and show my legs in public?"

"No, you know what I mean," said Zukisa.

In truth, there were no major issues dividing or threatening the town at this moment. Life in Lady Helen was so peaceful that Francina often wondered how Monica managed to find enough stories to fill the newspaper.

"You'd be the first female mayor in the history of the town," said Zukisa.

Francina had not thought of that. "What are we waiting for? Let's get to work on the posters."

While her mother-in-law went to collect markers and paper from downstairs in the shop, Francina confessed to Zukisa how she had tried to sign up Hercules as a candidate and, in doing so, become a candidate herself. "What I did was wrong, and I suppose I knew it, and that's why I never told you," she said.

Mrs. Shabalala returned with the supplies and the family sat down at the dining room table to design the posters.

When the residents of Lady Helen awoke the next morning, they learned that their beloved dressmaker was running for mayor and that, as the first female to hold this office, she would make the town even more beautiful than it already was.

✧ Chapter Twenty-Eight ✧

As part of her new health and wellness program, Monica had decided to walk to work if she didn't have to go far during the day to research a story. The distance from her home to the office was not more than a mile, but she had not accounted for the late summer heat, and so she was relieved each morning to reach the shaded sidewalks of Main Street.

"I think Francina will be good," Nalini said to her one particularly warm morning. Nalini, who was originally from Durban and always wore a sari, was looking at a poster on a lamppost outside her gallery, which she had yet to unlock.

Monica read the handwritten words on the poster and was shocked to discover that Francina was running for mayor. She had not said a word to her about it yesterday afternoon when Monica had arrived home from work. Why the secrecy? Nalini was correct in her estimation though;

after putting up with Monica's mother for so many years, Francina could handle anything. Monica could not wait to see her mother's face when she found out that the lady who had once scrubbed her floors and washed her dishes might become the next mayor of Lady Helen. The relationship between Francina and Monica's mother had changed since Francina established Jabulani Dressmakers. Mirinda Brunetti had never expressed an interest in Francina's creations when she was making them in the tiny servant's quarters of the Brunetti home in Johannesburg, but now that Francina had a list of clients as long as her tape measure, Mirinda couldn't get enough of her former employee's designs.

Monica walked on, seeing Francina's name on every other lamppost until she reached her office, and by then she knew that her first order of the day would be to set up an interview with the new mayoral candidate. In the three weeks before the election, there would, hopefully, be some newsworthy debates between the two candidates.

Dudu jumped up when Monica walked in. "Have you heard?" she asked. "Zak just called."

"I saw the posters on the way to work."

Dudu came around to the front of the reception desk. "I meant about Max Andrews. He's had a fall. The ambulance took him to the hospital. Zak said to tell you to come at once."

Monica did not bother going inside her office. Now, of all days, she needed her car. Dudu didn't have one; her husband brought her to work.

Fifteen minutes later, Monica arrived at the hospital, puffing and sweating after running all the way. Adelaide, a nurse Monica had interviewed years ago for a story on the hospital's burn unit, directed her to the hospital's one-bed intensive care unit. Daphne was just coming out.

"Max's son said you could go in," she told Monica.

Edward Andrews rose to his feet as she entered. Like his father, he had lost most of his hair except for a thin tufted row that ran around the back of his head from ear to ear, but Edward's hair was not yet gray. The town did not provide Edward, its only lawyer, with enough business to earn a living, so he spent three days a week in Cape Town, working as in-house counsel for an international oil company. Max had moved in with Edward the year Monica became editor of the newspaper, and Edward's wife, Ann, who had never been able to have children, had cared for her father-in-law as though he were a ten-year-old boy. In the beginning, Max had complained to Monica that he felt overwhelmed by her attention, but as his arthritis had grown worse and he was able to move about less, he had needed—and appreciated— Ann's care more than he ever would admit.

Now, Ann sat crying quietly in the corner of the ICU.

"How is he doing?" Monica asked Edward.

"Not good. Your husband told us to say our goodbyes."

Zak never placated a patient's family with half-truths, because time was so precious when death drew near.

"Dad asked me last night to invite you over for lunch on Sunday. He wanted to give you his memoirs to read."

"He finally finished?"

Edward nodded. "Yesterday. He fell during the night when he got up to use the bathroom. Ann was always telling him not to go by himself, to call her to help. She'd even given him a bell to ring. But Dad never wanted to wake us."

Max stirred in the bed and Monica stepped back to let

Edward go to his father's side. Max's eyes were shut. When Monica had first met him, his bright blue eyes and strong jaw had made her believe that he had been handsome in his youth. Now, after he'd had all his teeth replaced by ill-fitting dentures, his jawline had softened, giving his face a less rugged quality.

Monica leaned forward and touched his hand. His skin felt cool and dry. There was a bandage around his head, covering the injury he had sustained in the fall. An IV dripped slowly into a port on his wrist.

Max had not wanted to look at her portfolio of work on the day she'd come to interview for his job as editor of the *Lady Helen Herald.* He said he'd seen her on *In-Depth* and that her talent was indisputable. The reason he had wanted to meet her was to judge her character, and after she'd defended the profession of public relations against Max's unintended insult, he told her that she'd won his respect. He did not know then that the boys Monica had brought with her to the interview were the sons of a woman who had been a public relations officer, or he would never have said what he had.

During Monica's first year as editor, Max had infuriated her by hanging around the office, keeping an eye on her. But when she'd realized how hard it had been for him to give up the newspaper, she'd tried to keep him involved. He saw through her pleas for help with various projects, but gave it all the same. Now she wished she had visited him more often.

"Those are his memoirs," said Edward, pointing at a brown folder on the nightstand. "We brought the manuscript from home this morning, knowing you'd be here."

Monica opened the cover. On the first page, Max had written by hand, *To Monica, with respect, Max.*

Edward saw the surprise on her face. "He printed two copies. This one is for you."

She fanned through the pages. There were four hundred in all. These four hundred pages had kept Max busy for the last six years of his life. While Monica had been raising her boys, running the newspaper, falling in love and getting married, Max had been sitting in front of his computer, dusting off his memories.

"We'd still like you to come to lunch," said Edward. "You and your family."

Monica thanked him and promised that she and Zak and the children would be there.

"Once my father is gone, I will be the only one left of our family," said Edward. "I hope you never have to experience what that feels like."

Max's face was almost yellow against the bleached white pillow slip. Although Monica had not always been the best protégée, he had been an excellent and kind mentor. Over the past few months, Max had seen the newspaper he'd started degenerate into a community newsletter, full of frivolous stories, typographical errors and advertising, but he'd summoned Monica to his home only once, and then had quickly realized that reprimanding her would only exacerbate her depression. Instead, he'd offered his services to Dudu, but Dudu had been too polite to give work to an elderly man who was practically bedridden.

Monica wished that Max could read the latest issue, due out tomorrow. It would be the first decent one in months. But it did not appear likely that he would see it.

She bent over him and whispered, "I'm sorry, Max. It won't happen again." Then she looked at him in silence for a few minutes. The world was about to lose an honorable man; she was about to lose a dear friend.

It would feel strange going back to her office—his old office—now. He had taken his orange couch away, but there were still reminders everywhere of his ten years at the helm of the *Lady Helen Herald:* the light patches on the wooden floor where his filing cabinets had once stood, the masthead design that hadn't changed since the newspaper's inception, the letters to the editor page that he said should always contain the rantings of irate readers, if she was doing her job properly.

"Goodbye, Max," she said quietly. Tears coursed down her cheeks.

Edward handed her a tissue. "Thank you," he said.

"For what?" asked Monica.

"For keeping him involved. You will never know how much that meant to him."

Monica said goodbye to Ann, who was still crying in the corner. She waved at Zak on the way out.

She had not put things right with Max in time, but it was not too late to patch up her friendship with Kitty. Before she went back to the office, she would stop at Abalone House. Perhaps she and Kitty could sit on the porch with a cup of coffee as they used to. This time, Monica would ask to hold Kitty's baby, Jimmy, although now that he was walking, he might no longer be interested in occupying her lap.

❧ Chapter Twenty-Nine ❧

Francina was in her shop, sewing the final fifty beads onto Gift's dress, when the bell over the door jangled loudly.

"You won't believe what I'm going to tell you," said Mrs. Shabalala. She put her hands on her knees and breathed deeply. "I ran all the way from the bakery."

"What happened?"

"I was ordering the bread Zukisa likes, with the raisins, and Mayor Richard came into the store wearing a pair of red shorts. I'm not joking."

Red shorts were unusual, but that wasn't likely to cause a woman to run all the way home from the bakery, especially if she was, to put it politely, not built like an athlete.

"I hope his shirt matched his shorts," said Francina. The mayor's clothes didn't always coordinate.

"It was white with large yellow frangipani flowers, so no, it didn't match. But that's not my news. Mayor Richard said that last night, just after you entered the race for mayor, there was another entrant."

Francina put down her sewing. "Who?"

"Oscar."

"Oscar wants to be mayor?"

"Apparently so," said Mrs. Shabalala, now recovered from her exertion.

Oscar had been Francina's first tutor, back in the day when she was studying for the grade nine School Leavers certificate. The first thing he'd told her about himself was that he'd been named after a famous English playwright. He'd never read any of the man's plays, however, because Oscar didn't like stories that were set in one room. Oscar was an adventurer. He had sailed around the world and returned to the place of his birth after the end of a love affair.

It had been Hercules who had pointed out to Francina— incredibly—that Oscar was in love with her. That had been on a night when the two men had almost come to blows. After that, Hercules had become her teacher, and she rarely saw Oscar again. He'd offered his condolences after her father died, and at that time he'd also urged her to complete high school. Now, she could feel grateful to him, since she had that smart green matric certificate hanging in her home, next to the grade nine School Leavers certificate.

She and Oscar might have to debate each other in the run-up to the election. That wouldn't be a comfortable situation for either of them, or for Hercules. Francina had often wondered why Oscar had never gone off again on his travels. He had no family to keep him in Lady Helen, and the odd jobs he did—such as the fences he'd built around the cemetery, the statue of Lady Helen and the San paintings he'd discovered in a cave on the koppies—were often unpaid and voluntary. She'd heard that he spent his weekends tramping around the countryside, looking for the grave of Lady Helen, the founder of the town, who'd freed her husband's slaves and escaped from Cape Town with them in a stolen wagon. Many of the graves in the cemetery were marked only by piles of stones, but Oscar was sure that Lady Helen's would be clearly identified.

"So we have a three-way race," Francina said to her mother-in-law, whose incredulous expression suggested that she did not think Francina's reaction worthy of her sprint from the bakery.

Francina did not know that Hercules had told his mother about his altercation with Oscar all those years ago, but it was clear that she believed Oscar was not an ordinary competitor for Francina.

"Perhaps I should go from door to door to persuade people to vote for me," she said. "Oscar is popular around here."

"And I hear he fights dirty," said Mrs. Shabalala.

That was untrue; when Hercules had arrived in Lady Helen and made it clear that he intended to win back Francina's affection, which he had lost because of his depression over his late wife's passing, Oscar had dropped out of her life and never tried to get close to her again. From her mother-in-law's behavior now, it might be forgivable to think that Oscar was still interested in her—an impossible notion. Or was it? Had her mother-in-law heard something on the grapevine?

"Oscar is a perfect gentleman," said Francina. Romantic as it sounded, no man would love a woman from afar for years, especially if she was married.

"A perfect gentleman doesn't—" Mrs. Shabalala stopped herself.

"Doesn't what?"

"Nothing. I'm going to finish the marketing now. I just thought I'd tell you this news before you found it out from someone else."

"Thank you, Mama," said Francina.

When Hercules came home from school with Zukisa at lunchtime, he, too, had heard of the new development. "You have more to offer as mayor than Oscar does," he said.

Hercules was never unkind, and so this comment revealed his true feelings about the matter. He was upset.

"Perhaps he'd make a better bureaucrat," said Francina. "He has more time on his hands."

"You have to start thinking like a winner," said Hercules. "You can beat him."

This kind of talk was not at all in Hercules's nature. Had her husband and mother-in-law taken too much sun recently, or did he, too, know something Francina didn't? At least Zukisa was acting normally.

"I have detention tomorrow afternoon," the girl announced.

"Detention? You've never had detention before. What happened?"

"One of the boys in my class said that a dressmaker has no business being mayor, so I stapled his tie to his backpack."

"You did what?" Francina was wrong; her whole family was acting strangely.

"He insulted you."

"But Zukisa, we've taught—"

"Dad has already given me the lecture. You have to win this election, to show everyone."

Francina found it touching that her daughter would rush to her defense, but not by ruining a boy's property. Zukisa, of all people, should know the damage a staple could do to fine fabric.

"I think you should start getting out there and campaigning," said Hercules. "A block a night and you'll have covered the town by the time of the election. I'll devise a route map."

"I could bake cookies to give out," said Mrs. Shabalala, who had come down to the shop to call them to lunch.

"And I'll sew your name on little flags to give out," added Zukisa.

Francina put up her hand. "Do you really think this is all necessary? People know who I am."

"Oscar will be out there shaking hands and kissing babies," said Hercules, in a scornful tone that made it seem a disgusting practice.

"And can you imagine the getups we'll see Mayor Richard in?" added Mrs. Shabalala.

Francina had never imagined running in an election. In her village, authority was transferred through birth. If she had borne her first husband, Winston, a son, that boy would have eventually taken over as chief from his father. There were times, she was sure, when the villagers wished that the leadership was selected by democratic means, but no one would ever dare put this idea into words. Winston had the power to make his people's lives easy or difficult, and Francina had personal experience of both.

If the other candidates in this election were going to make an effort to win, then so should she, or it would all be a waste of her time.

"Okay, I'll do it," she said.

Hercules's affirmation was so emphatic that her suspicions were again aroused. There was more than one reason he wanted her to beat Oscar. She might have only one eye, but she saw everything.

That night, the family went to Mama Dlamini's Eating Establishment because Mrs. Shabalala had been so busy baking cookies for Francina's campaign she had forgotten to make dinner.

For once, Mama Dlamini herself was in the kitchen.

"It's good to see you in your own restaurant for a change," said Francina.

"I'll be here every day for a while," she replied.

"Oh, does that mean you didn't get the job?" Francina realized that, as usual, she had said too much.

Mama Dlamini smiled broadly. "I'm taking a well-earned rest, because in a week I begin as the permanent head chef of the restaurant at the golf resort."

Francina's family erupted in applause, causing the other diners to stare.

"You're the first people I've told," said Mama Dlamini. "I should run away and let you tell the town."

Francina nodded. "I understand why the townsfolk won't like it. But they'll get over it when you tell them that this type of opportunity doesn't come often to a woman from your background."

"Kind of like you becoming mayor," said Mama Dlamini.

"Exactly. We are the same, you and I. Women who have risen beyond expectation."

"Like old dough," she laughed.

"My mother is going to win," said Zukisa. "We're her campaign helpers."

"If there's anything I can do, don't wait to ask," said Mama Dlamini.

"You should remain neutral if you want to protect your business," said Francina.

"Sometimes loyalty is more important," she replied, looking pointedly at Hercules.

His nod was almost imperceptible. What was going on? wondered Francina. The only people who seemed not to be in the know were Zukisa and herself.

Later, when Francina went to wash her hands, she entered the kitchen to speak in private with her friend.

"Are you going to hire someone else to help here?" she asked.

Mama Dlamini's happy expression became troubled. "I'll have to. Anna can't work full-time, neither can your mother-in-law."

Francina told her that she had the perfect person for the job, but that Mama Dlamini would have to keep it secret until everything had been finalized, because Francina didn't want to get Zukisa's hopes up.

Mama Dlamini's eyebrows shot upward. "You want Zukisa to work here?"

"No, no. Her cousin, Lucy. She's working as a cook now in Cape Town."

Mama Dlamini was shaking her head before Francina had completed her sentence. "Francina, I don't need trouble. I've heard all about her."

"That's in the past. A person can change."

"No, I'll find someone else."

Francina was irritated. Mama Dlamini had never met Lucy, yet she had already judged her. Still, Francina was prepared to overcome her annoyance to plead Lucy's case.

"Give her a chance, please."

"No, Francina. I won't stop worrying, and that means I won't be able to perform well at my job."

Francina felt like telling Mama Dlamini that she had been given a chance to prove herself at the golf resort, so why not give Lucy the same opportunity? But she didn't. She went back to her table, vowing never to set foot in her friend's café again.

The following evening, Francina, Hercules and Zukisa set out on the campaign trail. Mrs. Shabalala, who had spent the morning putting the cookies she had baked in individual gift bags, declared herself unfit for the journey and elected to remain at home watching her favorite soap opera. As promised, Hercules had devised a route map and the first area he'd targeted was Sandpiper Drift.

The windows of all the low, whitewashed stone cottages were open to catch the breeze blowing across the lagoon from the ocean.

"Let's start with Miemps and Reginald," said Francina.

Their cottage, the last in the row, was different from the others only in that it had window boxes filled with red, orange and yellow geraniums. For almost as long as Francina could remember, Reginald could be found at this time of the evening sitting outside his house, watching the neighborhood boys play soccer in the street, or talking to their fathers. Now Reginald needed assistance to walk, and Miemps could manage only to get him out of bed and to a chair in the living room.

Francina knocked on the door, and within seconds, her friend opened it, wearing an apron.

"I'm sorry, are we interrupting your cooking time?" Francina asked.

"No, no, I was washing the dishes. Please come in."

Francina looked at Hercules. Entering people's houses was not part of the plan. Francina was supposed to tell whoever came to the door that she was running for mayor. She was to say why she thought she'd be good at the job, ask for a vote, and then hand out a bag of cookies and a flag, featuring the slogan *This Town Needs a Woman's Touch*.

"Reginald would love to see you," said Miemps. "Come in. I'll put the kettle on." She motioned for them to enter the cottage.

Francina gave Hercules a look that said *we have no choice* and followed Miemps into her home. A lamp was on, but the television in the corner cast the most light in the room.

Miemps's floral furniture had been covered in plastic for as long as Francina could remember, but she noticed now that the plastic had been removed from the armchair where Reginald sat. Perhaps he had finally complained, as Mandla had done, that the plastic made his legs sweat.

Reginald's face broke into a broad grin when he saw the visitors. "This is a lovely surprise," he said, trying to stand.

"Don't get up for us," said Hercules. He shook his hand.

"Just look at your little girl. She's almost all grown up," said Reginald.

Zukisa smiled coyly and fidgeted with the bag of cookies she'd picked out for Miemps and Reginald. Thankfully, she'd had the good sense to leave the rest outside on the bench.

Reginald's feelings would be hurt if he realized this was a professional visit.

"Gogo made some cookies," said Zukisa, handing them over.

"How kind," said Reginald. He shouted to Miemps, who had disappeared to the kitchen, to put the kettle on.

"Already done," she shouted back.

For the next hour and a half, over tea and cookies, the talk was of families, neighbors and life in general. Miemps looked after her grandson, Victor, every day while her daughter, Daphne, worked at the hospital and her son-in-law, Silas, wrote the underground newspaper he smuggled into Zimbabwe, and petitioned the South African government to admit his parents and sister as legal immigrants.

From the way Reginald's eyes lit up when he spoke of Victor, Francina could tell that he lived for the boy. It saddened her that her own mother saw Zukisa only once a year, when Francina and Hercules took her to visit the village in the Valley of a Thousand Hills. Francina's mother had other grandchildren; Francina's eldest brother, Dingane, had two grown sons who lived in the same village, and her other brother, Sigidi, and his white wife had three daughters who lived in Durban, a port city an hour and a half drive away. But Francina's mother had never grown close to Zukisa. How could the two of them have formed a bond when they saw each other for a mere two weeks a year?

Francina noticed that Reginald was tiring, and told Hercules that they ought to be heading home. It was already dark when Miemps opened the front door to let them out.

"Thank you for visiting. It really lifts Reginald's spirits to have company."

Francina was thankful her friend did not step outside, where she'd see the bag of cookies and flags waiting on the bench where Reginald used to sit.

"We'll come again," she said to Miemps. "Now you go inside and don't let this cool breeze into the house. You don't want Reginald to catch cold."

Nodding, Miemps said good-night and closed the door.

"Oh, Mother!" said Zukisa. "Look." She pointed at the paper bag she'd left on the bench. It had been ripped open, and most of the gift bags of cookies were missing, although some lay on the ground, torn and masticated. Zukisa began to cry. "A dog took them."

"Shh, it's okay," whispered Francina. She did not want Miemps to open the door again to check what the commotion was about.

They picked up all the cookie remnants they could find and wrapped them in the ripped paper bag.

"The dog didn't touch your flags," said Francina.

Zukisa sniffed. "Nothing turned out right tonight."

Francina put an arm around her as they walked down the garden path toward the road. "It's a pity about the cookies, but I think the night turned out just right."

They climbed into their car, which Hercules had left at the end of the road where they'd expected to conclude their campaigning for the evening, and drove home in silence. Zukisa was tired, but Francina was deep in thought. Seeing Reginald had reminded her that it was important to grow old surrounded by family, and since she could not have her mother and brothers near her, she would do everything in her power to bring Zukisa's aunt and cousin to Lady Helen, with or without Mama Dlamini's help.

⊰ Chapter Thirty ⊱

On the weekend, Hercules drove Francina and Zukisa to Cape Town to visit Zukisa's aunt. The previous weekend, Lucy had expressed hope that new medication would give her mother strength, but Zukisa's aunt was unchanged. As usual, Lucy's son, Xoli was not at home. His younger brother, Bulelani, was watching television.

"I'll make tea while you sit with Mama," said Lucy.

Hercules, who was uncomfortable being in any woman's bedroom, sick or well, hurriedly volunteered his services for any minor repair or heavy lifting that Lucy required in a home with no adult male, and boys who wafted in and out like the wind.

When Francina visited Zukisa's aunt, she talked about whatever came to mind, usually whatever she had done that week, orders she was working on, memorable meals her mother-in-law had cooked. Sometimes Zukisa's aunt would offer a comment. Sometimes she'd just lie with her eyes closed, listening. On the rare occasion when Francina ran out of things to say, she would sing the songs her choir was practicing at the time.

"Can you believe that Hercules has convinced the ladies of the choir to travel to a competition?" she asked Zukisa's aunt.

As expected, there was no reply.

"Yes, we're going to sing at a festival in Grahamstown." Francina chuckled. "But the choristers don't want to rent a minibus taxi, so two of them will drive their own cars. And they don't want to stay in a dormitory like my choir from Johannesburg always did. Oh, no, dormitories are not for them. So we're all staying in a hotel. Now that I'm a married woman with a business of my own, I can afford it."

She realized that this talk of staying in a hotel might not be appropriate when Zukisa's aunt and cousin were struggling to put food on the table. She would never have imagined that she'd ever be in a situation where she was able to make such a gaffe. In the past, she'd been the butt of such insensitive remarks. God had truly blessed her. But with this blessing came responsibility, and thinking of this brought back all her irritation with Mama Dlamini. Francina was trying to do the right thing, but her friend was being as stubborn as a cow that would not leave the kraal on a rainy day.

"We had dinner at Mama Dlamini's Eating Establishment this week," she said. "My mother-in-law forgot to cook because she was so busy making cookies for my campaign." Francina proceeded to tell Zukisa's aunt about her bid to become mayor of Lady Helen.

Lucy came in bearing a tray set with three mugs. She gave one to Francina and one to Zukisa, and set one down beside her mother. "Hercules is drinking his in the kitchen. He's trying to repair the light above the stove. I've replaced the bulb, but it still won't work."

Francina hoped her husband had turned the electricity off at the main switch. As far as she knew, electricity was not his area of expertise, and she worried for his safety.

"My sister-in-law was very good to that Mama Dlamini woman," Zukisa's aunt said.

Francina was doubly shocked; these were the first words Zukisa's aunt had spoken since they arrived, and Zukisa had never told Francina that her late mother had known Mama Dlamini.

"What do you mean, Zukisa's mother was very good to her?" she asked.

Zukisa's aunt cleared her throat. "My sister-in-law took in Mama Dlamini when she first arrived in Lady Helen. Mama Dlamini stayed with her for almost a year."

Francina was flabbergasted. "Did you know about this?" she asked Zukisa.

"She was just a toddler," said Zukisa's aunt. "My brother met Mama Dlamini in Cape Town. He was working in a fish canning factory and she had a food cart. She sold curry and rice to dock and factory workers at lunchtime."

"Mama Dlamini never mentioned to me that she knew my parents," said Zukisa. She sounded disappointed.

"Maybe she was afraid she'd upset you by talking about them," offered Lucy, holding the cup of tea to her mother's lips.

Francina, who had encouraged Zukisa to keep the memory of her parents alive, wondered if this was the case or if Mama Dlamini simply did not want to be reminded of her humble beginnings.

"Mama Dlamini never told me she'd lived in Cape Town before coming to Lady Helen," said Francina.

"Did she tell you why she left her village?" asked Zukisa's aunt.

Now that Francina thought about it, the answer was no. She and Mama Dlamini had struck up a friendship based on their similar positions in the Lady Helen community as pioneering female entrepreneurs. When either of them mentioned their villages, it was to speak about a letter from home, and their conversations were always about the present, not the past.

"The women of her village chased her out with sticks," said Zukisa's aunt.

"I can't believe that!" declared Francina.

"It's true. She told my brother when the police in Cape Town confiscated her cart for operating a business without a license."

"What did she do to upset the villagers?" Francina wondered if she'd regret asking this question.

"Mama Dlamini ran a shebeen in her village, where the men spent all their money on alcohol instead of saving it for their families."

Francina could not believe her ears. The woman who did not want to give Lucy a chance because she had once been a drunk had herself been a supplier of alcohol. And didn't Jesus say to remove the plank in your own eye before trying to remove the speck from your brother's?

"My brother felt sorry for her because she couldn't pay the fine," continued Zukisa's aunt. "She started afresh in Lady Helen, thanks to him."

Francina found herself smiling broadly. Setting out from

Lady Helen this morning, she had expected nothing more from the day than to keep a sick woman company and offer moral support to her daughter. Now she had been presented with the solution to her problem. She couldn't wait to get back to Lady Helen to have a little conversation with Mama Dlamini. For the rest of the morning, while Lucy talked of her fears for her two sons, Francina itched to tell her that very soon her worries would be over.

By the time Hercules announced that it was time to leave, having given up on the light above the stove, Francina had, in her mind, rehearsed every word she would say to her friend.

As soon as they pulled away from the block of flats, Francina told her family of her plan.

Zukisa leaned forward between the two front seats, joy in her eyes. "Do you think it can really happen?" she asked. "Do you think my family can come to live in Lady Helen?"

Francina wished she could open a window and let her jealousy fly away on the wind. "Yes," she said, trying not to betray her real feelings.

Zukisa unbuckled her seat belt so she could reach her to deliver a kiss on her cheek. "You're the best mother in the world."

Francina smiled. "Thank you, sweetie. Now buckle up again."

She had nothing to fear. She was Zukisa's mother and had been for many years. Lucy could never replace her or take away what she and Zukisa had shared, just as Francina could never eclipse the memory of Zukisa's birth mother.

When they arrived home, there was a message on the answering machine from Monica, asking if the family could come for dinner that evening. Francina guessed that she wanted to talk about the mayoral race. Since her mother-in-law had not yet started cooking, Francina telephoned to tell Monica that they'd be over at six.

Monica's mother opened the door to them when they arrived, on time, bearing cookies.

"Thank you," said Mirinda Brunetti, taking the cookies from Mrs. Shabalala.

Although Francina felt comfortable having Mirinda in her home for coffee and cake as they pored over fashion magazines together, she could not be herself when the situation was reversed and Mirinda was the hostess—even if it was in Monica's house. Francina had worked for the Brunetti household since Monica was nine. She'd scrubbed the ring from their baths, peeled their vegetables, washed their clothes, cleaned Monica and her brother's cuts and scrapes, and not once had they asked about her family, about her home. She had moved about the house like a phantom, keeping order, cleaning, listening, observing. When Monica's brother had been killed by a land mine while in the army, Francina had slipped in and out of Mirinda's bedroom, taking her food, clearing away her crumpled tissues, running her bathwater. She'd disposed of the empty liquor bottles that Monica's father, Paolo, had left next to the couch; she'd watered down the bottles in his liquor cabinet, apologized to the postman, the gardener, passersby—any black person on whom Paolo had vented his wrath.

Many years later, when Monica was shot in a carjacking and left to die on the side of the road, life in the Brunetti household took an unexpected turn. It had started with the questions. All of a sudden, Monica wanted to know if Francina had a husband, why she didn't have any children, where she was from. At first, Francina had been irritated because Monica hadn't needed this information for more than twenty years, and could certainly live without it for another twenty. Monica had given her a television to replace her little black-and-white portable. She'd asked if they could have tea together, and all of a sudden she'd wanted Francina's opinion on matters.

While this change had been under way, Francina noticed Mirinda's silent disapproval. Mirinda did not think it was appropriate for servants to eat with the family. She did not want Francina to sit on her sofa, set a teacup down on her coffee table. She did not want Francina leaning on the kitchen counter, laughing at something Monica said.

Mirinda had grown up in a different time and place than Monica. When Mirinda was little, in the small Karoo town of Laingsburg, she and all her fair-haired friends had been told that they were superior to the dark people who scuttled about the periphery of their lives. Their future was assured. They didn't even have to go to university if they wanted to get a good job, as they were owed a living by the sheer good fortune of their birthright.

Monica's childhood had been less certain. She and her brother had played in the garden, swum in the family's pool and ridden their bikes in the street, but every night the television news reported on cross-border skirmishes, dawn raids on African townships, arrests of dissidents, threats issued by exiled freedom fighters, and the violent crushing of mass protest by the powerful South African military. Monica's had been a childhood of privilege and lurking menace.

Hercules and Zukisa shared none of Francina's reserve about being hosted by Mirinda Brunetti, but Mrs. Shabalala, bless her heart, was a nervous wreck. She had lived her life surrounded by black neighbors, in one of the many square brick houses that had once belonged to whites who worked in the coal mines when Dundee was a boomtown. She'd shopped in areas of town where whites never ventured, and because her late husband had never wanted her to work outside of the home, she didn't have any contact at all with white people. Her husband had worked for whites, but it had not mattered to Mrs. Shabalala where their weekly money came from as long as it was on time. Her mind didn't conjure, as Francina's did, the memory of a strict madam and maid relationship, because there was nothing similar in her past.

Mirinda ushered them into the living room and invited them to sit. Francina had sat on this couch hundreds of times to watch television with Mandla or discuss the children with Monica, but not in Mirinda's presence.

"I hear you're running for mayor," said Mirinda, sitting down next to Francina. "I'm sure you'll win."

Francina wondered what Mirinda really thought of her aspirations.

"Is there anything I can do to help with your campaign? I'm afraid I don't have as many talents as you do, what with your sewing and baking. You know me, I'm not much of a cook."

Francina had never heard Mirinda talk this way; she was immediately on guard. She would rather be subjected to blunt rudeness than patronizing kindness.

"Did Francina tell you about the day I burned my son's tenth birthday cake? Francina whipped up a new one and decorated it to look like a fire engine," Mirinda said to Hercules.

He smiled. "She's good at helping people out of tight squeezes."

"She certainly is," said Mirinda.

Francina could tell from Mirinda's expression that she was no longer thinking about the cake. Her former employer had endured more heartache than a mother should have to bear. Perhaps Francina was at fault here; she was the one who could not get over the past and change. Mirinda wasn't being patronizing. This was just her way of reaching out.

"Zukisa has come up with a new dress design that I think will be perfect for you," said Francina, trying to sound as friendly as possible. If she managed to overcome her own reservations, she might find that the imbalance in her relationship with Mirinda was all in her own mind.

Monica came in from the kitchen with a platter of olives and explained that Zak was outside with the children, cooking the sosaties on the braai. Francina saw the look on her daughter's face. The skewered meat marinated in a spicy sauce was her favorite. Zukisa wandered outside to join Mandla and Yolanda.

"Have you had any news from Yolanda's mother?" asked Francina.

"She's not coming back," said Monica.

Mirinda shook her head in disapproval. "A mother who deserts her child doesn't ever deserve to have that child back."

Francina caught Hercules's eye and knew that they were both thinking of Lucy. Zukisa, she hoped, would not, in her excitement, blurt out Francina's plan to Yolanda and Mandla.

The front door opened and Monica's father walked in, carrying a fishing rod and tackle box.

"Paolo, you should leave all that outside," said Mirinda.

"Look who I found in the driveway," said Paolo.

Oscar appeared next to him. As soon as he saw Francina

and Hercules, the grin slid from his face. "I didn't know you had company," he said.

"The more the merrier," said Monica. "Come and sit down. This is a nice surprise."

There was an empty spot beside Francina on the couch, but Hercules stood to offer his chair, and then sat down next to Francina.

Ignoring his wife's directive, Paolo trudged through the house with his fishing equipment, and returned to bring in the bucket that contained his catch of the day.

"Snoek!" he exclaimed proudly. "A big one. Do you think it's too late to put it on the braai?"

Monica assured him that it was not, and he went to join his son-in-law, whom he adored, even though he had once told Monica that she shouldn't marry an Afrikaner.

Francina looked everywhere except in Oscar's direction, while Hercules could not keep his eyes off the man. Monica must have been aware of the tension in the room because she tried to make a joke.

"You two could have a dry run of your mayoral debate."

Everyone smiled except Oscar. "Actually, I came to see you," he said to Monica. "I found something while I was out on a long hike today."

"What did you find?" asked Mirinda. "Come on now. It's not fair if you keep it from the rest of us."

Oscar shifted uncomfortably in his seat. Francina felt sorry for him. He was probably wishing that he'd telephoned instead.

"I found a grave on a small koppie north of the golf resort." Oscar explained the exact location.

"You walked almost as far as Velddrif," said Mirinda.

Oscar shrugged. "It's what I like to do."

Francina saw Hercules studying Oscar's face. Perhaps he was thinking about all the intellectual pursuits he could accomplish in the time Oscar spent tramping about the countryside.

"Well, whose grave is it? A Bushman's?" asked Mirinda.

Oscar shook his head. "The tombstone was decorated by the San people—" he corrected Mirinda's use of the pejorative name for the nomadic tribesmen who had roamed these parts many years ago "—but the grave belongs to a European woman."

"You found it? You found Lady Helen's grave?" asked Monica in an excited voice.

Oscar nodded. "The paintings on the tombstone are of a lady in a long dress with a parasol. It can only be Lady Helen. I started to dig, but when I found the first bone I lost my nerve. Those archeology professors who came to take pictures of the San paintings up in the cave can excavate her remains to check if my theory is correct."

"Do you think her husband killed her?" asked Monica.

"No. I think that after her husband marched all the slaves she'd freed back to Cape Town, she continued to live here with the assistance of the nomadic San people."

"That's incredible," said Mirinda. "I don't know if I would have made the same choice she did."

"She probably didn't *have* a choice," said Monica. "She must have run away as soon as she knew he was coming. If her husband had caught her, he would have killed her rather than return to Cape Town with the woman who had made a fool of him."

Zak put his head into the living room. "Hello, Francina. Hello, Hercules. Oh, I didn't see you there, Oscar. How are things?"

"Oscar's staying for dinner," said Monica. She turned to Oscar. "You will stay, won't you?"

"I was just about to tell you all to come and get it before it's cold," said Zak. "Come on, Oscar."

Oscar shook his head, but Monica would have none of it. "You're not leaving after you've told us this exciting news. We have to celebrate."

Oscar's expression was more fitting for a man who'd been told he had to walk over coals if he wanted to get home, but he graciously accepted and followed Francina and Hercules into the dining room, where dinner was to be served, since it had turned too cool to sit outside.

As they passed around the bowl of homemade apricot jam that they had been instructed by Paolo to smear on their braaied snoek, Mirinda asked the two mayoral candidates if they would care to let the assembled group know the basic tenets of their campaigns.

Francina did not know the meaning of the word *tenets* and hoped that Oscar would be given the chance to go first, but he insisted on being a gentleman and letting her start.

"Francina believes we should not sacrifice the character of our town for commercial gain," said Hercules.

What a sweet husband, thought Francina, *to understand my confusion and step in to help.*

"What does she propose?" asked Oscar.

"Banning tour buses from Main Street," replied Hercules. "They clog it up, they pollute the air. Francina believes they should have to park outside of town."

Francina remembered discussing this issue with Hercules, but she had never decided on a plan of action or considered it part of her campaign for mayor.

"Shop and gallery owners on Main Street rely on tourists for a large part of their livelihood," said Oscar, looking not at Francina but at Hercules. "If we make travel inconvenient for tourists, they'll start going to other towns on the West Coast, and Lady Helen will suffer as it suffered before."

In the past, a group of Afrikaner farmers had moved into Lady Helen to breed ostriches and sell the feathers overseas, where they were highly prized in women's fashions. But the cooperative lost business to the large-scale operation in Oudtshoorn, a small town southeast of Lady Helen in the Klein Karoo, and eventually the farmers turned to the ocean instead. For almost sixty years, Lady Helen was a successful fishing port, but then deepwater trawlers belonging to large corporations started appearing, and the local fishermen could not compete.

"Art, scuba diving, shark watching—they all require outside interest," added Oscar. "As does fashion."

"Francina does very well without having to rely on clients from Cape Town," replied Hercules—a little too abruptly, she thought.

The two men stared at each other.

"More snoek, Hercules, Oscar?" said Monica, in an obvious attempt to dispel the tense atmosphere.

Francina remembered the time, long ago, when Oscar and Hercules had gone for each other's throats like wild dogs—in a figurative way of speaking. Hercules had just met Oscar and was not used to his straightforward way of talking. Now it seemed that Hercules had thrown off his usual cloak of decorum. And neither man seemed concerned to hear the tenets of Francina's campaign from her own mouth. Why were they behaving this way, years after their first clash? Francina and Hercules had built their lives together; they had a daughter now. And while Oscar had never married or, as far as Francina knew, dated, he had gone on with his life, doing construction work in the town and looking for Lady Helen's grave. After all these years, he could not possibly still be in love with Francina. Or could he?

For the rest of the meal, Oscar and Hercules were mostly silent, and Monica, Zak and Mirinda tried hard to lighten the mood at the table. Paolo, who was oblivious of the friction, entertained the children with stories of improbable fishing adventures.

Later that night, when they were alone together in their bedroom, Francina confronted Hercules over his behavior at Monica's house.

"What has gotten into you? You've managed to be civil to Oscar all these years and now this."

"I've been civil to him because we haven't had much to do with each other. Now all of a sudden he enters the mayoral race mere minutes after you entered. Come on, Francina. Don't you think it's a little suspicious?"

"Hercules, people don't pine away for years for someone they once cared about."

"Sometimes they do," he said softly.

She should have thought before speaking. On her first visit to Hercules's home in Dundee, long before they were married, Francina had discovered that Hercules had been sleeping with his late wife's nightgown under his pillow ever since her death fifteen years before. His deep depression had needed the care of a psychiatrist.

"That man is still in love with you."

"And if he is, what does it matter? I'm married to you. We have a family."

Hercules breathed out noisily through his mouth. "I just don't like it. What's he doing? Waiting for me to fall off a cliff, or to get sick?"

Francina wished that she had never entered the race for mayor so that her encounters with Oscar would remain as they had been for years: rare and brief. Young girls thrived on drama like this, but she had orders to complete, a child to take care of, a family to bring to Lady Helen.

⊰ Chapter Thirty-One ⊱

Oscar was not in church the morning after the disastrous evening with Francina and Hercules, and Monica thought she knew why. She caught up with him as he was leaving his house for a hike to the alleged grave of Lady Helen.

"What was that all about last night?" she asked, employing his typical straightforwardness.

"I don't know what you're talking about," he replied, shifting the weight of his pack on his back.

"Oscar, you and I have known each other for a long time. I'm sorry you still feel so much for Francina."

Oscar looked her straight in the eye. "I'm not. I'm only sorry that Hercules knows. Don't tell me it isn't healthy that I haven't gotten over her, because I know that. Don't tell me I'm wasting my life, because I'm not. I haven't met anyone who compares to her. I'll wait for her until she's free."

Monica could not hide the shock she felt. "But Oscar, she might never be free, or she could be an old lady by then."

He shrugged. "She's worth it."

"If you didn't want anyone to know how you feel, why have you entered the race for mayor?"

"I didn't know Francina had entered, too. I'm thinking of withdrawing my name."

Oscar was very invested in this town; its history was his passion. But if the race for mayor was going to stir up all his suppressed love for Francina, perhaps he was better off out of it.

"That's your decision," she told him, knowing that he would be disappointed with her careful response.

"I take it the *Lady Helen Herald* is not endorsing me?"

Monica attempted a laugh. "You sound like a politician already. The paper is not endorsing anybody."

She left him to carry on with his hike, and returned home to find Yolanda cooking lunch. Monica told Zak what Oscar had said and that she thought he should drop out of the race—and perhaps leave Lady Helen, too.

Zak disagreed. "His feelings don't appear to be causing him any harm. If I thought he was suffering from depression, I'd tell him."

"It can't be—"

"I know you want to help, but I think you'd be making a mistake to prod him to follow your suggested course of action. What you think is right might not be right for Oscar."

"But he's—"

"If this is the way he wants to live, then let him be."

Monica sighed.

"If you think about it, you'll agree."

* * *

Monica thought about it as she drifted off to sleep that night and as she readied Mandla and Yolanda for school the following morning. She still had not reached the same conclusion as Zak when she arrived at the office, but perhaps over a cup of Dudu's hot tea, she would come to see his point of view. Her thoughts, however, were interrupted by a telephone call from her friend Miemps, who was out of breath.

"The government finally processed our land claim, even though we missed the cutoff date. We've been informed that we can either go back or take the money."

Years ago, Miemps and Reginald had lived in District Six, a cosmopolitan neighborhood on the slopes of Table Mountain in Cape Town. In 1968, two years after the apartheid government invoked the Group Areas Act to declare Cape Town's city center and surroundings a whites-only area, the government began forcing District Six's "colored" or mixed race residents to move to low-cost housing provided by the state fifteen miles away, in a desolate, outlying area appropriately named the Cape Flats. By the early eighties, more than sixty thousand people had been relocated in a large-scale attempt at social engineering.

Some said that District Six had been demolished not because it was a vision of how an integrated South Africa might be one day, but merely because the view of the ocean from the slopes of Table Mountain was too highly valued to waste on working-class people. Miemps and her brothers needed only to step onto the veranda of their house to watch ships from all over the world come into the harbor.

More than just buildings were destroyed. District Six had been an urban neighborhood; many of its residents worked in the nearby Woodstock clothing factories, in central Cape Town, or at the Morning Market, which supplied fruit and vegetables to the whole city. There were no employment opportunities in the Cape Flats.

Every day for twenty-five years, Miemps's father had walked down Constitution Street to his job at a sweet factory in Cape Town, but after the move he had to spend more than two hours each day riding buses and trains. When he returned at night, the man who'd once played the trumpet in the church choir had barely enough energy to eat the dinner his wife had placed under a saucepan lid in the darkened kitchen.

In 2000, in a ceremony presided over by President Thabo Mbeki, the land was formally returned to seventeen hundred tenant families who had been evicted. There were tears as people who had not seen each other since the forced move were reunited. Some of these families had chosen to go back, others had elected to take the cash settlement. Miemps, Reginald and many others had missed the cutoff date for the land claim, but thanks to a group of activists, an extension had been granted.

"Congratulations, Miemps," said Monica. "So which are you going to choose?"

"The money, of course. If we left Lady Helen we'd be leaving a community that is like a modern-day District Six."

Monica was relieved to hear her answer, and told her so.

Miemps's voice broke. "Reginald cried when we got the news, Monica. I've never seen my husband cry. He says good things like this don't usually happen to people like us."

People like us. Monica felt herself choking up at Reginald's characterization of himself. How sad that some of the older generation would never shake off the terrible repression that had forced them to lower their expectations of life.

There was a lesson in this for her. No human being had the right to tell another where to live. She had seriously considered ignoring Zak's advice and telling Oscar that he should move to the city, where he was bound to meet someone and fall in love again. Through God's grace she had been saved from offending, and perhaps even losing, a good friend.

Chapter Thirty-Two

Francina saw the Cook Wanted sign in the window of Mama Dlamini's café and sighed. Since visiting Zukisa's aunt on Saturday, she had been rehearsing what to say to her friend, but she still didn't have a good opening line. She had intended to have this confrontation yesterday, after taking Zukisa to school, but when she saw Mama Dlamini talking to a tableful of tourists, she'd turned around.

Now, the bells over the door jingled as Francina entered the café.

"Seat yourself. I'll be there in a minute," Mama Dlamini shouted from the kitchen.

Francina had half an hour to say what she'd come to say before Anna, the waitress and sometimes cook, reported for work.

"Ah, Francina, it's you," said Mama Dlamini, rubbing her

hands on her apron. "I just put my pies in the oven. They'll be ready in twenty minutes."

Francina slid onto a stool at the counter, while Mama Dlamini cleared away breakfast dishes.

"It shouldn't be a surprise for me to see you at this time of the morning," Mama Dlamini scolded her friend.

Francina considered pointing out the obvious: that she, too, had a business to run. But she remained silent. None of the lines she had rehearsed to introduce this difficult topic came to her.

"Tea?" asked Mama Dlamini, filling the mug she had placed in front of Francina without waiting for her answer. "We'll have another cup when the pies are ready. Your mother-in-law will be here in two hours for her slice."

Francina could not remember how many times Mrs. Shabalala had vowed never to set foot in Mama Dlamini's Eating Establishment because she found the pies too tempting. There could not be another person in the world who had started a diet as many times as Francina's mother-in-law.

Francina wished she had asked Monica's advice on how to approach Mama Dlamini. Monica was good at getting people to do things without them realizing that they were being manipulated. Francina took a deep breath. She valued her friendship with Mama Dlamini too much to lose it, but in a tiny flat in Cape Town a woman lay dying, while her daughter tried desperately to make ends meet and keep her boys out of trouble. Just as importantly, Francina would make Zukisa happy if she succeeded in doing what she'd said she'd do.

"I have come to talk to you about Lucy."

"Not again, Francina. I've given you my final word on that subject." Mama Dlamini began wiping the counter.

"God teaches us to forgive."

"I can't trust my business to a woman who used to be a drunk. Alcohol can mess a person up forever."

"I imagine you should know about that."

Mama Dlamini stopped wiping the counter. "I beg your pardon?"

"You, of all people, should know that alcohol destroys families, and that children sometimes go without food because their parents have spent all their money on alcohol."

"I don't know what you're talking about."

"My friend, I know why you had to leave your village."

Mama Dlamini sat down. "Who told you? The only people who knew were Zukisa's parents, and they're no longer with us."

"It doesn't matter who told me. And you have to trust me when I say that I won't breathe a word of it to anyone."

"That was in the past. I've changed."

"Yes, a person can do that," Francina said quietly.

Mama Dlamini put her head in her hands. When she finally looked up, she said, "I was given a second chance. How can I deny Lucy one?"

"Thank you, my friend. I know you're a good woman. Now there's also the small matter of the family's accommodation. Are any of the tenants in your flats—?"

"Don't push your luck," said Mama Dlamini, wagging a finger in her face.

Francina laughed. The major problem had been solved, and although it would be difficult to find housing for the family in Lady Helen, she would figure something out.

A timer sounded in the kitchen and Mama Dlamini hurried to remove the pies from the oven. When she returned, she seemed surprised to see Francina still sitting at the counter.

"I'll take you up on your offer of a slice," said Francina.

"These are not your favorite. They're apricot."

"Ah, but your pies are the best in the world. Didn't you tell me that yourself?"

Mama Dlamini smiled as she cut two large pieces. "So we're going to be friends, as usual?"

"Of course," said Francina. "The past is the past."

Francina didn't have to wait long for a solution to the problem of the family's accommodation. The following afternoon, a customer mentioned to her that Lizbet DeVilliers and her husband were leaving Sandpiper Drift—for good this time. Lionel DeVilliers had helped Mr. Yang, the owner of the golf resort, trick the government into selling the land on which Sandpiper Drift was built. With the money Mr. Yang had paid him, Lionel had bought a large house in Bloubergstrand, across the bay from Cape Town, but he'd been forced to give it up when he'd narrowly escaped prison by testifying for the state against Mr. Yang. The word was that with Mr. Yang now out of prison, Lionel wanted to get far away from Lady Helen.

"But Lucy won't be able to make a down payment," said Hercules, when Francina told him her plan.

She looked at him pleadingly.

"Oh, no," he said. "We can't. That money is to send Zukisa to university."

"Lucy will pay us back. It won't take long. The Devilliers aren't asking much for the house because Lionel didn't do the greatest job rebuilding it after the bulldozers knocked it down. Please, Hercules. This is for Zukisa as much as it is for Lucy."

Hercules considered for a moment. "All right then. You'd

better save some of your persuasive talents for the debate against Oscar on Saturday. I've been analyzing the tenets of his campaign that he sent out in a letter, and I've devised responses to all of them."

Francina sighed. For a few hours, she had managed to forget about Oscar and the campaign. Still, the best was yet to come. First she would tell Zukisa, and after the dreaded debate on Saturday, Hercules, Zukisa and she would drive down to Cape Town to give Lucy and her mother the good news. It might not seem to be good news to the boys, but in the long run they would benefit from the move.

On Saturday morning, when Francina went onto the balcony to water her tomato plants, she could not see the small triangle of ocean between the buildings at the end of the street. Fog had rolled in from the sea overnight, and the temperature was noticeably lower, which was good, considering that she was wearing a new jacket and pantsuit designed by Zukisa for the occasion of the debate. Francina did not approve of women wearing men's clothing, but Zukisa thought it necessary for her mother to appear businesslike and efficient. Zukisa had spent all her free time working on this suit. Francina could not tell her daughter that she'd prefer to wear one of the dresses from her own wardrobe.

Sighing, she went back into her flat, closing the balcony door to prevent the dampness from coming inside and ruining Hercules's paintings.

"You'll be fine," said Hercules, tying his tie.

"Why are you wearing business clothes?" asked Francina.

"Zukisa told me that the husband of the future mayor has to look dignified."

"I wish the debate was over and we were on our way to Cape Town."

Hercules motioned for her to sit on the bed beside him. "We've rehearsed all the responses to every point Oscar could make."

Poor Mayor Richard had not featured at all in Hercules's preparations for this debate. In her husband's mind, this was a two-way race, and Francina suspected that sometimes he lost sight of the real goal, which was to be in charge of running Lady Helen.

When Francina and Hercules came into the kitchen, Zukisa was making bacon and eggs and telling her grandmother about a fashion design course in Cape Town.

"You don't need to study fashion. You need a university degree," said Francina, sitting down at the table. "Mama, you're up early. You look pretty."

"Thank you," said Mrs. Shabalala. "Zukisa got me up and picked my outfit. I think I look like the mother of the bride."

"You have to look elegant today," said Zukisa, serving the eggs on buttered toast. "We're on show this morning."

Francina groaned. "I don't like the idea of a public debate. Let's give it a miss and go to Cape Town."

Zukisa glared at her. "Mother, if you take part in this debate, I'll go to university."

"Wow! I have no choice then. Give me two eggs, please. I need the strength."

There was not a single soul around when they arrived at the hall of Green Block School, where the debate was to be held, and for a blissful second Francina imagined that the mayoral race had all been a bad dream. But then the school principal, Mr. D., who was to be the master of ceremonies, arrived to make sure that the chairs had been set out and the microphones installed.

"Do we have to use those?" asked Francina. She had never before spoken into a microphone.

"You may not need one, but I will," said Mr. D.

"Don't give me any difficult questions, please," said Francina.

Mr. D. laughed as though she was joking.

People had started to arrive and were filling up the seats in the front rows. Francina saw Mayor Richard talking to a group of elderly ladies at the back of the hall. His daughter, obviously, had not impressed on him the need for elegant attire. He was dressed in one of his trademark colorful shirts. When he waved goodbye to the ladies and moved down the center aisle toward the stage, Francina saw that he was wearing shorts. The collar of her shirt began to scratch her neck.

She saw Oscar arrive through a side door and shake Mayor Richard's hand. Then he moved toward her. Francina was relieved that Hercules was talking to Mr. D. and had his back to her.

"Here's to a friendly debate," said Oscar, holding out his hand.

Francina shook hands lightly with him.

"May the best man win," he said.

"You mean person," Francina corrected.

"Oh, sorry, I meant person."

Francina felt sweat forming at her hairline. Maybe it was an honest mistake, but Oscar had managed to irritate his opponent right before the debate. The points that Hercules had tried to drum into her suddenly came clearly to mind, and she could not wait for the showdown to begin.

"I'll see you up there," she said, indicating the stage.

She joined Hercules at her podium, where he was adjusting the height of her microphone. "I'm ready," she said.

Hercules looked her in the eyes. "You can do it."

There was not a question Francina could not answer or a remark from one of her opponents that she could not refute. Mayor Richard's answers were meandering, filled with anecdotes and weak jokes; Oscar's comments were concise and thoughtful, but delivered too efficiently, preventing his personality from shining through. Francina, however, lit up the rather austere interior of the school hall with her witty comebacks, amusing short stories and the sheer warmth of her personality. From her position on stage, she could tell from his slack-jawed expression that even Hercules, her staunchest fan, was astonished.

When Mr. D. declared the debate ended, Mayor Richard came over to congratulate Francina. She could feel Hercules's eyes on her as he waited for Oscar to do the same. But to her surprise, Oscar left the stage, ignored the audience members who wanted to shake his hand, and exited through the side door. Francina knew better than to make eye contact with Hercules or he would be able to tell that she had been watching Oscar.

For fifteen long minutes, Francina accepted congratulations and pats on the back from the residents of Lady Helen. Mandla told her she should be in the movies, and Monica said Francina's next goal should be the provincial government. The comment she most appreciated, however, came from Zukisa, who said she was proud and that she would go to university if that was what her mother and father wanted.

While Hercules and Zukisa helped Mr. D. return the chairs to the storeroom, Francina, feeling hot in her tailored suit, went outdoors for some fresh air. The fog had lifted and the sun shone brightly through a few wispy clouds. She found a spot in the shade from the overhang of a covered walkway and took off her jacket. Suddenly, she had the sensation that she was being watched, and she turned around to see Oscar sitting on a retaining wall, drinking a bottle of water.

"I didn't notice you there," she said, feeling self-conscious. She didn't want him to think she had come to find him. If only Hercules hadn't put this ridiculous idea in her head that Oscar was still in love with her. On the rare occasions she had run into him before, she had felt entirely comfortable chatting to him, but now she felt awkward.

"You were fantastic," he said.

She thanked him and told him he, too, had done a good job.

"I'm glad things have turned out well for you, Francina. You have your family—" she noticed he did not say husband "—your business, your high school certificate. You deserve it all."

And you, she wanted to say, why do you not have a family? Why have you not married in all these years? But she was afraid of what his answer might be. She tried to come up with a suitable reply.

"You're a good caretaker of Lady Helen," she said at last, wondering if it was the wrong thing to say because it trivialized his life and made him sound lonely. "I'm sorry, that didn't come out correctly."

He shook his head. "You're right. That's the sum of my life—taking care of a cemetery for nameless souls and traipsing across the countryside, searching for the grave of a woman who was not even one of my forebears. It's rather pathetic."

Francina was quiet. Oscar had opened up to her; a trite, polite response would not do. "You used to live life to the full. You traveled the world, met interesting people."

"But I didn't have anyone to share it with."

"It's not too late."

He looked at her a long time. "I wish you meant something else."

Out of the corner of her eye, Francina saw that Hercules had come to look for her. She prayed silently that he would have the compassion to stay away.

"Oscar," she began. Dare she say it? "Don't wait for me."

"Did you ever feel anything for me?"

Hercules was approaching, Francina saw. "Oscar, we've got to leave the past in the past."

He paused and she knew he was trying to interpret her answer. The truth was she had felt only respect and friendship for him, but there was no point in telling him that. If he inferred from her reply that she had once felt something more, what was the harm?

"I've got to go," she said.

He looked up and saw Hercules, and Francina discerned sadness in Oscar's eyes.

"You'll make a great mayor," he said.

Francina waved at him as she walked to meet Hercules, and was aware of his gaze following her as she went back inside the hall to find Zukisa and Mrs. Shabalala.

* * *

Hercules was quiet on the journey to Cape Town, and Francina knew that he was itching to ask what Oscar had said to her, but that he wouldn't in front of their daughter.

Francina had changed out of her tailored suit into a casual linen dress. Hercules had removed his tie. Mrs. Shabalala had chosen to stay behind, to cook a celebratory meal, while the rest of the family went to Cape Town. Tonight there would be two reasons to celebrate: Francina's success in the debate and the impending move of Lucy and her family to Sandpiper Drift. Lionel DeVilliers had already accepted a small down payment on the house and agreed not to entertain offers from any other interested buyers. Not trusting the word of a man who was known for his love of money, Francina told Hercules that Lucy needed to agree to take the job at the café and commit to the house this very afternoon or the residence could be lost to a higher bidder.

Lucy was not home when they arrived at the flat, but surprisingly both boys were there. The first thing Francina noticed was that Xoli smelled of smoke, and not ordinary tobacco. He deserved a scolding, which she would have felt at liberty to give if his mother had not returned from her exile in Johannesburg. The other boy, Bulelani, could not have been out with his brother, because he smelled of fabric softener, not smoke. Little Fundiswa was playing with her doll on the floor of her grandmother's bedroom and jumped up to hug Zukisa.

"Granny's tummy hurts," she said.

Francina went to Zukisa's aunt, who was lying on her side facing the window.

"It's not my tummy, it's my chest. It hurts to breathe."

Francina could not hold back. "We're going to get you some medical care," she said.

Zukisa's aunt shook her head. "I'm not traveling to the hospital in Cape Town to wait seven hours to see a doctor."

"You won't have to wait for this doctor, and he will help ease your suffering."

"And where is this wonderful doctor?"

Francina saw Hercules shake his head in turn, and knew that he was right to caution her. "I'll talk to Lucy about it when she gets home," she said.

They didn't have to wait long. Within a few minutes, they heard an argument erupt in the living room between Lucy and her eldest son. Lucy had apparently asked him to make lunch for his grandmother, but he had forgotten.

"Don't worry about lunch," Zukisa said to her cousin. "We brought cold roast chicken. Mother's giving some to my aunt."

"Thank you," said Lucy, glaring at Xoli. "You can clean up the kitchen then," she told him, but he ignored her and continued watching music videos on television.

"Why can't he be a good child like you, Zukisa?" whispered Lucy, taking her cousin's arm before entering her mother's bedroom.

Francina had hoped that the joy of being home with her family would soften some of the lines on Lucy's face made by years of hard drinking. But each time Francina saw Lucy, the woman was frowning with worry.

"Can I speak to you in the kitchen?" Francina asked her now.

"If it's about the doctor who's going to help me, I want to hear," said Zukisa's aunt.

"Doctor? What doctor?" asked Lucy.

In words rehearsed silently during the trip to Cape Town, Francina told Lucy of the job as head cook at Mama Dlamini's Eating Establishment, of the two spots at Green Block School for Xoli and Bulelani, of the care Lucy's mother would get at the hospital as an outpatient, and later, if needed, as an inpatient, and, finally of the whitewashed cottage in Sandpiper Drift.

When Francina was finished, Lucy sat down on the end of the bed.

"We'll go," said her mother.

"You're very talkative today," said Lucy, in a voice tinged with impatience. "I don't know, Francina. It's a kind offer, but I've just gotten used to life here in Cape Town."

Francina knew then that she would have to summon the fire and energy she had possessed on the stage this morning at Green Block School.

"If you don't come your boys are going to end up in prison—or worse," she said.

A look of shock appeared on Lucy's face.

"She's right," said her mother. "Those boys are up to no good, staying out all night, smoking, drinking, taking drugs."

"They haven't had the best example to follow," said Lucy quietly.

Fundiswa announced that she was hungry, and Hercules took her to the kitchen to see if the boys had left any of the roast chicken.

"And now's your chance to make up for it," said Francina. "Take them away from their friends who are a bad influence. Bring them to Lady Helen, where we'll all watch them like hawks until they're good boys again."

Zukisa, who until then had been silent, said, "Please say

you'll come, Lucy. My mother has gone to a lot of trouble to get you a job."

Lucy began to cry.

"What's this?" said Francina, taking her hand.

"You're so nice to me and we're not even family."

Francina caught her daughter's eye and smiled. "Yes, we are."

Zukisa would not stop thanking her mother and father on the way home to Lady Helen.

"I can't believe that my relatives will be moving into a house in Sandpiper Drift next weekend," she said over and over. "Do you think they'll be able to vote in the election?"

Hercules told her that they would. "Not that your mother's going to need extra votes," he added.

Francina sighed. She was remembering the sadness in Oscar's eyes. Becoming mayor had never been a goal in her life; she had entered the race in error. The debate had given her a taste of what it would be like to have people hanging on to her every word, and she could not lie; she had enjoyed it. But was that a good reason to become mayor? Was a decades-long passion for the town and its history not a more legitimate reason? Oscar had been absolutely correct when he'd said that her life was full. Responsibilities to the town would take her away from the family she had waited for for so long.

"I have something to announce," she said, interrupting Zukisa, who was talking about the curtains she planned to sew for her cousin's new house.

"Listen to your mother, sounding like the mayor already," teased Hercules.

"I'm dropping out of the race."

Hercules and Zukisa could not have been more shocked if she'd told them she was planning to hitchhike to Cairo.

"Does this have anything to do with Oscar?" asked Hercules.

"No," said Francina. "I mean, yes." She explained that Oscar would make a better mayor because he could devote all his time to the office.

"We'll help more at home," said Zukisa. "I'll take on more of the dress orders."

Francina turned in her seat and held her daughter's hand. "But I don't want to miss out on any of my time with you and your father. Yes, I'd have an office to myself and I'd make decisions for the town, but I'd always be wishing I was at home with you. What do you think, Hercules?"

"You beat him fair and square in the debate."

"Yes, and you'll be glad to hear that he knows it. I also have a family, which he doesn't. Let me give him this."

Hercules was silent.

"I'll still go to university, Dad," said Zukisa.

"If this is what you want, Francina, then so be it."

Francina smiled at her daughter, turned to face the front again and lightly touched her husband's hand on the gearshift.

"I'll ask Monica to find out from Zak if we can use the hospital's truck to move Lucy and her family next weekend."

There was a record turnout for the election the following Saturday, and when the majority of voters got over their disappointment at not seeing Francina's name on the ballot, they elected Oscar to be the new mayor of Lady Helen.

✄ Chapter Thirty-Three ✄

When autumn approached, Sipho usually wanted to visit the lagoon to check on the birds that gathered in large numbers to feed before the long flight up Africa and across the Mediterranean to their breeding grounds in Europe. This year, with Sipho in the United States, Mandla took it upon himself to report to his brother which birds left first, which ones left last and which ones struggled to keep up. For Mandla, their departure couldn't come fast enough, because he knew that his brother would return close to this time.

One Sunday, two months after Oscar had been elected mayor, Reverend van Tonder had to shout to be heard over the noise of the birds. His wife, Dalene, closed the church's windows, but even though the temperature had dropped over the past two weeks, it was soon too warm and stuffy in a confined space with so many people. So she opened the windows again, and her husband grew hoarse finishing his sermon.

Mandla, who attended the children's Sunday School and not the adult church service, was waiting at the door when Monica came to pick him up.

"Quick, I think today is the day," he said excitedly.

They hurried out to join the rest of the congregation on the banks of the lagoon. Two hundred people, dressed in finery and Wellington boots, were about to walk across the salt marsh. The birds that returned every year to the waters next to the Little Church of the Lagoon weren't intimidated by the crowd. They were used to an audience.

"Look, the gray plovers are going first this time," shouted Mandla. "Help me remember the order for Sipho, Mom."

They watched as the birds took off in a flock, the black breasts of their recently acquired summer plumage making them look like shadows against the stark blue West Coast sky. The sky grew dark as the pace of the migration increased. Knots, sanderlings, sandpipers and greenshanks all left at the same time, quickly followed by the long-legged whimbrels, curlews and godwits. The leaders were already some way off, nothing more than a smoky tracing in the sky.

"Godspeed," shouted Mandla. This was the farewell Sipho had used since he first saw the mass migration.

The godwits flapped their wings furiously to catch up to the rest of the birds, and in a few seconds merged with the dark mass passing over the lagoon and heading north along the Atlantic coastline.

People started to trudge across the salt marsh to cars parked on dry land. A loud screech went up as the seagulls that had been banished to the beach for the duration of the summer came wheeling around to take back the lagoon and feast on whatever food was left by the migratory birds.

"If the birds had waited one more week, Sipho would have seen this," said Mandla.

"Never mind, you can tell him all about it," said Monica.

Mirinda was cooking lunch when the family arrived home. She and Paolo had attended an early-morning service at the Catholic church. After the death of his son, Paolo had not set foot in a church. But this year, at the urging of his brother, he'd given in and started going again in Italy.

"The roast is in the oven. I just have to pop the vegetables in, too," said Mirinda. "Go put your feet up," she told Monica. "You look tired."

"I didn't sleep well last night. Must have been the curry we ate for dinner."

"Well, I'll do the rest of the cooking. Can you believe that this time next week Sipho will be landing?"

"Thanks, Mom, for changing your return date."

"We couldn't have left without spending time with Sipho. I want to hear all about his life in America."

Mandla was counting the days till his brother's return, but his happiness was tempered by the imminence of his grandparents' departure.

The following Saturday, Mandla stood in the international arrivals hall of Cape Town Airport clutching a sign on which he'd written his brother's name.

"He might not recognize me," he said when questioned by Yolanda about the need for it. "I've got a new hairstyle and I've grown two inches since he last saw me."

Mandla had been attending acting lessons in Cape Town for a couple of months, and because he'd dropped the American accent of his own accord, Monica was allowing him to grow his hair long. They would renegotiate when it was long enough to become dreadlocks.

"There he is!" shouted Mandla, pointing wildly in the direction of the automatic doors that hid passengers from view as they opened their bags for customs officials.

And there was Sipho, scanning the crowd for his family before he slipped into the stream of people heading for the exit.

Catching sight of them, he came over to the railing and said, "It's a good thing you had a sign, Mandla, or I wouldn't have recognized you." Laughing, he hugged his brother.

"I'm auditioning for a South African movie," said Mandla. "Mom's my agent."

"Is that so?" said Sipho. He kissed Yolanda hello, hugged his father and then allowed himself to be enveloped in his mother's arms.

Monica could feel from the intensity of his return embrace that he was happy to be home.

"Let's go," she said. "Your Nonna and Nonno are waiting for you at the house."

From the kitchen window, Monica watched Mandla bouncing around Sipho and her parents like a wild rabbit as they waited in the garden for lunch to be served. Although officially autumn now, there was no breeze and it was quite warm in the sun. Sipho had begged to eat outside so he could smell the fresh air of Lady Helen.

"The air smelled strange in Houston," he said.

Zak put an arm around Monica. He'd finished carving the

roast lamb and was waiting for her to put the vegetables into a serving dish.

"Sipho's being a good sport," he said. "Mandla has already made him watch his audition piece twice."

Monica smiled. "It's good to all be together for a change."

"It is."

Feeling suddenly light-headed, Monica leaned against Zak.

"What's the matter?" he asked.

"It must be all the excitement. Now let's get this food out before it's cold."

"Monica, is everything okay?"

"I'm fine." The feeling had passed.

"Perhaps you're anemic."

"Come on, Doctor, you're off duty now."

"Is your cycle regular?"

"Usually. I'm a few days late this month."

"A few days? Have you taken a test?"

"Come on, Zak. Let's eat."

"I'm serious, Monica. You should take a test."

She shook her head. "That's all in the past now, Zak."

"Please take a test. For me."

Sighing, she put down the dish of vegetables. "I threw them all out."

"I'll go and get one from the hospital."

"Not now, Zak. Lunch is ready!"

But he was out of the door, his keys jangling.

He returned as they were all beginning to eat.

"Monica, I've left it inside." He gave her a meaningful look. "Please go and check."

She dropped her knife and fork onto the plate with a clang. His insistence, which she had dismissed as sweet, was now irritating her so much that if the children and her parents hadn't been there she might have told him to sit down, be quiet and eat the lunch she had spent more than an hour preparing. But because she didn't want anything to spoil the day of Sipho's homecoming, she pushed back her chair and went inside, letting the door bang behind her to let Zak know she wasn't happy with him.

She took the test, left it on the bathroom vanity and went back to finish her lunch.

"And so?" asked Zak.

She finished chewing the food in her mouth. "I don't know. I didn't care to wait, with my lunch getting colder by the minute."

Zak got up and went inside.

"What's Dad on about?" asked Yolanda, with the exaggerated patience of a teenager.

But there was no need for Monica to search for a suitable reply because Zak came rushing out of the house waving a white stick in his hand.

"Two pink lines, Monica!" he shouted. "We're pregnant!"

❧ Chapter Thirty-Four ❧

From the kitchen window, Monica watched Mandla pulling funny faces at Lilly in her bouncer. Summer was drawing to a close, but the days were still warm enough to spend long hours in the garden. Two-month-old Lilly's favorite activity was watching the dancing leaves and shadows of the syringa tree. Monica could not have found a more dedicated helper than Mandla if she'd advertised in all the newspapers in the country. Sometimes he even tried to get out of school in order to look after his new sister.

Monica had returned to work, but she spent only half the day at the office. Silas had stepped in to take up the slack. Monica's parents had arrived in Lady Helen at the beginning of summer, announcing that they would not return to Italy when winter began. Although Monica had doubted that her mother's interest in her granddaughter would be sustained when all Lilly did was eat and sleep, she had to admit that she had been wrong. Mirinda was a doting grandmother, who also always made sure that Mandla knew he was just as important as the new arrival.

Sipho, who would turn seventeen soon, was the youngest in his first-year class at medical school in Cape Town, and was coping admirably. Every weekend he came home to Lady Helen, unless he had a test the following week. After his brief association with the popular crowd in Houston, he had settled into his final year at Green Block School and scored the highest marks in the entire country on his matric exams.

Most of his dormitory mates at the university stayed in Cape Town on weekends for rugby and soccer games or social activities, but Sipho preferred to be in Lady Helen with his family. He would observe Lilly from all angles, as though she were a new species he'd discovered while walking on the beach.

Sometimes Monica found herself looking at Lilly with similar awe. After years of desperately wanting this child, Monica had given up on ever having a baby of her own, and yet here was her daughter, all fat rolls and dimples, softness and heavenly smells—alive and real in her home. Monica felt that her life had been blessed beyond comprehension.

She went outside into the garden and sat down next to Lilly's bouncer.

"She likes my surprised clown look best," said Mandla. "She laughed at that one."

Monica knew that Lilly was too young to laugh, but she did not tell Mandla this.

Mirinda came out of the Old Garage and took the chair next to Monica. "Your father's having a nap."

"Babies are tiring," said Mandla in an earnest voice.

Monica had found that she needed to be extra quiet when feeding and changing Lilly's diaper in the middle of the night because Mandla, who had once been a heavy sleeper, woke at every sound since Lilly's birth.

"I thought I'd find you all out here," said a voice at the kitchen door. It was Francina.

With Monica not working in the afternoons, Francina had given up her usual shift watching Mandla after school. Instead of throwing herself into taking on more dress orders, as Monica had expected her to, she often wandered over to have tea with Monica and check on Lilly.

"Zukisa's watching the shop," she explained.

Although Zukisa had finally given in to her parents' requests to go to university, at the last minute she had begged them to allow her to study part-time so that she would be able to remain involved in the running of Jabulani Dressmakers. Francina had to admit that she had been surpassed by her daughter's design talent. All the publicity the shop had recently received in national magazines was due solely to Zukisa's vision. It had been because of Zukisa's skill that a certain film star chose Jabulani Dressmakers to make her gown for the wedding of the year in Johannesburg. It had been Zukisa who the reporter from a television fashion program had come to interview.

From her part-time studies in business administration, Zukisa would learn how to expand the business if she wanted to, but Francina knew that her daughter's first love would always be design. Zukisa was an obedient daughter; she would complete her degree and Francina would hang her certificate in the shop next to her own for completing high school. Nobody would ever be able to say that the women of the Shabalala family were not educated.

"You didn't tell me you'd been cast in another movie," Francina said to Mandla.

He shrugged. Since the release of the film he'd made in Los Angeles, Mandla had starred in two local productions and had been offered a role in a television soap opera, which he'd turned down because he "wanted to concentrate on serious drama."

The American movie had earned him several mentions in reviews—often in favorable comparison to Steven, the main child actor.

"I don't want to be like one of those typical child stars," Mandla was fond of saying, "who are overexposed and end up on game shows."

Monica knew that one day he would leave South Africa to pursue his dream in Hollywood, but she was grateful that he had agreed to attend university in Cape Town first.

"I almost forgot," said Francina. "I brought you some pie. It's in the kitchen."

Mandla jumped up and ran inside before she had even completed her sentence. He came out with his cheeks bulging like a chipmunk's.

Mirinda got up. "I'll make tea and bring us all out a piece of pie before someone I know finishes it."

"Don't tell Mama Dlamini," said Mandla. "But Lucy's pies are better than hers."

Lucy was running the café as though she had been there for years. In fact, she was so good at it that Mama Dlamini only came in once a week, to approve the menu. Although Mama Dlamini had never admitted that she'd taken some of what Monica had said in her outburst in the café to heart, Mr. Yang had started encouraging the resort guests to frequent businesses in town, and both Monica and Francina suspected that this development had been upon Mama Dlamini's urging.

In her personal life, Lucy had suffered two major heartbreaks. Her mother had passed away three months after the family's move to Lady Helen, and her eldest son, Xoli, had been arrested by Lady Helen police for possession of *tiktik*—the local term for crystal methamphetamine. He was now in a juvenile detention facility in Cape Town. Freed from the influence of his brother, Bulelani was flourishing, both at school and on the sports field, where he was proving himself to be a star player for the Green Block soccer team. Little Fundiswa was devastated when her grandmother passed away, but she had quickly grown close to the mother she had known only briefly in the first year of her life. Lucy often told Francina it was the healing love of her daughter that kept her humble and on her knees in prayer.

Mirinda came out with the tea and poured a cup for each of them.

Lilly started to cry, and Mandla picked her up and swayed back and forth, as he had seen his grandmother do countless times.

"What a good big brother," remarked Francina.

"Sipho and Mandla are both good with her," said Monica.

"It's a shame Yolanda's missing out on Lilly's first year," said Mirinda.

Yolanda had decided to split her years at university between her mother's and father's countries of residence. This year, she was taking classes in Sydney. It had upset Zak that his daughter chose to go back to the mother who had deceived her into leaving South Africa. But with all her faults, Jacqueline was still Yolanda's mother—and Yolanda's new little brother, Marcus, was an added attraction.

Mandla missed Yolanda, but, with her gone and Sipho at university in Cape Town, he made the most of his monopoly over Lilly.

Monica looked at her mother, at Francina and then at her baby asleep in Mandla's arms.

"We've come a long way together. Haven't we?" she said.

Her mother nodded. "Through some bad times, too."

The three women sat in silence, thinking about the death of Monica's brother, Monica's near-death experience in a carjacking and the death of Mandla's birth mother, Ella.

"Who would have thought that we'd still be together after all these years?" said Francina.

Mandla handed his sleeping sister to Monica, and they all watched as she snuggled into the crook of her mother's arm. The baby girl was the first of Monica's family to be born in Lady Helen. Though it was common in this country to move around in search of work, Monica hoped that, years into the future, newcomers would come across Lilly, surrounded by her children, grandchildren and great-grandchildren, in this little town that had given each of them a fresh start in life.

* * * * *

QUESTIONS FOR DISCUSSION

1. Discuss the relationship between Monica and Zak in the light of the following excerpt: "Positive, negative. Two mundane little words, so undeserving of the impact they might have on the lives of a yearning couple."

2. Discuss Francina's relationship with her adopted daughter and how the traditional values of the Zulu nation threaten to tear them apart.

3. Discuss the following excerpt in the light of the title of the novel: "Monica the individual wanted to say (to Sipho), 'Don't go, stay here with me.' But Monica the parent had to weigh her words. She didn't want Sipho to one day regret the opportunity he had passed up."

4. Francina and Hercules have markedly different ways of looking at people and at the world. How is this demonstrated during their quest to find Lucy?

5. Discuss the trajectory of Monica's emotions throughout the book with regard to her own infertility.

6. Why does Francina not approve of Mama Dlamini's intent to become chef at the golf resort?

7. Referring to the AIDS pandemic, the following is noted in the book: Hercules said that one day this would all be "a chapter in a history textbook, the kind that he used

to teach his pupils. People didn't realize, he said, that they were a part of history in the making, and that the course of history could be changed." Why do you think that some countries manage to make a great impact in the fight against AIDS, whereas in others the number of infected people continues to rise?

8. Why does Francina drop out of the race for mayor?

9. Sipho and Mandla are attracted to life in the United States for different reasons. Discuss the divergent ways in which each boy adjusts to his new environment.

10. We are told that "Francina had worked for the Brunetti household since Monica was nine. She'd scrubbed the ring from their baths, peeled their vegetables, washed their clothes, cleaned Monica's and her brother's cuts and scrapes, and not once had they asked about her family, about her home." With this in mind, do you find the present-day relationship between Monica and Francina realistic? Can you think of any instances in your own life in which the relationship you have with a person now is not as it always was?

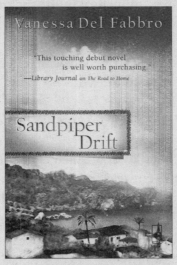

SHE *SEEMED* TO HAVE IT ALL

ROBIN LEE
HATCHER

Alicia Harris says she's happily married and expecting a baby—
but only the last part is true. She can't bear to disappoint her
grandfather by telling him she's two months away from single
motherhood. Then Grandpa Pete drops in unexpectedly to
spend the holidays with Alicia and her *husband*, and Alicia
needs to find a fill-in—*fast*. Childhood friend Joe Palmero
fits the bill, and is willing to play along. Still, the longer they
spend playing their parts, the closer Alicia and Joe come to
discovering what love, faith and marriage truly mean.

Bundle of Joy

Steeple
Hill®

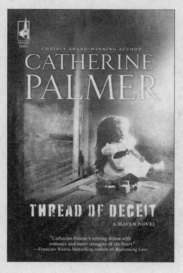

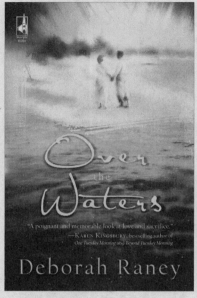